A Tori Mulligan Mystery

Vetted for Murder

D.W. EARNHARDT

Independently published.

Cover Design: Melody Simmons

www.bookcoverscre8tive.com

Interior Formatting: CPR Editing

www.carmenrichterwriting.com/cpr-editing

For my husband and daughters. I love you more than you know.

For Triple Trouble–Mama, Rachie, and Kelly–y'all are the best.

And for H.S.–Thank you for being my favorite technical advisor!

Killing Craig was turning out to be harder than I'd imagined. He was a terrible husband and a liar to boot – but shooting him didn't feel right and it was messy. Poison could work, but was it too cliché? Whatever I chose, he had to die... and soon. Maybe I should—

"This is NOT working, Percy. Not at all."

My chunky orange and gray cat snuggled up beside me, then purred in agreement with my assessment.

"I'm running out of time and ideas on how to kill him. Got any suggestions?" I asked him. "I've got to have this done by tomorrow night!"

He purred louder, hopped down, and weaved between my legs.

"You are cute...but zero help," I muttered. *Victoria Ellice Mulligan, get yourself together. You gotta get this done!*

Thursdays were my usual days to murder someone, but only on paper, of course. I'd always wanted to concentrate on writing, so moving back to Craven to work for the Mountain Gazette brought me a little closer to my dream. Inheriting the house that I now called home didn't hurt, either.

Alberta "Bert" Diggs, my mother's youngest sister, used to own my 10-bedroom farmhouse. When she bought it back in the late 70's, she'd named it The Nestled Inn—and ran it as the most popular B&B in town for almost 45 years. Two years ago, she passed away and left it to me. It included 20 acres of land, a pool, a pond, and several old farm buildings that could be used for weddings and other events. However, I hadn't yet screwed up the courage to rent out the rooms as she had. If I could figure it all out, I could be an inn keeper by day, and writer by night. *Maybe one day.*

For the moment, I just needed to finish my latest story for Murder Mystery Corner and get it to my editor before tomorrow's deadline. That was more than enough pressure for the time being.

The setting sun spun shadows through my open windows, and the rush of a late November breeze blew the week of unopened mail off of my living room table, scattering it on the floor. I scooped up the mail, shut the windows quickly, then heard a faint knock.

The only people who usually came by this late were my parents, my best friend, or my closest neighbor, Mr. Fisher. He came at least once a week to see if I'd seen his Bull, an escape artist aptly named "Moodini". One time we found the bovine deep in my woods with one of his horns caught in a low lying oak branch.

I took a quick look through the peep hole, but it wasn't Mr. Fisher, my parents, or my best friend. No, it was Anna Webster, my boss—the owner of the Gazette. *Great. Just great.*

"Hi Anna! I thought you were out of town until tomorrow?" I tried to sound happy to see her, but my poker face was worse than Pinocchio's.

Anna shoved off her fur-lined hood, revealing her signature blue-dyed pixie cut. She was 31, but looked closer to 21. "Hi Tori. Sorry for just dropping by."

"No worries—come on in." I glanced at the pile of clean

clothes on the wooden bench on the other side of the living room, thankful that I'd transferred it from the couch a little earlier. At least most of them were folded.

"I was just about to order some soup and biscuits from Jo's café," I said. "Can I get you something? I think she's made a new scone recipe."

"Wow. I haven't had good scones since my mom visited from London last year. But no—food is the last thing on my mind right now." Anna hugged her arms tightly to her chest. "I really am sorry for popping in unannounced. It's just—I need to talk to you about something important. Can we sit down?"

Uh-oh. Here we go. "Look…I know I'm struggling this week, but I'll have the story in on time. I still have 24 hours."

"That's the least of my worries," Anna said, "and maybe the least of yours."

I folded the menu from Jo's Café that I'd been drooling over. Supper would have to wait.

Anna took a seat on the edge of the leather couch near the fireplace, and I sat across the room on the comfy, blood-red love seat. It was my favorite seat in the house, usually. But at that moment, I was so tense that the cushion under me felt like a giant brick.

Anna took off her jacket, revealing a slightly wrinkled, periwinkle t-shirt. I'd never seen her in anything other than her perfectly-put-together business attire. Her face was more pale than usual and her eyes were red, as if she'd been crying. Until now, she had never let down her reserved veneer.

Anna took a deep breath, fiddled with the zipper on her jacket, then finally spoke again. "I didn't want to tell you like this, Tori—but you should start looking for another job."

"You're firing me?"

"I'm sorry." She dropped her head to her chest. "We don't have the advertisements we need to keep our heads above water, so the Gazette is dying slowly and painfully. The humane thing is to just hit the "kill" switch and move on. So that's what I'm going to do." She sighed again and fidgeted with the silver and turquoise bracelet on her right arm. "I'm closing up shop."

"But we've been doing great these last few months! We can't just give up without a fight. Have you thought about--"

"I've thought of everything," Anna said. "I'm sorry. I really am. But—I have no choice. So there's no need to worry about the column for this week. It's over, Tori."

My mind churned as I paced the hardwood floor; there had to be a way to save the paper. But how? Our advertising budget was maxed out and we'd been a skeleton crew for the last four months.

I was the only other full-time employee at the Gazette. On top of writing Murder Mystery Corner, my duties included the Obituaries column, the weekly Foodies review, and the calendar for "local activities". It was nothing like my last job, but it did have a lot less baggage. At least until now.

Anna owned the paper and handled most of the front page stories as well as the advertisements. She was 18 years younger than me, but usually handled things with the wisdom of someone who'd been in the business for ages. And though we'd had some disagreements over minor issues with the content, I usually knew when to push and when not to. But this wasn't an office discussion over whose restaurant should be covered next, or if a bereaved and salty widow should be allowed to include details of her deceased husband's affair in his obituary. No, the imminent death of this small local newspaper felt more like murder.

"Hold on! I have an idea!" I ran to the kitchen and pulled a faded business card from the front of the fridge and offered it to Anna. "This is Dad's accounting firm. I am certain that he can help us find ways to cut costs and save the business."

"Unless your dad is a miracle worker, there's nothing he can do." She waved the card away. "I've already contacted a realtor."

"It just seems so… sudden."

"Not really. I've been thinking about it for a while. I'm barely making the building loan payments." Anna paused, as if editing her words before speaking them aloud. "I have personal debt, too, Tori. I am drowning."

She didn't expound on the personal debt—and I didn't ask her to. I instinctively knew better. There are many things in life that polite southerners don't talk about unless invited into the conversation. And finances? Number one on the list. I stood up and started loading my dishwasher instead. I hated cleaning, but at least it was something I could control.

The clanging of the dishes filled the uncomfortable, sad silence between us. "After that write-up in the Charlotte Observer, it seems that Craven Mountain is the new "in-place" to visit," I said, trying to find something positive in the situation. "Maybe you'll get a quick offer."

"I hope so. There are too many ghosts here."

"You and Blake are leaving town? Why not just go back to teaching English at UNC Asheville again?" Anna had worked there on a teaching visa before marrying Blake. "Y'all could commute and stay right here in town."

"That is not an option. And no, I don't want to talk about it." Anna abruptly gathered her things, then headed toward the door and stopped. "I'm really sorry, Tori. I wish things could have been different."

"My grandpa used to say that miracles happen when we aren't looking for them, so I'm going to pray that things turn around."

"You can pray all you want to, but I gave on up miracles a long time ago." Anna flashed a sad smile, then hurried out the door, down the steps, and into her gray Mercedes.

Fighting the urge to burst into an ugly cry, I picked up the phone and called the best cook in town. She also happened to be my best friend: Josephine "Jo" Parker.

As soon as she answered the phone, I lost it. Between sobs, I explained everything.

"I'm coming over as soon as I've given the boys their list of chores and a good lecture. They've been living like a herd of swine, and I ain't having it." Jo's raspy voice was a tad more southern than mine. "I'm bringing double chocolate brownies and ice cream. Calories don't count on days like this."

"From your lips to God's ears," I mumbled.

"Yes and amen! See you in a few!"

Jo lived one road over on her own 5-acre mini farm, so I didn't have to wait long.

I barely had time to change into my plush, polka-dotted pajama pants with the stretchy waist before I heard Jo's familiar voice wafting down my hallway. With full arms, she made her way into the kitchen. Several containers, precariously topped up to her chin, threatened to topple. I moved toward her and caught one of the smaller bowls as it escaped from the stack and hurtled toward the floor.

"Nice catch!" Jo plopped the rest of the containers on the counter, grabbed two bowls, and started building our sundaes. "Chocolate almond crunch ice cream plus the perfect corner-brownie. Good for what ails you." She topped the desserts with homemade hot fudge and mini white chocolate chips.

As I stuffed my face with the ice cream, I detected a faint whiff of Kahlua. "New recipe?"

"Yep!"

"I know that I'm biased, but your ice cream is the best medicine."

"At the risk of sounding too big for my britches…I know. I'll start serving it at the restaurant next week."

We enjoyed the brownie Sundaes in silence for a while, but it didn't last long. It never did.

"I am so mad at Anna," Jo mumbled. "She has continued to work you at all hours, then complain that she doesn't have enough money. Every time something has needed to be done, you took care of it, not Anna. She might have paid you a good wage for being the editor of one or two columns, but not four.

You are the reason she's been afloat this long!"

Jo never had an issue sharing her opinion, especially if she was feeling protective. She oozed southern sass.

"I know you're just mad for me, but you don't need to be mean about Anna. She's actually a really good business woman."

"Really? Then why is she losing the business? And why didn't she give you more than a 24-hour notice?"

I sighed and dug into the last few bites of my sundae. We fell into a small silence again, but I broke it this time. "It's not like she murdered anybody, Jo. She's just trying to keep her head above water." We'd already cut the paper production to three times a week. Maybe Anna was right. Maybe it was a losing battle.

"I'm sorry," Jo said, not sounding sorry at all, "but I'm just speaking the truth—and the truth ain't always easy. Anna might have worked hard to get the paper off the ground, but now she's managed to drive it into an early grave—and she's taking you down with her."

"This isn't exactly making me feel any better."

Jo didn't say another word; she just scooted her chair back and went to get more ice cream.

I didn't like the way she'd been talking about Anna, but Jo wasn't wrong about the balance of work at the paper. More often than not, Anna had expected me to cover any breaking news... including the black bear wine caper at the Scott Family Winery a couple of months ago. Drunk bears and unhappy store owners made for good front page news and good sales, so we needed as many exciting news stories as we could get. But those exciting stories were few and far between. And when I'd first been hired, Anna was robbing Peter to pay Paul for a few months—so maybe it had all just caught up with her.

"If I can't talk about Anna," Jo said, "then let's move on to your next adventure. I've heard there is a manager position open at the ski resort, but I figure that won't be high on your application list."

"After the epic ski lift fall and subsequent leg break of 1997? Definitely not." *My leg still gets a little stiff in freezing weather.* "I guess I could work at another paper, but I'd have to head toward Boone for that."

"Hold on—you just gave me an idea!" Jo ran her hand through bottle-blonde hair. "What if you got a loan and bought the paper from Anna? You could be your own boss!"

"I can't afford it, Jo. I don't want to invest and then lose it all. If Anna couldn't make it work, why would I be able to?"

"Because you've got a great head for business, just like your dad. He could help you figure out how to make it work. And people around here know you and love you. They'd buy the paper just to support you, and of course, your fabulous reporting skills."

"But I don't have the cash to invest." *And I wasn't sure the paper was where I'd want to invest my money if I had it.*

"You could always put the Inn up for collateral."

"You're kidding right? Aunt Bert would roll over in her grave."

At the will reading, Aunt Bert's lawyer had given me a deed to the house with a short list of bullet points. In the letter, Aunt Bert reminded me to keep a watch out for the Sasquatch she was convinced lived on her property, but she also begged me not to sell the house to anyone outside of the family. Thus, putting it up for collateral was too risky of a situation. I didn't want to lose it.

"So what are you going to do?" Jo asked.

"The only thing I can do: start looking for a new job. And I'd rather not go to bed without at least seeing what's out there. Be right back—I need my computer."

I ran upstairs to find my laptop covered by the same squishy blob of fur who had been little help to me earlier in the day. "You've got to move, Percy."

But the 12-year-old feline seemed to have other ideas, none of which included obeying me. He meowed, rolled over, then started to give himself a leisurely bath, all while still on my laptop. I scooped him up and laid him gently in the middle of my queen-sized bed. His colors matched the comforter—my latest Goodwill find—giving him a camouflaged effect.

"You can come downstairs if you'd like," I told him, "but I've got work to do."

He stopped licking long enough to give me a disgusted glance that instantly reminded me—*you can't spell scathing without "cat"*.

An hour later, Jo and I had only found three jobs that might work. There were two front desk receptionist jobs, one at the Valley View Vet Clinic and one at the Craven courthouse. The last job was in the human resources department at Grace Hospital—the smallest hospital in the state. None of them made me jump for joy, but I needed a job.

"I think you should apply for the front desk job at Valley View," Jo announced. "I've heard the ladies in the café talking about it. You love animals, so you'd be perfect!"

"I'm not so sure about that." Sebastian Westminster was the owner and only vet at the clinic. He'd lived in Craven Mountain all of his life, but acted like he'd been born and raised where they didn't say "y'all". Plus, he'd been known to pitch a hissy when he had to wait more than five minutes in line at Jo's café or any restaurant in town. Definitely not my favorite person.

"But you'd only be dealing with people and mostly small animals. No more bear wrangling."

"Yeah, but I'd have to deal with Sebastian, day in and day out. He's worse than a bear."

"Actually, you wouldn't have to. I heard there's a new vet coming on board…and he's single."

Jo was smiling deviously. I knew that look—and didn't like it at all.

"I was told that he's moving here from Wilmington. From the beach to the mountains? He's going to need someone to show him around."

"You can stop now…"

"If he's a widower, then that means he is marriage material."

"Jo! That's awful! Don't you think that's a wee bit insensitive?"

"If I was telling him, yes. But I'm not; I'm telling you."

"I wish you weren't."

"I'm just saying that y'all might hit it off. Keep an open mind, my friend."

Jo's idea of an attractive, eligible man didn't match mine. But to be fair, after the last few years of dating several Mr. Wrongs, I didn't always trust my own instincts, either. Still, I had no desire to be set up by Jo or anyone.

"I am looking for a job, *not* a man."

"They are one in the same, aren't they?" Jo held up the gold ring on her left hand and grinned. "But don't tell Hank I said that!"

The doorbell rang, interrupting our laughter. I opened the front door to a tall, bearded, husky man.

"Speaking of the devil…" I said.

The soft-spoken fella in front of me was anything but a devil—and he was the perfect match for Jo. His calm demeanor and patience balanced out her high-strung tendencies, and that was good for everyone, including the general public. He'd served as one of only six police officers in the Craven Mountain community for the last 20 years.

"Come on in. We've got cookies and ice cream, thanks to your lovely bride."

He took off his cowboy hat and made his way toward the kitchen. He filled a small bowl with the sugary goodness, then plopped on the couch next to his wife.

Jo kissed him on the cheek. "Are the boys getting their rooms clean?"

"I cannot tell a lie…so I choose not to answer that." He pulled out a postcard and passed it to me. "This was put in our mailbox by mistake."

I scanned it, then quickly threw it in the trash can beside me before Jo could see that it was a coupon for the vet clinic.

"Yeah. We got one and I threw it out, too," Hank said. "We don't need it."

"I'm confused," Jo said. "What is it?"

"It's nothing," I mumbled. "Just a useless advertisement."

"It's from Valley View Vet Clinic," Hank said, obviously unaware of the earlier conversation about the incoming vet and my efforts to avoid more of it.

Jo jumped up and grabbed the postcard from the trash. As she read it silently, her eyes got wide, then she pointed at me. "You know what this means!"

"Yes," I said, "that the vet needs to know its target audience a little better. Poor Percy is already half the cat he used to be."

"No, Tori! This is a sign. A clear sign!" Jo plopped back on the seat and kicked her legs up on the table. "I told you so."

Hank looked from Jo to me, confused—then suddenly stood up. "I don't know what is going on, but I'm going home." He kissed Jo on the top of her head and headed toward the door. "I'll see you when you get home, sweetie."

Then he tipped his hat toward me and smiled. "And please don't kill my wife, Tori. I'm kind of fond of her."

He sprinted out the front door before Jo could express her opinion with a flying pillow.

"By the way," I said, trying to divert her attention from the idea lodged in her brain at that moment, "when is your next date night? I know the boys don't need a babysitter anymore, but I miss seeing them. They can come hang with me."

"It's Friday, like always. But don't try to change the subject. You know that the mail from the vet is a *sign*."

"No, it's a useless coupon. Nothing more, nothing less."

Jo sat back in her seat, arms still crossed. "But what if you're wrong? What if you are supposed to apply there? What if this is the job you are supposed to have?"

"It's not."

"But what if it is?"

Jo liked to argue, but I knew how to get her off my back. "I will apply at the other two jobs first. If they don't pan out, then I'll apply at the Vet's office."

But even if they offered me the job, the answer would be no. *I would tell Jo that part later.*

"I've got a good feeling about this one!" Jo said.

"Mmmm-hmmm…I bet you do." Suddenly, I felt a yawn coming on and couldn't hide it. "I need to get to bed."

"Same! I've got early shift at the café tomorrow."

She left four small brownies for me with firm instructions. "Eat two…and call me in the morning. And don't worry, God's got good plans for you, including a fabulous job."

"I know," I replied, stifling another yawn, "I'm just hoping He lets me in on those plans, preferably sooner than later."

I locked the doors, threw away our bowls, then grabbed the coupon off the table and chunked it back in the trash. I covered up the brownies on the stove with plastic wrap, then headed up the stairs. When I opened the door, Percy had barely moved from where I'd placed him earlier. I checked his food, water, and litter box. Then moved him to the other side of the bed. He protested a bit, but settled down quickly.

It felt late, but it was only 9pm. I whipped out my computer and looked at the blank applications that I had downloaded earlier. After two more hours of work, I had completed and submitted one to the hospital and one to the courthouse. The hospital job had good benefits and would never be boring, but I didn't relish the thoughts of working around tons of germs. However, working at the court house also sounded interesting and the pay was comparable. I plugged in my computer and shut it down, then turned out the lamp on my side table and snuggled under the covers. No deadlines meant an early bedtime…but it also meant no job. My thoughts swirled, but I drifted off much quicker than I thought I would.

It felt like I'd only been asleep for a few minutes when I heard something loud and dramatic downstairs on my porch. I peeked out the window and the early sun shined in my face. *Morning already?* The sounds grew louder, forcing me to refocus on the matter at hand.

I grabbed my bat and my phone. If it was a bear, I was at least going to be prepared. And if it tried to come in my house, well…I didn't want to think about that. As I got closer to the door, the loud noises stopped, and suddenly, a whimpering filled the air. If it was a bear, something was wrong with it.

The tall window beside the back door was the perfect place to sneak a peek of the porch critter. I slowly pushed aside the red and black plaid window dressing—then dropped my bat in relief.

I cracked open the door and stepped onto the porch, slowly reaching out to the humongous, wrinkly hound dog on my porch. She sniffed me quickly, then licked my hand, covering it in slobber. Her droopy eyes were anything but sad; on the contrary, they seemed to be "smiling", and her tail wagged so hard that she knocked over the small vase of dying mums on the side porch table.

I wiped the wet kisses from my hand onto the dog's reddish fur. By the looks of her hanging belly, it was clear that she had puppies somewhere. Her prominent features screamed "bloodhound".

"You are a happy girl, aren't you? What's your name and who do you belong to?"

It didn't take long to find her name on the small, pink metallic charm hanging from her collar, but the owner contact info had rubbed off.

"Holly, huh? That's appropriate for this time of year!"

The dog's ears perked up at the sound of her name, then she rolled over for belly rubs. As I obliged, I noticed an infected injury on her back leg. *Not good.*

I picked up my phone and called Jo again. "I know it's early, but I've got another problem…a big one…"

Jo and her 16-year-old boys arrived within minutes of my early morning call. The twins were in love with animals and had proven to be great pet/house sitters for me in the last few months.

"They are old friends already," Jo whispered.

The teens were playing with Holly in the fenced area of the backyard. When she plopped on the ground, the boys did, too. Then Holly rolled on her back and wiggled all over.

"There is definitely enough of her for two laps at a time," I said. "You should take her home."

"You know we can't. Hank is allergic!"

"Hank can take meds."

We were talking in hushed tones, but her scrunched-up eyebrows made her position clear.

"This is not about me or Hank; this is about that sweet dog," Jo said. "Holly is hurt, has puppies somewhere, and the temperature is supposed to drop below freezing tonight. What are we going to do?"

"We need to find the puppies, then take them all to the vet. I don't know where she came from, but I think she may have been living in the woods."

"You've got 20 acres, that's a lot to cover. What if Holly hid her puppies in one of your aunt's old buildings? Or maybe the cave near the river?"

"That makes sense. There are several places she could have used for shelter. Maybe the boys could follow her to the puppies if she'll let them."

"Yes! And once we get them to the vet, maybe they can put them up for adoption." Jo grinned. "And you could also turn in your application while you're there."

"Not that again…"

"You know I don't believe in coincidences, Tori. Holly chose *your* home to come to. She needs to go to the vet—it's like she knew you'd take her! And…we only have one vet in town who just happens to be offering a half-off spay coupon. You lost your job and the vet is hiring. Connect the dots!"

"I don't believe in coincidences, either, but the half-off spay coupon is not a dot." I made a mental note to pull it back out of the trash...again. Holly was going to need it. "The only dots in this room? The excessive freckle population on my face."

Jo groaned. "You're impossible!"

Holly suddenly stood up, then whimpered.

"I think she's trying to tell us something," Grady said, rubbing Holly behind the ears. "She's probably upset about her puppies. Where are they, anyway?"

"Well, that's the mystery. But we have a proposition for you that could help us solve it." I explained the plan. "Are you up for it?"

"Yes!" The boys said, high-fiving each other.

"But you've got to be careful. Some of those old buildings are rotted and should have been torn down years ago!"

"Your mom's right, so take your time," I said. "And if you find them, call us and give us your coordinates so we can come help carry them back here." Both boys were tech savvy and had no problems sharing GPS coordinates. "The hardest part will be getting Holly to let you follow her."

"Tori—can we keep one of them as a reward?" Grady asked. "We'll take good care of it!"

"I think that's a great idea!" I said, jumping in. "You are both great with animals and have wanted a puppy for years. And these will be available for adoption—for free! Plus, we do not believe in coincidences around here. Right Jo?" I smiled playfully. "Connect the dots."

Jo's glare could have peeled the freckles off my face.

Holly seemed to know what we were saying and waited for the boys at the edge of the woods. While the boys followed her, Jo and I looked for a basket and blanket for the puppies. None of my wicker clothes baskets were puppy friendly or big enough for Holly.

"I have an oversized plastic pool in the garage that I just haven't been able to let go of," Jo said. "At least it will have babies in it, again. Be right back!"

I found a giant plush blanket and threw it in the dryer, just to freshen it up. It didn't smell bad, just dusty. Percy stared at me from the top of the washing machine. "Stop looking so worried," I said. "I'm not gonna keep Holly or her puppies."

He didn't look like he believed me.

About 30 minutes later, we saw the boys coming back, each carrying something. Holly marched right between them, never leaving their sides.

But something was very wrong. I could feel it.

Jo and I ran to meet them. "Why didn't you call us?" she asked.

"There were five puppies in the first small barn in a cluster of buildings, about

ten minutes inside the woods," Booker said softly. "These are the only ones that made it." He showed us the sleeping black and white puppy in his arms, and Grady showed us the one he had wrapped up in his jacket. It was red like its mama.

Jo and I broke into tears.

"Holly kept nudging the others and trying to help them," Grady said, "but…it was too late."

"We thought it was best to bring the healthy ones back here

with Holly." Booker wiped his eyes. "We'll go back and bury the others after you've got her inside."

It didn't take long for the boys to do what needed to be done and get back to the house.

"We buried them inside the barn," Grady said.

"And put a few big rocks on top, just to make sure no other animals try to, ya know, dig them up." His voice cracked.

"Yeah, I know," I said. "You did good."

"Holly doesn't want to hear the details," Jo said. She put her hands over Holly's ears. "And neither do I. I'm about to cry again."

Holly didn't seem to mind the car ride to the vet as much as she minded the boys holding her babies. She didn't growl at them, but constantly checked on her pups with whines and nudges.

When we arrived at the vet, I attached the make-shift lead to Holly's collar that Grady had fashioned from an old jump-rope. We headed to the front desk and explained everything to the raven haired, pale-skinned woman behind the counter: Luna

Hale.

"Hi, Luna! I know we don't have an appointment, but this sweet hound mama needs some help. It's a bit of an emergency." I made the request with as much "show us some mercy" in my voice as possible, but Luna didn't look up or respond in any way.

I lightly tapped the counter. "Hello?"

Luna finally looked up long enough to snarl at me, then pointed to the sign on the window: *No walk-ins.*

"Can't I just make an appointment with you right now?" I scanned the room again to see if someone had come in after us, but they hadn't. "You don't seem to have any other customers."

The heavily tattooed 23-year old tapped the appointment policy on the glass window, then looked back down at her phone.

I felt my face getting hot. "So if I call you, then I can make an appointment for today?"

Luna put her phone down, looked up again, and crossed her arms.

Jo must have sensed my frustration because she jumped in and took over.

She stepped up to the counter, then reached in her pocket book and pulled out a $20 bill.

"Maybe you can fit us in now?" Jo slipped the money across the counter to Luna. "This lil' furry mama has a bum leg, and her puppies really need to be checked out."

Luna kept her hand in the open position. "My tattoos aren't going pay for themselves, hon."

Jo narrowed her eyes and slapped another $20 in Luna's hand. "Here ya go, *sweetie*." The ice daggers in Jo's voice must have made at least a minor impression. Luna retracted her hand and pocketed the cash, then she handed me a clipboard. "Looks like an appointment slot just opened up, so fill out the front and back of each sheet, then bring them back to me."

The boys held the puppies and Jo took care of Holly while I penned in the information on the patient sheets.

"Maybe she's got a chip," Grady said. "They can check for that while you're here."

"Good idea! Maybe there is someone out there still searching for her."

I was about to take the finished papers to Luna when we heard two people arguing and stomping down the hall. I could hear them loud and clear, but was surprised to recognize Anna's voice as the angriest sounding of the two.

They rounded the corner, expletives flying, but didn't notice the group of us staring at them from the waiting room…until Holly bayed.

Anna and Sebastian both swiveled their attention our way. Anna's face went pale, but a sardonic smile filled Sebastian's face.

I immediately tried to break the tension. "Soooo…" I said, holding up Holly's sweet, but very wrinkled face, "would either of you be interested in a free dog?"

"No. I've had my fill of bitches today," Sebastian said softly, turning to look at Anna.

Quick as lightning, Anna pulled her hand back and slapped him, leaving an immediate mark. She dropped her hand to her side and stared at Sebastian with the heat of a thousand southern suns, daring him to respond.

He rubbed his crimson cheek and spoke through his teeth. "Go home, Anna, before I call the police and have this room full of witnesses tell them how you assaulted me."

His hands were clenched by his side, and I wasn't so sure he wasn't going to retaliate. I started to jump up, but felt Jo's hand on my arm. "I've got Hank on alert," she whispered. "He can be here in a minute if we need him!"

After a few more seconds of intense staring, they both seemed to have had enough. Anna marched toward the door, slung it open, then turned and pointed in Sebastian's general direction. "You better watch yourself. You're not the only one who can play dirty." Then she waltzed out, slamming the door behind her.

Rarely was I at a loss for words, but my tongue was definitely tied.

The clock struck 10am. I didn't realize how long we'd already been here. This was not supposed to be an all-morning trip.

Grady cleared his throat. "I'm sorry to be the bearer of more bad news, mom…but we still have to feed the animals and make sure Hamlet and Piggly Wiggly have their worm medicine."

"And we promised Mr. Fisher we could help with some chores today," Booker said. "Remember?"

"Yes, I remember. Do you remember that there's also a little thing called school work?" Jo had her mama voice on. "Go ahead and feed the animals, but Mr. Fisher and the deworming can wait until after you're done with school."

Our local dual enrollment facility had been shut down for a couple of months due to a fire that gutted the entire building, so the boys' school was completely online until the repairs were made. It had been a wild semester, to say the least.

Jo texted Hank and asked him to pick up the boys.

"Sorry, Tori," Grady said. "But we can help tonight if you need us."

"I'll let you know," I said, "but I hope they're going to let me leave the dogs here."

I was sure the staff could find them all a good home. I was glad to pay for the shots and anything else they might need, but boarding them here would be the best option, at least for Percy and me.

Jo handed Holly's leash to me and walked the twins out. "I'll be back in a bit!"

Sebastian marched toward Luna's desk. His voice was loud and clear…and mad. "Do you have last month's recordings downloaded yet? I asked you for them a week ago."

"I've been a little busy," she replied, cool as a cucumber. "This isn't exactly my normal job. I'm still learning the ropes."

"But I was told you were a whiz at computers and technical stuff. Was I misinformed?"

She breathed in deeply through her pierced nose, then tapped her fingernails on the desk. "I'm better than anyone here."

"Then get me that footage! I need to know how our merchandise is sprouting legs and disappearing. I'm losing money and I want to know who's responsible!"

"I'll get it to you tomorrow."

"No, you'll get it to me tonight. Capeesh?"

Who knew a vet's office could have so much drama?

At that moment, the front door swung open again.

I held my breath, sure that it was Anna on her way back in to add assault charges to her morning to do list, but the woman sashaying into the clinic was definitely not my boss.

Fortyish-year-old Sophia Westminster's jet black hair was pulled into a high ponytail that accentuated her diamond-studded sunglasses. She wore an oversized (and probably over-priced) sweater and leggings paired with knee-length high leather boots. Sophia marched right in, not once looking my way. Her eyes were glued to her husband of 7 years. She looked as if she wanted to frown, but couldn't. Sophia's unnaturally taut cheekbones and smooth forehead were obviously not the result of a joyful demeanor. None of us were sure how many surgeries she'd had, but they certainly hadn't made her happy.

"I called you twice." Each of Sophia's words exited her mouth with staccato.

"Hello, dear. I didn't expect you for another hour." He opened his arms to her and flashed his perfect pearly whites.

Sophia did not return his embrace; instead, she reached in her purse and pulled out a stack of papers. "I don't think you want to do this here, do you?"

Sebastian straightened his jacket and dusted off his shoulders, then followed Sophia down the hall. The slamming of Sebastian's office door echoed down the hallway.

"I bet that's about Sebastian and Anna," Luna said, sticking her head out from the office window. "I wondered how long it would take her to figure it out. She's madder than a hornet."

I gave Luna a bewildered stare. "You must have your facts wrong. Anna's married."

"Come on now…" She looked at me, then raised an eyebrow in surprise. "You really didn't know? Man. I'm shocked. Nothing stays secret in a small town."

The argument between Anna and Sebastian definitely seemed more like a lover's-tiff rather than a simple business argument. I tried to think of the last time Anna had talked to me about her husband or said anything about their relationship. The only time I could remember recently had been last night in my living room. And yeah…it seemed a little tense.

"I hope you're wrong about them," I said. "I just can't believe that Anna would cheat on Blake."

"Believe what you want," Luna said, retreating back to her position behind the counter. "I've got work to do."

Somehow I found that hard to believe.

Five minutes later, the front door opened and Jo came back with a puppy in each hand; both boys were gone. "The twins said they'd be glad to hang out with the dogs tonight."

"I see how it is," I said. "They've taken top spot. Am I suddenly chopped liver?"

"Yes. That's probably why Holly seems to love you so much."

The bloodhound was laying on the floor beside me, her head on my feet.

"What did Hank say about the slap heard round the world?" I asked.

"I didn't tell him about it. The boys probably will, though. I just informed him that there was some trouble brewing between Sebastian and Anna. But he said unless one of them wants to press charges, there's nothing he can do."

"I've never seen Anna like that. Not even when the mayor tried to sue us for posting a picture of him with an open mouth full of BBQ at last year's Founder's Day Festival."

"Hah! I remember that!" Jo lowered her voice. "Speaking of memorable moments, did you get any info on why Anna felt the need to smack him? Other than the reasons everyone else has?"

"Sort of…maybe…not really?" I shrugged.

"Well that was a whole lotta nothing."

"I know, but what I do know is gossip. Nothing substantiated."

"Well, you can share it with me when we finally get out of here."

After another 10 minutes, Luna stepped out from behind the desk again.

"Your exam room is ready," she said. "Down the hall, take a right onto the other hall, then it's the last door on the left."

When we entered, a familiar young face was waiting for us. She had glasses on the top of her curly head of hair, a giant smile filled with braces, and looked a lot like her Uncle Hank.

"Suri!" Jo hugged her. "Hank and I are so proud of you. How long have you been working here now?"

"Five months!"

"How do you like it?"

Suri looked around and made sure the door was shut tightly. "Let's just say that it's been…wild. This place is worse than the soap operas Grandma used to watch."

"We'd love to hear all about it," Jo said. "Come by the house next week. I'll make your favorite cookies."

"Deal!" While Suri read over the sheet that I'd filled out in the lobby, the two puppies whimpered and tried to wiggle out of Jo's arms. Holly made a beeline for them.

"They're probably hungry," I said. "Can Holly nurse them?"

"Of course!" Suri grabbed a blanket from the cabinet and put it on the floor for Holly to lay on. The puppies latched on quickly.

While the puppies got a mid-morning snack, Suri gently checked the wound on Holly's leg.

"It's not as bad as it looks," she said. "After Doctor Westminster examines her, I'll wash her leg and bandage it for you. You will probably just need to apply ointment for a couple of weeks to stave off any further infection."

"A couple of weeks?" I was sure she could hear the mixture of surprise and angst in my voice. "But I was hoping y'all could check for a chip, board her, and find her a home this week."

Suri sighed. "I'm sorry…but that's not how it works. We can check for a chip and advertise on our adoption board in the waiting room, but we don't keep them here. You are the responsible party…not us. Also, our kennel is closed for the next couple of months. Not enough staff and not enough supplies."

"Well that's not what I'd hoped to hear."

"You can always take her and the puppies to the county shelter. But you need to know… it isn't a no-kill shelter."

Then that's not happening.

Sebastian came in right at that moment. He was all business, not once addressing the previous kerfuffle in the lobby, and his cheek wasn't red anymore. He didn't say anything to us as he poked around Holly's belly, checked her ears and eyes, and looked in her mouth. After he was done, he stood up and leaned against the wall.

"Your dog is obviously part bloodhound. They might also have some other type of hound in them, so these puppies are going to be big," he said. "I'd say they are about 3 weeks old."

"That makes sense," I said. Then I told them about the strange yelps and howls coming from the woods over the past couple of weeks. "I figured it was just coyotes."

"Coyotes sound nothing like dogs," he drawled. "Just because something sounds or looks the part, doesn't mean it is."

Oh…we know, I thought. Westminster's handsome outer appearance sure didn't match up with his personality at all. "But I bet coyotes are nicer than some humans."

I felt Jo's elbow in my arm, but Sebastian didn't act like he'd heard me. He gave Suri a few curt instructions about

Holly's leg, then opened the door. As he walked out, he paused and looked over his shoulder with a glare. "For the record, you might not find coyotes to be nearly as nice as you think." Then he slammed the door behind him.

"Sorry, not sorry," I said with a shrug. "He's a turd-muffin."

"Don't mind him," Suri said. "He's just salty because he'll be here well past closing. I heard him say that he's got lots of paperwork to do. He mentioned something about finishing up some forms before Dr. Williams starts on Monday."

Jo raised an eyebrow and smiled at me.

I did not smile back.

"Well," Suri said, wrapping Holly's leg in a sterile bandage, "the puppies appear to be very healthy. I'm going to deworm them today, but they'll need shots in about 3 more weeks. If they have any problems before then, bring them in right away."

"Anything else we should know?" I asked. "I'm not exactly a dog person."

"Puppies are usually weaned between 3 ½ and 4 ½ weeks, then you're going to have to feed them puppy food."

"But what do I feed Holly? Does she need a special kind of food since she's a new mama?"

"She's probably been eating whatever she can sink her teeth into. However, you should get her a solid dog food, maybe even let her eat some puppy food. But make sure she doesn't ingest any grapes, onions, or chocolate. Especially dark chocolate."

"Poor baby," Jo said, rubbing Holly's head. "So none of my chocolate chip cookies for you, sweet girl. I'll have to come up with a special doggie treat."

"Seriously?" I asked. "Not getting attached are you?"

"No. I have lots of customers with dogs," Jo said. "So making a doggie treat is simply a smart business decision."

"Sure it is."

As we bantered back and forth, Suri pulled out a special wand and ran it over Holly's body. "No chip," she said. "Sorry, y'all."

The drive home seemed much quicker. We pulled in the driveway around 11:00, but it felt like lunch time to me.

"I could eat something," I said. "And I could sleep for a few hours."

"Same." Jo handed me the puppies, then helped Holly out of the backseat and followed me to the front door.

I slowly unlocked the front door. "Wait here. I need to make sure Percy is out of sight."

I peeked in, but no Percy. "The coast is clear!"

But as soon as we stepped across the threshold and got halfway down the hallway, Holly stopped, stared, and started baying.

Jo and I followed her gaze. King Percy sat on his perch, cleaning himself and taunting Holly from the top of the antique upright piano at the end of the hall.

"Give the puppies to me," she said, holding out her arms, "and you get Percy out of here."

"Are you sure? They are pretty wiggly."

"I had twins," Jo said, "this is nothing."

I transferred the puppies to her arms, then herded the stubborn cat up the stairs to my room. I promised him a few treats later that night if he agreed not to aggravate poor Holly. "She's a stressed new mom," I said, as if he could understand me. "Have some compassion!"

I shut the door behind me, but not quickly enough. "Percy! NO!"

"What's going on?" Jo yelled.

But by the time the last word escaped my friend's lips, her question had been answered by the determined kitty skidding down the stairs. He landed about three feet away from Jo, Holly, and the puppies. The wrinkly canine's eyes locked on to the cat, and Holly pulled out of Jo's full hands.

I ran as fast as I could to stop the impending fight, but

Holly and Percy were faster. It didn't take but a few minutes for the furry duo to wreak havoc on my living room, kitchen, and hallway. Finally, Holly cornered Percy near the backdoor. But when the 20lb cat hissed and clawed at Holly, the giant, slobbery dog turned into an over-sized chicken. She scrambled back to Jo and the puppies.

"You just had to show her who was boss, didn't you?" I scooped up Percy in my arms. "You didn't need to do that. She's just visiting."

Percy purred, unfazed by the entire affair. I took him back upstairs, making sure that he was curled up on the bed before I shut the door firmly behind me.

When I got downstairs, I found the puppies insisting on Holly's attention and lunch.

Jo put the puppies down and they followed Holly over to the make-shift whelping area.

"It's going to be just the right fit," Jo said.

Somehow, Holly knew the repurposed kiddie pool was for her. The blanket was the perfect size and she scratched it into the position she wanted, then circled a few times before settling down. As the puppies moved in to nurse, Holly kept a wary eye on the direction of the stairs.

"Don't worry, girl," I said. "Percy is upstairs for the rest of the day."

The puppies made quick work of their lunch, then Holly cleaned them. The two wrinkly babies made sweet snuffling noises as they tried to get as close to her as they could.

"What are we going to name them?" Jo whispered, as if talking too loudly would break the magical moment in front of us.

"I am not naming dogs that I'm not planning to get attached to. If you want to adopt one, however…"

"No. I don't want to. But I guess we are stuck with them until they are weaned and old enough to be adopted out."

"Yeah, and I definitely can't leave them outside in the cold.

But Percy is going to be a problem."

"How about the garage? Once this cold snap leaves, you can keep them out there."

"True! And in the meantime, I can put them in my study. It has a door that leads outside, so I won't have to walk them through the house."

"Sounds like a good plan to me!"

It wasn't long before Holly and her puppies were asleep in a heap.

"I'm gonna take a cue from the pups," Jo said, waving as she headed toward the front door. "Nap time."

"Me, too, but I have to do some laundry first. Also, I want to text Anna and make sure she's okay. After this morning's blow-up, well, I'm concerned about her"

"Oh yeah! You never told me what you found out!"

I explained the little bit of info I'd gleaned from Luna. "… and that's when Sebastian's wife sauntered in, telling him that she had paperwork for him to sign. She was not a happy camper."

"Oh! I saw her outside! She was giving Kevin an ugly look. I guess he's not her kind of people."

Twenty-two-year old Kevin Clark had helped lots of folks in Craven over the last few years since graduating high school. He did yard work and was good with overall handy-man type things. But when some of his clients' items disappeared last year—Kevin became the missing link. No one pressed charges, but they stopped hiring him when everyone put two and two together.

"I didn't see him come in," I said.

"That's because he didn't. At first I thought he was scoping out the unlocked cars. But then I realized he'd stopped at Luna's and put something in the front seat."

"How did you know it was Luna's car?"

"She's at the café all the time and her license plate is cute: Moonpie. It's a nod to her name and her favorite food," Jo said. "She comes in for a slice of pie every Friday afternoon.

Interestingly, the last two Fridays she's had company. And her company happened to be the person putting stuff into the front seat of her car."

"Kevin? Really?" I thought about the two of them—and it made lots of sense.

Kevin and Luna both had multiple tattoos and piercings and seemed to be mad at the world. Maybe they wanted to be mad at the world together. *Weirder things had brought people together.*

"Didn't Luna graduate with Suri?" I asked.

"Yup," Jo said. "But they never ran in the same circles. Suri tended to want to stay out of trouble. Luna seemed to run towards it."

Jo and I ate lunch while talking for another two hours about the morning's events and how it all worked together.

I yawned, then so did she.

"It's almost 2 o'clock!" Jo said. "My nap is long overdue."

"Same. Morning came way too early today."

After Jo left, I grabbed the purple and black crocheted blanket from the chair and snuggled up on the couch. My mom was great at crochet and made me something new every year, but this was the blanket I got the year I left for my first overseas teaching job at 30 years old. The blanket had traveled with me for 10 years in Scotland, Ireland, Wales, all over Europe, and then back home to NC. I worked 5 years at ASU as a creative writing instructor, then got the job at the Craven Gazette. I wrapped the blanket around me and felt the beautiful weight of the years I'd been able to spend doing what I loved.

Just as the hound family in the corner had already done, I felt myself relax, then prayed for a peaceful sleep for all of us.

A strange sound woke me from a weird dream about bears, banshees, and blind dates. I looked around, my eyes adjusting to the afternoon light streaming through the side window. The puppies whimpered in the corner, but Holly was gone. A crash from the kitchen signaled her location.

"Noooo!"

I jumped off the couch, smacking my right leg on the small side table. I ran through the pain and reached the kitchen just in time to see the conniving canine chowing down on trash-can cuisine.

Without a thought, I ran over, held Holly's head with one hand, stuck my hand in her mouth, and pulled out a chicken bone. When I turned around, I saw more kitchen carnage. And on the floor in front of the stove? The brownie plate—licked clean.

I picked up the phone. "Jo—we have another problem."

Ten minutes later, the puppies were snuggling with the boys on the couch. They waved as Jo and I headed out to the door. They'd finished their school work and dewormed the pigs, but Mr. Fisher said they could help him tomorrow with his animals.

"Shouldn't we call first to make sure someone is at the clinic?" Jo asked. She held open the back door of my truck's king cab while I put Holly in the backseat and secured her. The truck was over 20 years old, but it was more reliable than most modern vehicles.

Jo continued. "It's almost 5:30 and we won't get there until closer to 6. Also, according to the sign I saw today, they close at 3:30 on Fridays."

"Yeah, but remember what Suri said? Sebastian was upset because he had to work overtime with a lot of paperwork."

"I'm sure his day will feel much more productive to have two hysterical women show up on his door with a dog who may—or may not—be sick."

"Look—Suri said *no* chocolate, but Holly ate the four brownies that were left on the stove. You used milk chocolate and dark chocolate in that batch, Jo." I held up two fingers. "Not one…but two types of chocolate!"

"Fine. but did the chicken bone have grapes and onions on

it? If not, why in the world did you put your hand inside of that dog's mouth?"

"I read the papers that Suri gave us. Bones are bad for dogs, too."

"My grandma had dogs when I was growing up. They ate anything and everything my grandma gave them. I think you're being paranoid."

"But if Holly dies and we didn't at least try to get her to the vet," I said, "do *you* want to have to tell the boys?"

Jo breathed in sharply, glaring my way. "That's below the belt."

"Well? Do you? 'Cause I'm not gonna do it!"

For a moment, neither of us spoke. Then Jo sighed and climbed in beside Holly and patted the back of my seat. "What are you waiting on? We've got a vet to get to!"

While I tried not to get a speeding ticket, Jo called the office—three times.

"I keep getting his voice mail," she said. "What if he's not there?"

"Then we call Suri. Maybe she'll know what to do."

"We should have called her first!"

"Probably," Jo said dryly, "but it's a little late now."

When we pulled into the parking lot, there was a sole vehicle: Sebastian's signature Hummer in his clearly marked parking spot.

"Told ya!" Jo said.

"For once, I'm glad you were right." Holly, on the other hand, didn't seem to care either way. The trip had been unremarkable, other than Holly's rumbling stomach and occasional gaseous emissions, causing us to roll the windows down for over half the ride.

"She stinks to high heaven but I don't think she's in pain," Jo said. "I really do think she's going to be okay."

"True, but I'd rather be safe than sorry." I tried to help Holly get out of the car with dignity, but it didn't work. Holly's long limbs made her trip over the leash and land on my feet.

"You're about as graceful as I am," I said, brushing the dirt off of her fur.

"Let me do the talking." Jo held up her wallet. "If he doesn't want to help us, he might need the same form of persuasion that Luna did this afternoon."

I pointed to Sebastian's giant vehicle. "Do you really think he needs an extra $20?"

"Hmmmm. Then maybe we can turn on the water works? Or maybe we remind him that you can write a horrible review of his clinic?"

"I don't work for the paper anymore, remember?" I said, "But even if I did, blackmail is not on my list of professional duties."

"Um, Tori?" Jo pointed to the slightly open front door. "Maybe he just forgot to close it behind him?"

"And just in case he didn't, maybe you should call Hank."

"Not yet," Jo said. "I don't want to add more to his plate if there's nothing really wrong."

"Fine—but we stick together!"

The lobby was black, but a small light shined somewhere down the hallway.

"Sebastian?" I called his name a few times.

No answer.

"This feels a little creepy," I said.

"He's probably just deep in his paperwork and didn't hear us."

"But we could hear the yelling from his office earlier today. So he should be able to hear us now!"

We walked down the hallway until we found his office, located beside the exit door. A brass plate bearing Sebastian's professional name hung from a wire basket, which hung securely on the door frame. There was a light shining out from under the door.

"Hello?" I said.

No one answered.

I turned the handle, and pushed the door open. "He's not here." I started to walk in, but Holly moved in the doorframe, blocking my entrance. It was then that I noticed her hackles were standing on end.

"This isn't good," I said.

"Maybe she's just smelling all the other animal smells from earlier today," Jo said. "She is a bloodhound. She probably has a fantastic sniffer."

Suddenly, we heard the jingling of the bells that hung over the front door lobby.

Holly pulled on her leash, away from Sebastian's office, and led us back to where we'd started.

"Whoa!" Jo said, but Holly didn't listen. She just kept on running.

"Maybe she's caught his scent! Sebastian?"

"Not Sebastian—Duncan Williams," someone said. "And the police are on the way."

We stopped, face to face with a tall, handsome, and angry looking stranger.

"Duncan Williams? As in Dr. Williams?" Jo started laughing. "This should be interesting."

"Did you hear me?" he asked. "I said that I've called the police."

"You didn't need to do that," I said, pointing to Holly. "We're here because of an emergency."

"Save it for the cops," he said.

"I can understand how bad this looks, but let me start over. I'm Tori Mulligan. This is my best friend, Jo." Then I pointed to the hound dog beside me. "And this is Holly. She's a rescue."

"And how is that relevant?" Dr. Williams stood in front of us and crossed his tanned arms. He had a face full of scruff, but it made his gray-green eyes pop.

"Holly ate chocolate and tried to scarf down a chicken," I sputtered, trying to make his unimpressed scowl disappear. "We brought her in to make sure she's going to be okay. We aren't here to loot the place."

"And I'm just supposed to take your word for this?"

"Yes. Yes, you are," Jo interjected. "But it would make the whole situation much easier if Sebastian was here to vouch for us."

"I don't see him anywhere and I'm not inclined to believe the story of two intruders."

Holly seemed to understand what was going on and inched up close to Duncan. He bent down, held out his hand, and waited.

Holly covered his hand in slobber, just as she had done to me when she first showed up on my porch. "A stray, huh? She's pretty friendly and tame for a dog that doesn't have a home."

I watched as he gently scratched under Holly's chin. The stern and stressed-out doctor looked to be about my age, maybe a smidge older. His wavy black hair had streaks of silver running through it. If he wasn't getting on my nerves at that moment, I would have thought he looked distinguished.

"Where did you find her?" he asked, breaking into my thoughts.

"It's a long story, but she found me, then Jo's sons found her puppies. We were told to bring them in if we had any problems."

"She looks fine to me. Where are her puppies? And how did you get in after hours? I thought they closed at 5?"

"Actually," I said, "it's 3:30 on Fridays. And we got in because the door was open."

"You aren't exactly making your case any better," he said. "It's almost 7pm." He looked at his watch. "But if your story is true, where is Sebastian? And why hasn't he come out to back up your story? With all the racket we've been making, he's obviously not in the building."

"Not to be crude, but maybe he got sick and is in the bathroom," I said. "Or maybe he's out back?"

"Or what if he's hurt somewhere?" Jo continued my train of thought. "I saw this show last week where a guy had been attacked in his office and was only saved because the night cleaners came in early."

Duncan cleared his throat. "You know you're not making yourselves look any better."

"Wait…what?" Jo looked confused. "We aren't trying to make ourselves look good or bad. We are just here to help Holly!"

A horrible odor filled the air. Jo and I both pulled our shirts up over our noses and giggled like two kids.

"Do intruders usually bring a gassy bloodhound to tag along on their break-ins?" I asked. "Cause if they do, this dog is missing her calling."

"I'm beginning to think she ate a skunk instead of brownies," Jo quipped.

Duncan uncrossed his arms and ran his hand through his hair, no longer holding back his laughter. "If you are burglars, you are the worst I've ever seen."

"We could be burglars if we wanted to be!" Jo said with fake outrage. "We just choose to use our creative energies for good."

I parked myself on the floor next to Holly. The problem of the missing Doctor was worrisome, but the more pressing issue for me was laying in my lap at the moment.

"Since you believe us, can you please take a look at her?" I asked. "Sebastian is obviously unavailable for our impromptu visit."

"Maybe someone picked him up and took him out for supper," Jo said. "It is about that time."

"I wasn't thinking about food until you said something," I said. "Thanks, a lot."

As Duncan leaned down and checked on Holly's stomach and vitals, I noticed how at peace Holly seemed. Even when Duncan used his stethoscope to check her vital signs, the sweet canine mama didn't seem to mind.

"Was it dark chocolate?" he asked.

"Yes. And milk chocolate," I replied. "About four brownies

worth."

"How much does she weigh?"

"As of this morning, she's 102 pounds."

He poked around her belly a bit more, then gave her a good scratch. "She might feel a little sick tonight and tomorrow, but even with that amount of chocolate, I think she will be fine. But just in case, we should probably induce vomiting. That, however, will require medicine. Once we find Dr. Westminster we can go from there." He sounded serious, but also impressed. "You did the right thing by bringing her in. If she was a smaller dog, that chocolate could have done much worse damage."

"But she's still nursing the two puppies. Will it hurt them?"

Before he could answer, the front door burst open.

"FREEZE!" a familiar voice ordered.

Holly ran up to Hank while Jo and I put up our hands in the air with little enthusiasm.

"Hi, Sweetie," Jo said, unbothered by the gun being pointed at us. "How was your lunch?"

"Hi Hank!" I said. "Long time, no see."

Duncan's hands were fully in the air, and he was fully confused. "What am I missing here? And why does this sound like a reunion instead of a police intervention?"

Hank holstered his gun. "I'm gonna take a wild stab in the dark and say that you're Duncan Williams, right? New vet in town? And the one who called in the burglary?"

"Yes, but I only called because of those two," he replied calmly. "And now I feel at a disadvantage. You all seem to know more about me than I do you."

Hank shook Duncan's hand. "I'm Hank Parker, husband to Jo and neighbor to Tori." Hank then pointed to Jo and me. "And all you need to know about these two is this: they are trouble makers—but it seems that you've already figured that out for yourself."

"Yeah, your warning is a little late," Duncan said, smiling, "but thanks, anyway."

"We do tend to get in a bit of trouble," I said, "but not with the law."

"Not usually," Jo corrected.

Hank smiled and pulled out a notebook. "Now that the niceties are out of the way—if you two lovely ladies will please explain why you are trespassing, then I might not arrest you. Talk fast. I just took lasagna out of the oven at the station."

I held up my hand. "I can explain. It all started when Holly decided to take a chance on chocolate..." I explained again how we ended up at the clinic after hours and described Duncan's appearance on the scene around 6:30.

"Hang on a second..." Jo cocked her head to the right, as if a heavy idea had suddenly struck her, knocking her off kilter. She pointed to Duncan. "If closing time is 3:30 on Fridays, why are you here? We were told you didn't start work until Monday."

"Word really does travel fast in a small town," he said with a smile. "Sebastian texted me this afternoon and said come on down and get my office ready. I was in the middle of unpacking some boxes and putting my bed together. He said to just come when I could, as long as it was before 8pm. He needed to give me my key."

"And *where* is Dr. Westminster?" Hank asked. "His Hummer is out front."

"That's the million-dollar question," Duncan said.

"We've called his name and made plenty of noise," I added. "If he was here, he would have answered by now. Don't you think?"

"Makes sense to me." Hank wrote something down in his small notebook, then walked down the long, main hallway with a purposeful stride.

Jo, Duncan, Holly, and I followed suit.

"He may have gone to check on the big animals," Duncan said. "Sebastian told me that they sometimes have horses and other livestock outback."

"Maybe you're right. Maybe he used the emergency exit," I

said, pointing toward the door.

Hank put his hand on his gun holster, but his gaze was directed toward Jo and me. "Stay here."

Jo ignored his directive and started to follow, but Hank wasn't having any of it.

"I'm serious, honey. You and Tori stay here. Something doesn't feel right." Hank looked at Duncan and raised an eyebrow. "Care to be an honorary deputy for a bit?"

"I thought you'd never ask," Duncan said. "Lead the way."

"Hey now..." Jo's expression did not exude unicorns and sunshine. "What about us?"

"You have the hardest job of all," Hank said, as he walked out the door with Duncan. "Stay out of trouble." Then he pulled the exit door shut behind them.

"Can you believe those two?" Jo crossed her arms and narrowed her dark brown eyes. "Acting as if we are poor, helpless females! Who says we can't help find a missing person?"

"Um Jo? Holly's gone, too!"

We searched the hallways frantically for the furry, third member of our party for the next few minutes.

"For such a big dog, she sure does know how to sneak away quietly," I said.

"Probably just exploring the place. She is a hound dog, ya know. Her nose leads the way."

"That's what worries me. I don't want her getting into anything else that could hurt her. Let's check the rooms on this hall."

Jo fanned herself dramatically and batted her eyes. "But will we be able to stay out of trouble? What if Sebastian and Holly are being held hostage by a mutant herd of angry horses? Whatever will we do without Duncan and Hank to protect us?"

"We can be salty about it later...right now we need to find Holly!"

We checked the unlocked rooms, including the break room and x-ray room, and both bathrooms.

"We should check the rooms behind the office and down the other hall."

"Shhhh," Jo whispered. "I can hear her! That way!" She pointed toward the front office space. We snuck closer, being careful not to spook her. "There she is! Grab her!"

I hustled to catch her, but Holly snatched something from the low-rise cabinet, then scooted out of my grasp and dashed back into the hallway. We chased her down the second short hallway, and the last door on the right was open. Beside the door jamb was a "radiation danger" sign...but Holly couldn't read. She ran in anyway, then slid under a table in the far right corner of the room, tearing into the treasure she'd snagged from the office table.

"I'm not sure what that is," Jo said. "but she sure seems to like it!"

"But what if it's a chocolate candy bar or something?" As I moved in to snatch the food from Holly, she scooted out from under the table. Then she zigged, zagged, and made it across the room with the snack still firmly in her mouth.

When I finally got her cornered, Holly plopped in front of the closet and spit out an empty wrapper.

"No ma'am!" I said, giving her a good back rub. "Are you just trying to make yourself even sicker?"

Jo scooped up the wrapper and read the ingredient list. "Beef, corn, whey..." She turned it over and looked on the front. "It's beef jerky for dogs, Tori. Perfectly safe."

I didn't reply. Instead, my focus was on Holly and the fact that her nose was stuck to the bottom of the closet. Suddenly, she started scratching at the door and baying. A shiver ran down my spine.

I turned the closet door handle and opened it a smidge; the door felt as if something heavy was pushing on the other side. I pulled the door a little bit more and—

Sebastian Westminster's lifeless body rolled out of the closet, landing at our feet.

Jo screamed and jumped back, pulling me with her, and Holly's bay had turned into a whimper.

I swallowed hard, trying to find any moisture in my mouth. "You better call Hank," I whispered. "They are definitely looking in the wrong direction."

It didn't take long for Hank's police back-up to get there and shuffle us out of the building. Jo, Duncan, Holly, and I stood back as the investigating team took over the scene. The vet's office was blocked off by "crime scene" tape and they were taking pictures of everything.

Hank and two of the other policemen were deep in conversation. They kept looking over at us and shaking their heads.

"I don't think this counts as not getting in trouble," Jo whispered.

"From what I've heard tonight, Sebastian didn't seem to be the nicest of guys," Duncan said dryly. "But I didn't think you'd resort to this."

"You know we didn't kill him!" Jo's loud whisper garnered a quick glance from her husband. She lowered her voice a bit. "It's not every day that we find a dead body around here, and this is definitely a first for me!"

I saw the smirk on Duncan's face. He'd gotten under Jo's skin pretty easily. She was usually the one who did the teasing.

My phone buzzed and I looked at the caller ID; I pushed it to voice mail. It was not an appropriate time to tell my mom that I'd found a dead body. But I'd never been the kid who could keep secrets from her parents; I'd call her as soon as I could.

"Speaking of criminal behavior," Duncan said, "when we were looking out back, Hank let it slip that you were his first arrest."

"He might have over-sold that story," I said. "I was young, stubborn, and determined to change the world."

"For some reason, I don't find that surprising." A small smile crossed Duncan's face again. "It sounds like an interesting tale."

Truth be told, I was never arrested, just detained for trespassing—and got a good talking to. The best part? My "almost-arrest" ended up bringing Hank and Jo together. I was about to share that part of the story, but Hank walked over, interrupting the weird foray into my past. He looked very concerned.

"It's late and we still have a ton of work to do here before we can leave. I'll need all of you to come to the station tomorrow and give an official statement."

"Me, too?" Jo asked. "Can't I just give it to you over breakfast?"

"Especially you. I can't show you any special treatment during the investigation. So Florence will be taking your statement tomorrow to make sure there is not even a whiff of impropriety." Hank flipped through the notebook in his hand. "I need to find Sebastian's wife and break the news."

I felt Jo giving me a sideways glance.

"I saw that," Hank said. "Do you know something that I need to know, Josephine?"

Oof. He used her full first name. He only pulled that out when he was in work mode or they were mad at each other.

"I can honestly say that I did not talk to his wife or hear anything she said in the clinic," Jo replied, keeping her face as solemn as possible.

"Uh-huh." Hank sighed. …then gave me a questioning look.

"How about you, Tori?"

I shrugged, hoping my face was as stoic as Jo's. "I don't know anything for sure. I just know that she didn't seem to be a happy camper this morning, so it's best if you ask her directly."

I didn't even mention Anna's outburst. I figured that was better coming from her first, too.

"And you, Duncan?"

"I just found out where the restrooms are," Duncan said. "I certainly don't know any office gossip. If Holly could talk, she'd be far more help than me."

"Well," said, Hank, "I'm thinking about borrowing Holly for the investigation."

"I doubt she'll be able to tell you anything," I said, laughing. "She's not yet mastered anything but 'woof'."

"Funny. Real funny." Hank rolled his eyes and pointed to the taped off room. "Obviously she has an excellent nose and might be able to help us out at some point."

Homeless hound to Police dog? That wouldn't be too bad, I thought.

One of the other officers held up his hand to get Hank's attention.

"Give me a minute!" Hank shut his notebook and sighed, then stared at all of us for five, serious seconds. "Tomorrow morning at the station—8am."

Hank leaned in toward Jo and she kissed him on the forehead. "Be careful," she said, "I'll put a plate for you in the fridge."

Jo, Duncan, and I chatted as we walked Holly back to my truck. As Holly stopped long enough to scratch something on her backside, it hit me that I still didn't know what to do about the puppies.

"Duncan, you never answered my question about the puppies—should we let Holly keep nursing or should we use bottles?" I asked. "And what about inducing her to throw up? Don't we need medicine?"

At that moment, Holly started acting weird. She dropped her

head, took a few steps, then stopped. She did this three or four times, all the while opening and closing her mouth like her jaw was about to unhinge—making the same noise Percy does every time he has a hairball. Then she inched closer to Duncan…and hurled. She barely missed his boots.

"Poor baby!" I said.

"The answer to your second question is no," he said calmly, taking a few steps back. "That should do the trick. As for your first question, bottle feed for a few days. The toxins could still be present in her milk supply. Holly won't be happy about it, but it's better to be safe than sorry." He explained what we needed for the hungry pups. "If they'd let me back in the office, I might could find some supplies. But…"

"Yeah, that's a problem," Jo said, "and all the stores are closed."

"Maybe Mr. Fisher can help! He had a litter of puppies a few months ago and the mom died," I said. "So maybe he still has the supplies."

"Who is Mr. Fisher?" Duncan asked.

"The owner of the smartest bull in town," I said.

It didn't take me long to text Mr. Fisher, so I explained about his farm while I waited on a response. "Moodini is the sweetest bull you'll ever meet. But he likes to escape every chance he gets and nothing Mr. Fisher does can contain him. Moodini never goes far, but my property is his favorite place to roam."

"So what you're saying is…Moodini is bullheaded?"

Jo and I both groaned at his pun.

My phone dinged. It was a reply from Mr. Fisher. "He says he'll drop off some bottles on my porch in the next ten minutes. He's got an unopened can of formula, too."

"As long as it's in date, one can should be plenty for the next few days," Duncan said.

"Whew!" Jo said. "Crisis averted!"

"I need to apologize," Duncan said. "I'm sorry for calling the cops on both of you back there. We had a lot of issues with break-ins at my last job. Usually drug-addicts looking for whatever they could find."

"Drug addicts?" Jo asked. "What in the world could they possibly find attractive in a veterinary office?"

"You'd be surprised," Duncan replied. "Some of the medicine we use is considered off-label and can be used by humans, too. Addiction can make people do weird things."

I thought back to my brother and the war he'd waged on his own addictions...and lost. I didn't want to open that can of worms, though, so I quickly changed the subject. "Sorry to swerve the subject—but I'm starving."

"And my stomach just growled in solidarity," Jo said. "How about we swing by and grab something from the café and eat at your house? If there's any Hot Russian Tea left, I can snag that, too." She turned her attention to Duncan. "Would you like to join us, sir?"

I whipped my head to the right and hoped she was the only one seeing my glare.

"I don't want to intrude," Duncan said. "I can just grab more food from JT's Truck Stop. But I'll gladly take a rain check."

I felt like a jerk.

"You wouldn't be intruding." The words slipped out of my mouth before I could stop them. *What am I doing? My mama raised me to be hospitable—and he's new in town. Nothing wrong with being kind.* "No one should have to endure JT's food more than once in their lifetime. Besides, it's been a long day for you, too, and Jo's food is the absolute best."

"Plus," Jo said, "you should go ahead and meet the puppies. They are going to be your clients soon."

"You've twisted my arm—and my stomach thanks you!" He pushed his glasses back on his face. "What's the address?"

"Well, I have to swing by the café to grab the food, but Tori needs to get home to feed the puppies ASAP." Jo paused only long enough to take a breath. "What if Tori and Holly ride with you and show you the way? You're not from around here, so it can get very confusing in the dark. Some of our street signs aren't on google maps."

"I'm okay with that if you are?" he asked, looking directly at me.

I handed the leash to Duncan and held up my first finger. "Excuse us just a minute." Then I grabbed my best friend by the arm and led her out of earshot.

"We just found a dead body, and you're trying to play matchmaker?" I paused, then took a deep breath. "Given the circumstances, don't you think this is a little...weird?"

"Seriously?" Jo put her hand to her chest as if she'd just been shot. "I'm hurt that you would think that about me. I'm not that callous."

She sounded hurt...but I wasn't fooled. "This is me you're talking to, Jo."

"Fine," she said, dropping the fake emotional distress. "But don't play the "dead body" card. You write obituary columns and then turn around and write about the best doughnuts in town."

"But the dead people in the obituaries have never fallen out of a closet and landed on my feet!"

"Fair." Jo sighed, then put both hands on my shoulders and looked me in the eye. "It's not the dead body that's bothering you the most, T. And we both know it." She nodded toward Duncan. "I know why you don't want me to set you up with anyone, so I'll stop. But if first impressions mean anything, he does seem like a decent human being. You've always tried to make outsiders feel welcome—so here's your chance."

"But what if he's a weirdo? I didn't bring my Taser."

"I don't think you'll need a Taser. Look."

I followed Jo's gaze. Duncan was bent down, talking to Holly and rubbing her belly. She seemed happy to have his attention, and he seemed happy to have hers.

"See? He's really good with Holly and she seems to like him," Jo whispered. "And you know that dogs are usually very good judges of character, even if we aren't."

She had a point.

"Fine. Holly and I will ride with him. But if he starts foaming at the mouth or something…"

"You make him sound like a werewolf. But hey, if the fur fits..."

She always knew how to make me laugh. I could never stay mad at her for long.

Jo held out her hand, and I reluctantly dropped the keys in it. We both strolled back over to Duncan.

"See y'all in about 30 minutes," Jo said. Then she waved, climbed in my truck, and promptly sped out of the parking lot toward town.

Duncan, Holly, and I stood there for a minute, but Duncan broke the silence. "How about we get home to those hungry puppies?"

"Yes. That." I took Holly's leash, secured her in the backseat, then climbed in the front of his old Chevy truck. "It's not far from here, but I hope you don't get car sick. It's a bit curvy."

"I'll be fine. Which way?"

I gave him a quick round of directions. "We should be there in about 20 minutes."

"Okay," he said, "but I need to clear something up."

"What's that?"

"I promise that I don't drool, bite, or get car sick. And I have never, ever foamed at the mouth."

"Huh?" *Oh.* He'd overheard my description to Jo. "Um… sorry about that."

I was glad it was dark so he couldn't see my red face.

Duncan laughed. "You don't need to apologize for anything. I know that I'm not a weirdo, but you don't. And I get it. If it helps, most of my friends and family don't think I'm a weirdo, either."

"Most?"

"My Uncle Porter thinks I'm weird because I don't like Red

Velvet cake, tomato sandwiches, or Duke's mayonnaise."

"I'm with you on the tomato sandwiches and red velvet cake. But if you don't like Duke's—" I said, unable to stifle my laugh, "then your uncle is right; you're definitely a weirdo."

For the next few miles, we bantered about mayo and its place in southern cuisine, interspersed with my occasional directions. We drove by a plethora of farms, fields, and wineries, including the Scott Winery, the Smith Family farm, and the oldest church in town, Diggs' Chapel. A minute or so later, we came to a T-Stop, across from the Sharpe Strawberry farm.

"Is that what I think it is?" Duncan asked, pointing to the field across the road. "If not, I may need to get my glasses changed asap."

I didn't even have to look up. I knew exactly what he was asking about. In the middle of Billy Dicken's old corn field stood a giant wooden silhouette of a "Wood Booger" (aka Sasquatch), surrounded by three wood and metal baby sasquatch silhouettes. Duncan's car lights hit them at just the right angle and made the art pop.

"Take a right here. And yes…it is what you think it is. We have several of those pieces around town. It started out as a joke, but now the town counsel uses them to draw in tourists and get them to explore the area."

"It's certainly a unique way to interact with your public."

"It gets even more interesting in October when we have the Wood Booger Festival."

"Wood Booger Festival? That sounds…different."

I heard the laughter in his voice.

"It's a lot like other Sasquatch festivals around the state, and it's actually a lot of fun! We have pumpkin-chunkin', a wood-booger costume contest, and plenty of vendors willing to sell you stuff you don't need."

He slowed down near Cardinal Lane. "Do I turn here?"

"No, turn left on the next street, Brevard Street. My house is the last one on the left. Please ignore the bags and boxes of stuff on the front porch. Goodwill hasn't yet picked it up."

"Decluttering?"

"Something like that." I didn't mention that it had been a year and a half since I'd started unpacking and I still wasn't done. That detail seemed unnecessary.

"Before I moved, I did the same thing," he said. "Letting go was hard. My daughter helped me sort it all and decide what I really wanted to bring with me. She just turned 25 and has started her own company. She helps folks get organized." He paused for a moment. "If her mom could see her now, she would be ecstatic. She was always trying to get me to purge."

For a moment, I saw him rub his ring finger. But there was no ring, just a very strong tan line. I wondered how long ago he'd stopped wearing it. I understood the language of grief, and he was speaking it. I wondered what happened to his wife, but I wasn't about to ask.

"Are we close yet?" he said.

"My house is the next one on the left. There's a sign out front, so you can't miss it."

He turned at the giant B&B sign by the road: *Nestled Inn, established 1976.*

We drove down the dirt and gravel road that led to the Inn. It was about 1/10 of a mile, but felt longer. When we arrived at the end of the tree-lined road, he did a double take.

"This is your house? It's a wee bit bigger than I imagined. Is there anywhere particular I should park?" he asked.

"Pull around the driveway and park in front of the porch," I said. "And yeah. It's pretty big." *Especially for one person, a cat, and three visiting canines.*

Holly whined as soon as we got her out of the car. Grady and Booker were waiting on the front porch with the pups.

"These little guys are hungry. They've been acting like they've not eaten all day!"

I scooped up the box Mr. Fisher had left on my doorstep. It had a note on top: *Call me if you need anything!*

*"*I hope you're hungry, too," I said to the boys. "Your mom is bringing enough for a small army."

"I thought she was on a date with Dad," Booker said. "Weren't they going to a play or something after you took Holly to the vet?"

I avoided the question and introduced Duncan to the teens.

"Dr. Duncan Williams, this is Booker and Grady, Jo and Hank's sons. Grady and Booker this is Dr. Duncan Williams. The newest vet at Valley View Veterinarian Clinic."

The boys and Duncan shook hands, then we all went inside.

As I opened the box, Duncan explained about dark chocolate, dogs, and the problem with Holly's milk.

"I can feed them," I said to the boys, "or you two can."

Grady and Booker jumped at the chance.

I thought Holly was going to be upset about the situation, but like most tired moms, she seemed relieved to have a moment to herself. While Grady and Booker fed her babies, she plopped in the bed and went straight to sleep.

It didn't take long for the pups to finish and fall asleep, too.

"You'll need to keep an eye on them or they'll try to latch on, but don't let them do it for at least three days," Duncan said. "They are still babies, though, so she might not be happy with you about it."

"Guess my next job is constant puppy-sitter?" I looked at the sleeping mama and wondered how upset she would be if I kept her babies from her.

"At this age," Duncan said, "they can be fed every four hours or so and should be weaned soon."

I looked at my watch. "I might need some help tonight, boys. Would you be interested in spending the night and helping out with the pups?"

They both agreed.

"I am trying hard not to get attached," Booker said. "But I've already come up with a list of names."

"Speaking of names," Duncan said, clearing his throat. "I

have to apologize, guys. I'm having a very hard time telling you apart."

"No worries. It won't take long once you've been around us for a little while. But for the record, I was born first and I'm better at math than Booker."

"If we're setting the record straight," Booker said, touching his perfectly brushed hair, "then you should know that I'm the better looking twin, and better at everything else."

"As long as there won't be a quiz later, I think I'll be okay." Duncan looked over at the now satisfied puppies. "Other than being identical twins, looks like you also have a gift for taking care of animals. You've done a great job tonight."

"We're both thinking about going into veterinary medicine and opening our own clinic one day," Grady explained. "Dr. Westminster's is the only one in town. Dad says they could use some competition."

"Your dad makes good sense. So if you're serious about it and want to shadow me sometime…let me know."

"Seriously? I'm not sure Dr. Westminster will be okay with having us around. Our science class got a tour of the clinic one time, but he didn't seem to be the mentoring type."

"Um," I said, "Dr. Westminster isn't exactly on staff anymore."

"Did he retire or something?" Grady asked.

Duncan swiveled in his seat and looked at me.

I didn't know what to say, so I went with the first thing that popped into my head. "It's a long, long story—but Dr. Westminster had an accident."

Both brothers scooted up to the edge of their seat, hanging on our every word.

"An accident, huh?" Booker raised an eyebrow. "Sounds suspicious."

He sounded just like Jo.

"Yeah, you look like mom did the day she accidentally ran over Mr. Fisher's favorite hen," Grady said. "Must have been a really bad accident."

It was a foul fowl memory, but it paled in comparison to what we'd seen together today at the clinic.

"I would tell you," I said, "but I don't want your dad to get mad at me for sharing too much. Doesn't he usually say that crime scene details are not for public consumption?"

"Crime scene?" Grady narrowed his eyes, like he'd just figured something out. "I thought you said it was an accident."

I slapped my hand on my forehead. *So much for keeping it under wraps.*

Thankfully, a beep from the front yard jolted us out of the moment and I felt my phone vibrate with a text. "Your mom's here," I said. "And she needs you to help her bring stuff in."

As the boys headed out, I made my way to the kitchen to get paper plates.

"Can I help with anything?" Duncan leaned on the tiled kitchen island. "I'm good at setting a table."

I pointed to the dishwasher. "Clean forks and cups – top rack."

He hummed while putting out the silverware and tumblers. I thought that I recognized the tune, but didn't want to make him self-conscious. I wondered how he seemed so relaxed in a home he'd never visited before with people he'd just met. *Must be nice.*

Jo and the boys made their way back into the house, with bags of dogfood and people food.

"Make way! Coming through!" Jo plopped her bags on the counter and sighed. "Y'all better be hungry. There's enough here to feed a small army."

"Told you!" I said to the boys.

But she needn't have worried.

Except for the occasional "soooo good" and "pass me a roll, please", there was very little said as we dug into the scrumptious café meal. Thirty minutes or so later, everybody in the party was stuffed…and there wasn't much left.

Holly, on the other hand, had hobbled up to the table with her empty dog bowl in her mouth.

"Do y'all see this?" I asked. "She's asking for seconds!" Mr. Fisher had left her a small bag of food, too.

"Smart girl," Duncan said. "She was definitely somebody's dog."

"I just wish we could figure out who that somebody is," I said, rubbing her long snoot. "You *are* a working mom…so maybe just a little more."

I scooped another cup from the giant bag of food in the corner of the kitchen. The bag of cat food sat right beside it. "Percy might want a refill, too," I announced. "Be right back."

I ran upstairs and checked his bowl, but he had barely touched his food. "I know you're mad that the dogs are still here. But you're gonna have your house back soon."

He rolled over on his back and meowed at me.

"You've been here by yourself a lot today; I'm sorry. I'll bring treats once everyone is gone. K?" As I closed the door behind me, I saw him heading toward his food bowl. *Maybe he'd forgive me…but probably not tonight.*

When I got back to the table, Jo was scooting back from the table and motioning to the boys. "Since y'all are done, go on home and get your sleeping bags, toothbrushes, and whatever else you might need."

"Grady needs some new deodorant," Booker said. "I think he's scaring the puppies."

"Hey now!" Grady punched his brother lightly in the shoulder.

"Stop it!" Jo made a face. "You both smell bad. Get yourselves clean before you make your way back over here, but don't take all night."

"Yes, ma'am!" They said it unison, then continued to punch each other in the arm as they walked toward the door.

"Aren't you forgetting something?" Jo asked. "Here!" She threw the van keys toward both boys, but Grady caught them.

"See you soon, boys!" I said. "Be careful and watch out for crazy drivers!"

Jo started filling up the sink with warm water, but was still in "mom" mode. "Those boys are gonna drive me batty," she muttered.

"Just like their dad?" I asked.

"Just like their dad!"

"Well," Duncan interjected, "speaking from a man's point of view right now, I feel outnumbered!" He pushed himself away from the table. "Can I help with the dishes?"

"No need," Jo replied, holding up a soap-bubble covered hand. "This is sort of my specialty. But maybe you can help Tori put up the leftovers?"

I held up a few different containers that I'd already started filling up. "Would you like anything to take home with you? We've got biscuits, bacon, and cookies."

"No, but I think that's my cue to say 'goodnight,'" he said. "Despite the weird way we met, I've had a lovely evening. Thank you for inviting me."

"I hope that didn't sound like I was shoving you out the door," I said.

"I didn't take it that way at all. I'm tired and tomorrow is going to be a long day." He put his hat and jacket on. "And for the record, you two would make terrible burglars—but you make a mean batch of cookies!"

"And for someone who doesn't like Duke's mayo," I said, smiling, "you'll do in a pinch."

I was glad that he hadn't turned out to be the sourpuss I thought he was initially.

"You don't like Duke's?" Jo asked. "What about Hellman's? As long as you're not a Kraft fan."

He grimaced. "Guilty as charged."

"Oh lawsy! You might have to give up your southerner card for that kind of talk," Jo joked. "People have lost it for less!"

"Well, I'm originally from Pennsylvania, so that's not a

problem." Duncan headed toward the door. "Again…thank you for a lovely end to a very difficult day. I'll see you both bright and early at the police department tomorrow."

I closed the door behind him, then came back inside to find Jo sitting pensively at the table.

"So how do you think Sebastian died?" Jo asked. As long as talk of death didn't involve her family, Jo's love of "all things mystery" kicked into play. "Sebastian was over 6 feet tall and at least 200 pounds. He wouldn't have been easy to move. And dead men can't lock themselves in closets."

"It wasn't locked, just closed. So there is a small chance that he could have been hiding from someone…then just died of a heart attack."

"Has Agatha Christie not taught you anything? This is definitely a homicide."

"I didn't say that you're wrong. But does it bring you comfort to know that a murderer is walking the streets of Craven right now? Because it doesn't make me feel good in the least bit!"

"No. No it doesn't." She nodded to the sleeping dogs in the middle of the kitchen floor. "But you've got a three-way alarm system now. You don't have to worry!"

I heard footsteps on the front steps and a hard knock on the door, but Holly didn't move a muscle, and the puppies stayed snuggled up to her.

"Oh yeah, she's a real watch dog," I said. "Look at her in action."

Jo shrugged. "She can sense who's at the door, so she isn't concerned. That just proves that she knows more than you give her credit for!"

I couldn't argue with Jo when she had her mind made up.

The boys came in with wet heads, backpacks, sleeping bags, and pillows.

"Did you come prepared for a night or a fortnight?" I asked, trying to keep my laughter in check.

Graham held up a bag of chips, dip, and a Tupperware

container. "We have snacks for us…and a little something for Holly, too."

"Is that from my fridge?" Jo asked. "That better not be the beef bone I set aside to make more broth tonight."

"No ma'am," Grady said. "Mr. Fisher called and told us to swing by and pick it up for Holly; it's chicken and rice. He says it's good for upset tummies—in people and dogs."

"Why didn't he call me?" I asked.

"He said you were probably up to your eyeballs in puppy problems," Grady replied.

He wasn't wrong.

By this point, Holly had woken up and had her nose in the air. Then she came over and sat obediently at the twins' feet.

"Can we give it to her?" Booker asked. "We already texted Suri. She says that as long as it's not made with garlic or onion, it should be fine."

"And we already called Mr. Fisher back and asked what was in it—and there was nothing that could hurt her."

The boys' sweet puppy-dog stares and Holly's droopy, tender eyes melted my heart.

"Fine—you can give it to her. But first," I said, pointing toward the back door, "take Holly out for one last walk before bed."

"Yes, ma'am!" they said. "Be back soon!"

While they were gone, I fessed up to Jo. "So I messed up. The boys know about Sebastian. I tried not to tell them, but they are suspicious like you and Hank."

"Don't worry about it. They'd know before the night was over anyway. Besides, they're not babies anymore, even though I want to protect them like they are."

She was right. "By the way, Duncan offered to let the twins shadow him at the clinic."

"I knew I liked him," Jo said. "And I can tell that Hank does, too!"

"I think you're right." Hank was a good judge of character,

most of the time. "Did you see how he acted toward Duncan? I've not seen him warm up to someone that quick in a long time."

It usually took Hank a while to talk to folks he didn't know. He didn't trust easily. Part of it was because of his introverted nature, but the other part was because of his job. On the other hand, Jo could make friends with a porcupine if we put a pair of gloves on her.

"So back to Sebastian," she said. "We all agree that it was *not* a natural death. I didn't see any blood, though, so I'm assuming that he wasn't shot or stabbed."

"But there are plenty of other ways to kill someone without weapons," I said.

"You're right. But who would want to do it…and why?"

"I think there were plenty of people who didn't like him."

"But only one person acted like she would have killed him on the spot yesterday."

"Anna couldn't kill anyone, even if she sounded like she could."

Outwardly, I sounded confident. But inside, my mind was a swirling tornado. *Why had Anna been so mad at Sebastian? Maybe she did have an affair like Luna had suggested.*

Grady and Booker came back in before I could tell Jo what Luna had told me about the affair. I had offered the teenagers the opportunity to take turns sleeping in one of the extra rooms, but they both wanted to sleep in the office with the dogs. They could both fit on the sleeper sofa, but it was older than me, so I wasn't sure how comfortable it would be.

"My back would not be happy," Jo said as we closed the study door behind us. "Neither would my legs, my shoulders, or any of the rest of me."

"Same." I had made the decision many years ago to never sleep on the ground again unless I had no other choice; a sleeper sofa was only one step above that scenario.

For the next hour, Jo and I discussed the different ways we

thought Sebastian may have kicked the bucket.

"Unless there was a goose-egg on the back of his head that we didn't see, I think it was drugs or some sort of poison," I said. "But your husband probably won't tell us. And not even your powers of persuasion can get him to break the law."

"I couldn't even get him to make my last speeding ticket "disappear"."

"At least you can count on him to do the right thing," I said. "There are a lot of men who can never be accused of having integrity." I was thinking about Sebastian, but didn't say it aloud. I was raised not to speak ill of the dead…even if it was the truth.

The grandmother clock on my mantle struck midnight; I stifled a yawn.

"We've got to be at the office by 8am or your hubby might come looking for us."

"Okay Cinderella," Jo said, "but swing by the café and pick me up on your way, please. I have to be at work at 6 to make sure the breakfast shift workers are doing their jobs."

It was going to be a short night.

After locking up, I grabbed a few treats from the pantry for Percy. *A promise is a promise.* I headed up the stairs, wondering how long it would take to get to sleep.

I didn't have to wonder very long.

The morning light shined through the bedroom window, and I hit the morning alarm twice before Percy started curling up under my chin, begging me to get up. I still had an hour or so before I had to pick up Jo and head to the police station.

I snuck in the study and did my best not to wake up the boys or the puppies. Holly, however, was ready for a walk. Afterwards, I got her back in the house and offered a fresh bowl of water and some food. As she ate, I finished up a "to do" list for the boys.

I heard a door open and the shuffling of tired teenager feet.

"Hungry?" I said. "You know where everything is."

They mostly grunted, then shuffled off to the kitchen to find some good breakfast food. They came back with waffles, leftover bacon, and a plate of donuts.

Holly meandered over their way, then sat in between them, drooling.

"Here are the instructions from Duncan about feeding times, and you know where the remote controls are," I said. "Got any questions?"

They assured me they would text if they needed help. "It's Saturday and our rooms are finally clean, so we can stay as long as you need us."

"I have to take a quick shower and get dressed. I owe you both." I ran back upstairs and filled up Percy's food and water bowl, then cleaned his litter box. "And now...time to clean myself!"

He just stared at me for a hard 20 seconds, then meowed.

"Enjoy your breakfast or lay there like a lump on a log," I said. "Your choice."

He yawned, then curled back up into a ball.

"Lump on a log it is."

I had just finished my shower when my cell phone rang. It was Anna.

"Hi Tori," her voice sounded even more upset than it had when she'd sat in my living room and fired me. "I hate to call so early, it's just...I need to talk to someone I trust."

I looked at the clock. I didn't have time to stop and chat. "I would love to talk," I said, "but I'm about to head to the police department. I'm not sure when I'll be back. Can I come by the office this afternoon?"

"Why are you going to the police department?" she sounded very concerned. "Are you okay?"

"I need to give my statement about Sebastian."

"Sebastian? What are you talking about?" She sounded as on

edge as she had in the clinic yesterday afternoon.

Oof. She hadn't heard.

"Well," I said, trying to use the gentlest words possible, "You might want to sit down."

She was quiet, so I kept going.

"Sebastian is dead, Anna." I quickly told her some of what had happened, but left out the gory details. "Suffice it to say, it was not the night he—or we—expected." I sighed as I pulled on my socks and shoes. "If we had just arrived sooner, he might have still been alive."

There was still silence on the other end. I thought maybe the line had gone dead.

"Anna? Are you still there?"

More silence.

"I just can't believe it," she whispered.

"How about I come over once I'm done giving my statement? I'll bring lunch."

"No…I'm sorry. I can't do this today. I just…can't."

Then she hung up.

"Well…that was bizarre," I said to Percy.

Percy, however, didn't seem to care about anything other than snoozing in the sunrays shining through my window.

"At least Holly listens when I talk," I mumbled.

Percy's eyes shot open, and he glared at me—then promptly fell back asleep.

I grabbed my Sherpa-lined denim jacket and headed out the door. Jo was probably getting antsy.

I thought about my puzzling conversation with Anna all the way to the café. Twenty minutes later, Jo buckled in.

"What took you so long?" Jo looked at her watch. "I was sure you'd be early and grab some breakfast."

"Sure you did," I said, recognizing that teasing tone in Jo's voice. "Plus…there were complications."

Jo opened the small cooler in her lap. "Good thing I thought ahead." She whipped out a homemade pop tart pastry. The filling was plum jelly with a scrumptious jelly and sugar glaze. "You can spill the details in between bites."

"**S**o she never told you why she needed to talk to you?" Jo asked.

"Nope. I thought she was calling to say she'd changed her mind about the paper."

"Hmmph. As wacky as she's acting, I don't know that you should go back to that job. I know you love it, but she doesn't seem stable. There's always the vet clinic job, ya know."

"Don't start, Jo."

"I'm just saying that you'd make a much better front desk receptionist than Luna."

"Speaking of Luna," I said. "I thought of something on the way to sleep last night that didn't make sense. Why are they advertising for a front desk person if they already have one?"

"Maybe she needs some time off? Or is quitting? Or maybe they just need extra staff?"

"Or maybe she is getting fired," I said, "but doesn't know it yet. She doesn't seem like the best fit for the job."

"Oooh!" Jo snapped her fingers and pointed, an idea clearly in the works. "Or maybe she knows that she's getting fired. And maybe she is angry about it…angry enough to kill her boss."

"You've already made her into a suspect? That was quick."

"Well, she does take bribes."

"That doesn't make her a murderer," I said. "However, I did hear Sebastian mention something about having her come back that night to bring camera footage, but I'm not sure what that was all about."

Luna wasn't exactly a paragon of virtue, but I wasn't convinced she was a murderer…yet. "Maybe we should talk to her," I said.

"I don't know if we can afford to do that," Jo said, laughing. "We might have to take out a loan."

"You have a point."

"I could always offer her an entire pie if she'd agree to chat with us."

"We should give it a shot. Is there a particular time she comes in?"

"Usually right after the clinic closes."

"Hm…I wonder if she was there yesterday afternoon."

"I don't know, but I can find out." Jo whipped out her phone and pulled up an app. "Equipment has been disappearing around town, so at my husband's behest, I installed one of those doorbell thingees. It's come in handy. We caught a raccoon trying to break in a few nights ago, but he was wearing a mask, so we couldn't identify him."

"Funny. Real funny." Her pun wasn't much better than Duncan's earlier joke about Moodini.

"I can go through all the recordings here." She searched through the footage as we pulled around the next corner. Craven's cramped police department was located at the end of Main St., right after Mr. Fuji's exotic fish store, *The Picky Ichthy*. I parked in the adjacent parking lot across from the Farmer's Market, a local and tourist favorite. It was closed on Sundays, but open the other days of the week, come rain or shine. There weren't a lot of cars here, but the regulars had already been here and gone. It would pick up again around 9:30 or 10, when the tourists decided to roll out of bed and stroll through town.

"The Farmer's Market would be a great place to hang posters about Holly," I said, as we walked past the pumpkin lined sidewalk. "I can get them printed tomorrow. Maybe Mr. Fuji will let us hang some in his store."

"Give me some for the café, too," Jo said. "I bet we'll find her a home in no time."

Hank met us at the door of the police station, but his demeanor was even cooler than the stormy weather coming in. He was definitely in work mode.

"Come on in," he said, "this shouldn't take long."

Duncan was in an uncomfortable looking wooden chair in the far right hand side of the office. He smiled and stood as we came in the room. There were only a few men who still did that sort of thing as a sign of respect for women. I was impressed.

"I know this isn't how you wanted to spend your Saturday," Hank said. "But it's important that we do this by the book." He settled in his chair behind his faux mahogany desk and opened up a folder with the name "Westminster" on it.

"Our team was at the crime scene until well after midnight." Hank rubbed his face and stifled a yawn. "We rarely have violence around here; the last time we had a dead body that wasn't from natural causes was a couple of years ago."

"What happened?" Duncan asked, leaning in and resting his arms on his knees.

"A local man had a run in with his unruly Billy goat and the mountain lion that was trying to eat it," Hank said.

"A billy goat and a mountain lion were the murderers?" Duncan looked to Hank, Jo, and then me. "He's kidding, right?"

"It was less murder," I said, "and more of an unfortunate accident." I'd helped cover the story.

"That doesn't sound like a fun way to bite the dust," Duncan said, "but I don't guess there's ever a fun way to do that."

Hank walked to the door and got the attention of the front desk officer, Florence Dickens—the first and only female on the

Craven police force. "Hey Flo...can you take my lovely wife to one of the other interview rooms and get her statement?"

"Why can't I stay in here with them?" Jo asked.

"The same reason I explained last night—if the chief drops in, I want him to see that we are following the rules to a "T". Interviewing my wife could be seen as a conflict of interest," he said. "The chief has been stressed lately and I don't want to add anything to his load."

Chief Robby Furr had been in his position for at least 10 years longer than Hank had been on the squad. He'd hinted at retirement, but no one knew for sure when that would be. And even though Hank was the senior officer, that didn't mean he'd be a shoo-in for chief when the time came.

"While you are getting Jo's statement, I'll get Tori and Duncan's," Hank said. "Shouldn't take too long."

Jo waved as she followed Florence around the corner and out of sight.

Hank asked Duncan to hang in the lobby while I gave my version of the previous night's events, then we switched places and Duncan gave his. A few minutes later, Hank invited me back into his office to sit as he finished typing up each of our statements.

He was a much faster typist than I expected. "Did Sebastian give you any indication that someone else might have been with him when he called you, Duncan?"

"He seemed really upset and spooked. Said he thought he'd heard someone, but figured it was just the creaking of an old building. When I got there and saw the door was open—and saw Jo and Tori...well, I jumped to conclusions."

"Understandable." Hank pushed a button on his keyboard, then the printer in the corner of his office made a sputtering sound and spit out the papers. He scrounged in the drawer for a couple of pens, then handed us the printed statements. "I need you both to sign those. If anything else comes up or I have more questions, I know where to find you."

I signed my name and shoved it back across the desk.

Duncan did the same.

"I know you didn't know him well, but do you know anyone who might want to hurt Sebastian?" Hank asked, looking at Duncan.

"No, but he did say the sale of the company wouldn't make anyone happy but the two of us."

"Interesting," Hank said. He jotted down a few notes. "So how did you come to be the new partner at the clinic, anyway?"

"We apparently have some mutual friends in the vet business. He heard I was thinking about opening my own practice. So he reached out to me after we met at the regional convention a few months ago. He said he was looking to retire early, and wanted me to buy into the business right away." Duncan shook his head and laughed softly. "Forgive the pun, but Sebastian was like a dog with a bone. He was determined to win me over, and showed me all the profits he'd made in the last ten years."

"That good, huh?"

"Yeah. Very good. And he was prepared to pay my moving expenses and rent a house for me the first year."

"Sounds like a desperate move on his part, but a sweet deal for you," Hank said. "Looks like you took him up on it."

"Actually, I didn't. I don't like to be in debt to anyone or give them a reason to hold something over my head. So I didn't agree to let him pay for my move or my rental. I wanted to do this on my own terms."

Hank smiled. "I feel that."

So did I.

"We signed the initial paperwork two months ago with his lawyer, Todd something. I can't remember his last name," Duncan said. "He told me that he didn't want the staff to know about the buyout. Said it might make them worry about their job security."

That's strange. I'd never known Sebastian to care much about anything or anyone but himself.

"Then how did they know you were coming?" I asked. "Jo told me on Thursday."

"He said he told folks that I'd been hired as a new vet, but didn't want to give details about my partnership until my official first day on Monday."

"You said he wanted you to sign some paperwork. What was it?"

"Maybe tax stuff? Not sure. He did mention something about inventory, but didn't go into details.

"Anything else?"

"Hmmm—all of our conversations have been short and sweet. He didn't share anything important about himself, but I got the distinct impression that he was dealing with some personal stuff. He seemed on edge, even during our phone calls."

Hank jotted down the info in his notebook. "Tori? Got anything to add?"

I bit my thumbnail. I'd tried for many years to stop, but couldn't seem to shake the annoying habit. It was especially frustrating when I wanted to keep something under wraps.

"I've seen that look before—last Saturday night at your dad's Texas Hold'em game, to be exact." Hank stood up and sat on the side edge of his desk. "Care to share with class?"

"Nope," I said. "I'm not a gossip."

"But you are a witness to events that happened the day of the murder. I need to know if anything significant occurred."

He had a point. "Anna and Sebastian got into a small argument. Hardly worth mentioning."

"How small?"

"I mean…um…" I stuttered over my words. "He called her the "b" word, and she slapped him." My voice volume got softer and softer until he had lean in to hear what I had to say.

"Uh huh. Anything else that's hardly worth mentioning?"

"He said that he'd have her arrested if she showed her face there again."

"Her response?"

"She said that he wasn't the only one who could play dirty."

"Sounds like a threat to me," Duncan mumbled.

"A veiled threat…but a threat nonetheless," Hank said. Then he wrote it down in his little notebook.

"You can't really believe that she'd kill him?" I said.

"I dunno," Hank said. "But it does sound like she had a bit of a temper. Maybe it spilled over and she killed him in a fit of anger."

It wasn't a far-fetched idea. But I still didn't believe it.

Hank looked at his notes, then sighed. "I've not been able to find Sophia Westminster, yet." He looked at me. "You said she wasn't happy that morning. What happened?"

"As soon as Sophia sauntered in, she waved some papers around—they seemed to be as good as a leash. Sebastian followed her down the hallway without a backward glance."

"Interesting," Hank said.

Yeah. It was.

We heard laughter and a knock on the door.

Hank opened the door and we met Florence and Jo in the lobby.

"All done," Jo said. "And Florence said she might take one of the puppies when they're ready to be rehomed!"

I did a small happy dance right then and there. "You are my hero, Flo! You'll have to come over in a week or two and pick out the puppy you want. And what if we do lunch, too?"

"I said *might*," Flo iterated. "I still need to think about it."

"Ooh…I'll bring lunch from the café for all of us," said Jo.

"I think you should take one of the puppies, too," Florence replied, looking at Jo and Hank. "You could make it an outside dog."

"Anyway…" Hank cleared his throat, then looked toward Florence's desk. "Got anything else for me remotely related to the case?"

"Not this one." Flo handed Jo's signed statement to Hank and smiled. "I'm catching up on the paperwork for the latest burglary on Friday night. We found a partial bloody print on some broken glass. I'll have it on your desk as soon as the lab gets the results back to me."

"There was a burglary and a murder Friday night?" Duncan grimaced. "I thought small towns were supposed to be wholesome places full of whimsical kindness and colorful locals?"

"I guess it depends on the day," Hank said dryly. "And Friday was more like a weekend in Vegas."

Hank's phone started ringing. He hurried back to his office. "I hope to be home in time for supper," he yelled over his shoulder, "but no promises!"

Duncan walked out with us, but stopped just outside the police station. "I am meeting with my lawyer, Judd Kinston. Do you know him?"

"Yeah! Judd is one of the good guys. Probably one of the most honest people that I know." I'd dated him once in high school, but neither of us had sparks and declared ourselves to be friends, instead.

"An honest lawyer?" Duncan looked surprised. "That's refreshing."

"Hey now!" Jo said. "My dad has been a defense lawyer forever. He doesn't take on many cases these days, but he's the best of the best. He actually mentored Judd."

"I'm glad to know there are still some good ones out there." He held up his car keys and shook them in the air. "I better get going. I'll catch up with you ladies later!"

Duncan headed down the road in a slow jog, then disappeared around the corner toward the direction of the small public parking lot behind the Police Station.

Jo shook her head. "If you ever see me running like that, then you better run too...because I can guarantee you that something is chasing me."

"All I need to do is outrun you," I said, "but we both know that's not gonna happen."

The wind whipped around us, carrying our laughter away with the flying leaves. I was thankful for the scarf I grabbed before I left the house, especially since we needed to run a few errands.

"The Book Nook first?" I asked, knowing the answer.

"Yes, please! Maybe I can find another good cookbook."

"You really need to write your own. You could sell a ton."

"Yeah, I know. And you need to open up the Nestled Inn."

"Maybe one day for both of us…but today is not that day."

The Book Nook had only been around for five years, but it was definitely one of our favorite places. The owner, forty-year-old Allison Clark, always made sure to stock the store with new releases and the books of local authors. And for the last year, she also held an open-mic night on the third Thursday of every month for anyone who wanted to share their work. And if you got to the open mic night soon enough, you could get your name in the drawing for a free book. Those nights were usually packed.

Allison greeted us as we entered. "We just got in some new yoga books and CDs if you're interested?" She sounded cheery, but had puffy eyes and a sad smile.

"Well, we know how to do downward dog," Jo replied, "but we don't know how to feed one."

"Weaned puppies, in particular," I said. "We're clueless."

Allison came out from behind the counter. "I know just what you need. Follow me!"

She led us back down the long biography aisle, took a turn down the fantasy aisle, then past the end caps filled with the latest and greatest best sellers. We stopped at the back right corner bookshelf. "There are several different books on dog care, but most of them have the same info. The ones on the top shelf are the most current."

Allison headed back toward the front of the store, and we started our search. None of the titles sounded interesting until a familiar name jumped out at me. There were three other titles by the same author.

No...it can't be. I checked the back of the book, looked at the bio pic, then handed it to Jo. "You've got to see this."

"Well, well, well!" She read the jacket flap of the book. "So Duncan is an author and a vet? Why doesn't that surprise me?"

"It surprises me a little. He doesn't seem like someone who could sit still long enough to write a book." I didn't see him sitting behind a desk for long periods of time. He seemed more like the outdoorsy type.

"Well, let's buy it and ask him about over supper. If Hank gets home in time, we can all meet at the café." Jo took the lead and we headed toward the front of the store. "The boys won't mind puppy sitting as long as we bring food home for them."

When we walked up to the counter, there was a weird vibe in the air. Allison was blowing out a stick of incense, but the strong aroma didn't quite cover up the other odor. The door to Allison's office opened, and her 22-year-old son emerged.

"See you later, mom." A goofy look covered Kevin's face; his eyes were bloodshot.

"Where do you think you're going?" she asked sharply. "You know the rules."

"They are your rules. Not mine."

Then he stormed out the door, taking part of the sickly sweet smell of marijuana with him.

The slamming of the door made the bells at the top of it clang in momentary anger. Then Jo, Allison, and I watched through the oversized store front window as Kevin jumped into the passenger seat of a black SUV. It squealed out of the parking lot.

Allison rang up the book in silence. "That will be $17.65." she said flatly. And with that, she plopped down in front of her computer and stared blankly at the screen.

It was clear that Allison didn't want any discussion, so Jo

and I left as quickly and quietly as we could. The bells rang behind us, too, but not with the same fervor as they had when Kevin had stormed out.

Back on the sidewalk, we talked in hushed whispers.

"So—Kevin's problems seem a lot more serious than the last time Allison and I chatted."

Jo nodded in agreement. "That boy needs an intervention. He used to be friends with Hank's niece, Suri, but she stopped hanging around him about a year ago."

"I thought he'd been getting some help? Wasn't he sent to in-treatment therapy?"

"Yeah. But being "clean" only lasted a little while. And after a month of being back home, Suri suspected he was doing harder stuff than weed."

"Oh no!"

"Yeah. And when he stole her wallet, well…that was the end of their friendship."

I felt horrible for Kevin and Allison. They had started attending our church when Allison's husband was going through cancer treatments. When he lost his battle a couple of years ago, Kevin seemed to lose his way, too.

"We're here," Jo said, jarring me out of my thoughts. She pointed to the front door of Fred's Feed-Seed-and-Pet Supply. "Holly has no idea how much of a sucker you are, but she will after today."

Over the next half hour, I found treats for Holly and some new toys for Percy. And after a back and forth with myself, I decided to buy a giant dog bed, one that would hold Holly and the puppies—at least until the puppies got a little bigger.

"If we find Holly's owner, then I'll give it to them—or as a gift to whoever adopts her," I explained. "She deserves a comfy place to live, but she can't stay with me forever."

"That's what you keep saying." Jo pointed to a green bin full of dog beds. "The bed on top is huge."

"It's perfect!" I said. "And look! They have special toys over there for puppies!"

"Mm-hmmm," Jo muttered, shaking her head. "We better go before you spend all your savings on your temporary house guest."

At the front counter, Fred didn't look happy. "Cash or check only."

I always forgot he didn't take cards...and I rarely carried cash. I did, however, have at least one check left in the checkbook, but it was in my truck. "I'll be right back!"

I left Jo in the store, rushed down the sidewalk, then headed to the parking lot. My checkbook was deliberately hidden under a pack of gum, a pack of dried up wipes, and some straws at the bottom of the console between the two front seats. My door lock hadn't worked in months; I needed to get it fixed. I stuffed the checkbook in my back pocket, closed the door, the headed toward the crosswalk. My phone rang. It was Anna.

"Hello?"

I heard nothing but quiet sobbing.

"Anna? Are you there?"

More sobbing. Then dead air.

She'd hung up.

I ran back to the truck, then called Jo and told her to meet me out front. "Please ask Fred to hold my stuff. I'll come get it tomorrow. I'll explain when I pick you up!"

When I pulled up in front of the store, Jo was carrying my pet supplies. "Turns out that I had enough cash. You can pay me back later...in cheese straws."

"I can definitely do that." I didn't bake much of anything, except for cheese straws. And every year at Christmas, I made several batches and gave them as gifts. They were Jo's favorite—and she always asked for a double batch.

"Can you drop me off at the café?" she continued. "One of

my staff called in sick and I need to fill in until the next shift. The flu is going around. I just hope none of my other workers get it!"

"Of course, but listen…Anna called again." I explained the situation as fast as I could because Jo's cafe was just around the corner. "She hung up just as quickly as she'd called…but she never spoke."

"Nothing?"

"Not a word."

"She could be in shock about Sebastian's murder."

"Maybe. She seemed genuinely surprised when I shared the news with her this morning," I said. "And did you notice how Hank seemed very interested in Anna's love-life? I think he's making her his top suspect. Even if you don't like her, you can't think she's a murderer."

"You're right…I don't like her. And she did kill the paper. But I can't see her wielding anything other than the sword of perfect grammar."

"I'm going to call her back," I said. "If she doesn't call back, I don't know what I'll do."

The café was packed, so I let Jo out as close to the front of the restaurant as possible.

"Call me later!" she yelled. "I'll need details!"

I stopped at the small, refurbished and repurposed mill house on the corner of Church Street. A brass plate with the words "Craven Mountain Gazette" hung on the door. There were no cars in the parking lot, but I used my key to check inside. Her car could be in the shop again, so maybe Blake had dropped her off.

But Anna wasn't in her perfectly decorated office, the bathroom, or even in the small kitchen in the back. I called her phone again, but she didn't answer. I decided to drive to her house. If she was there, she could just need to talk.

On the way out, I ran into Luna, literally.

"I'm so sorry!" I bent down to gather boxes of cookies, brownies, chips, cheese curds, and other snackish items that I'd knocked out her hand. She'd been to Toasty's Shop and Stock. Toasty's was stocked like most grocery stores, but everything was locally sourced. It was a bit pricier than the "big box" stores—and worth every penny. "I should have watched where I was going."

"Ya think?" her voice dripped with disdain.

For someone who hadn't even hit 30, she sure had a lot of

bitterness oozing from her pores.

"Here." I held out the rescued bag of goodies and offered a smile. "I think I got it all."

"Thanks." She snatched it from my hand, then turned on her heel to go. "Try not to ambush anyone else!"

"Wait!" I ran to catch up. I had an opportunity, I didn't want to waste it. "I have a question for you."

"What?"

"Did you happen to see or hear anything out of the ordinary the afternoon of Sebastian's murder?"

"You mean other than him being slapped by his lover?" She narrowed her eyes. "Are you working with the police?"

"No."

"Then why would I tell you anything?"

She had a point.

"You're right. I'm sorry. I shouldn't have been so insensitive. I'm just trying to digest everything that's happened. It's been a rough few days." I hoped I sounded as empathetic as I did in my head. "And working with Sebastian? Ugh. How did you stand it for so long?"

"I gave my notice last week," she said. "I hated it."

"Why did you hate it so much?"

"Why do you want to know?" Her eyes were still suspicious. I had to come up with something.

"I saw the advertisement for the job in the paper and I'm looking for a career change. This one seems so…interesting!" It wasn't a lie. I was looking for a change. It did look interesting… *but it just wasn't the right job for me*.

"I've read your columns in the paper," she said. "And I don't think you're interested in my job any more than I think Craig is going to make it out alive in your next installment. You're just trying to dig for information. But I know my rights. I don't have to talk to you."

And with that, Luna took off running.

"Well that went over like a ton of bricks," I mumbled to

myself. *We would definitely have to bribe her with pie.*

I texted Jo and let her know what happened. She was busy with the midday morning crowd, but promised to call later. I jumped back in the car and headed toward Anna's house. I was already running later than I wanted to be.

Anna and I were not the kind of friends who had regular dinners together, but we were work friends. Thus I'd only been to her house twice. Both times were when her car was in the shop and she'd needed a ride to the office. I double checked my GPS to make sure I was heading in the right direction.

As I drove, my mind tripped over all the questions forming in my brain about Anna's call. Why didn't she speak? Why was she sobbing? Why didn't she answer when I called back?

I took a right at the Craven Community Garden, then took another left, one road down from that onto Rosebud avenue. Her house was on the right, directly across the street from the statue of Nathaniel Craven, the founding father of the town.

I pulled into her three car driveway and parked beside Anna's gray Mercedes. I walked up to the door and knocked.

No answer.

I peeked in the bay window. Anna's living room was in full view and I could see her laying on the couch. "Anna! Open the door!"

But Anna didn't move.

I prayed and jiggled the door handle—

It was locked.

I ran around the back of the house to see if her back door was unlocked.

"Shoot! This is locked, too!" I started praying and looking around at the windows. I remembered her saying something about leaving them cracked a little for the fresh mountain breeze.

The second window I checked was cracked enough for me to get a handle and pull it the rest of the way open. "Thank you, Jesus!"

I crawled in the window, landing in her mudroom. I tripped

over the end of a rug and caught myself on a metal table.

I ran through the house to her living room. But even with all the noise I'd been making, Anna didn't respond. She was still in the same position I'd seen her through the window.

At first I wondered if she'd picked up the flu and was just sleeping hard. But her skin wasn't hot with fever. I channeled my first aid training and checked for a pulse and breathing. Both were faint, but she was alive.

Then I felt something under my foot. A Jack Daniels bottle top? It matched the empty bottle on the floor. I prayed as I tried to wake her.

She didn't move a muscle. She needed help…and she needed it now.

I tried to use Anna's phone to dial 911, but it was locked with a password. I looked around, but couldn't find a house phone.

I unlocked the front door, then ran to my truck and grabbed my phone out of the passenger seat. As I hurried back up the driveway, I heard a vehicle slow down as it got closer to Anna's mailbox. I turned around, but the black SUV sped off.

My phone rang—it was Hank.

"I'm so glad it's you!" I said. "I'm with Anna and--"

"Perfect!" he said, cutting me off. "I've called her several times but she's not answering. Can you please tell her that I need to speak to her? I was hoping to—"

"HANK!" It was my turn to interrupt. "Anna can't talk. She needs an ambulance. I think she's overdosed!"

"Address?"

"262 Rosebud lane. Her house is directly across from Craven's statue!"

He immediately called out the address to Florence. "Get them over there stat!"

I was back in the house before Hank started talking to me again.

"I'll meet you at the hospital," he said. "They'll be there soon."

He was right. They arrived in record time.

"Next of kin?" the younger of the three EMTs asked.

"Her husband is next of kin," I said, "but I don't have a way of getting in touch with him."

Blake wasn't home and I had no idea when he would be. I didn't know his number and Anna was in no shape to give it to me.

"Do you want to ride with her and talk to her?" the older EMT named Andy asked. "It sometimes helps them to hear a familiar voice."

"Yes! But I need to go grab her keys and purse. I think I saw them on the table." I didn't tell them that I also had to go close the window that I'd left open on the back porch.

I closed it, locked it, and grabbed her purse and keys. I locked the front door behind me on the way out, then climbed in the ambulance with Anna and the EMTs.

I talked to Anna all the way to the hospital. I told her about Holly and the puppies and anything else I could think of. Anna didn't open her eyes, but I hoped she could hear me and understand.

After several pot holes, twists, and turns, we arrived at the ER.

I climbed out, prepared to go into the hospital with Anna, but the EMTs stopped me. "I'm sorry, but you can't come back," Andy said. "We'll call you when we know more."

As I waited by the door, I heard the doctor say something about pumping Anna's stomach. *That doesn't sound pleasant,* I thought, *but it's better than dying.*

Another hospital staff member quickly directed me to the lobby. There were only a couple other people there and they were glued to their electronics.

"The best seats are near the TV," the nurse said. "It helps the time go by faster."

She wasn't wrong. I'd already watched two episodes of MASH when an ER nurse came out. I couldn't make out his last name, but his first name was Will.

"You're the one who found her?" he asked, looking at her chart.

"Yes," I said, explaining the situation. "Her husband doesn't know yet and I don't have his number."

"Can you use her phone to call him?"

"Her phone is locked." On the way over, I had tried to send a message, but I needed the password for that, too. "How is she?"

"It's against the law for me to give you any information without the patient's consent or her next of kin's permission; I'm sorry." He shoved a pen in his pocket and pursed his lips. He seemed agitated, but I didn't take it personally. "And since she's not able to communicate yet, my hands are tied. Again, I'm sorry."

I understood, but didn't like it. "Can I at least see her when she wakes up?"

"I'll see what I can do. If you'll wait here a bit longer, a nurse will update you as soon as possible."

I waited in the ER lobby by myself and fell asleep. I was gently awakened by Will. "You can see her now," he said. "She's resting."

I quickly followed him through a maze of hallways and double doors. We stopped at room 315. "We want to watch her for another 24 hours. And please remember—no more than three visitors at a time."

I sat in the chair near her bed, but dozed off as the afternoon sunlight warmed the room. I woke up when I heard someone tapping lightly on the door.

It was Hank. "I'm sorry I'm late. I've been trying to get in touch with Sophia. She's not returning my calls and she's not been home when I've stopped by." He lowered his voice to a whisper. "How is she?"

"She's not woken up yet." I motioned for him to follow me back in the hall and shut the door quietly behind us.

"They won't give me details because I'm not next of kin.

But I don't have Blake's number, and we can't get into Anna's phone to find it." I sighed. "They did say they wanted to watch her for another 24 hours."

Hank held up his phone. "I have Blake's number right here. We used to golf together."

He dialed the number, but no one was there. He hung up without leaving a message.

"I'll try again in a few minutes," he said. "but I don't like to leave news like this on voice mail. I'll send his number to you, too, just in case I can't get him before I leave," he said. "Also, if she wakes up after I leave, please call me. I need to talk to her about Sebastian's death." He paused again, then raised an eyebrow. "Luna told me about Sebastian and Anna's affair. She said she told you, too."

I shrugged. "Yeah, but it's just gossip."

"Maybe, but she thinks the scene in the lobby was a break-up."

"I mean…it could have been, but you'd have to interview Anna to know that for sure."

"I intend to," Hank said.

"And," I said, "you should talk to Luna again before you take her word as the gospel. She tends to need her palm greased before making appointments for people. I don't think she's trustworthy."

"Apparently, my wife doesn't trust her, either. But I can't overlook this, T. If it's true, then Anna and Sebastian's little break-up gives her motive. But if she's got a solid alibi, then she's probably off the hook."

Probably?

Hank's phone rang, bringing our discussion to an abrupt end. It was Florence.

They didn't talk long, but it sounded important. When they hung up, Hank grabbed his hat and walked to the door.

"Florence has got a few more hints on Friday's burglary, so I need to get back to the office," Hank said. "Please let me know when she wakes up."

I went back in the room, shut the door, and sat back down beside Anna's bed.

"If you don't soon wake up and clear your name, you'll be front page news…and not the good kind." I didn't know if she could hear me or not, but I hoped somewhere my words struck a chord.

A few moments later, I heard a moan—then watched as Anna moved her right hand. It wasn't much, but it was something.

"Anna? Can you hear me?"

She moaned again.

I didn't waste any time; I ran out into the hallway and yelled for a nurse.

"She's awake, but groggy." Maygan said, looking at me. The young nurse had a kind, quiet voice. She wrote her name on the whiteboard on the wall beside Anna's bed then poured her patient a glass of water. "She might not be able to express herself well until she wakes up completely. Were you ever able to get in touch with her husband?"

"No. He hasn't picked up and I didn't want to leave a message," I said. "But when I do, do you have any information that I can share?"

"Well, her vitals look good, but that's all I can say." She looked down the notes on Anna's chart, then back at me. "You're the one who found her, right?"

"Yes."

"I can say this," Maygan replied, lowering her voice, "you saved her life. Any later and you would be calling her husband with much different news."

When the doctor finally came in to talk to Anna, he asked me to step out. I called Blake again. It rang a few times and then...

"Hello?"

"Blake! This is Tori. I've been trying to get in touch with you!" It took a few minutes, but I explained everything. "Anna's having a hard time concentrating right now, but I'm sure she'll be glad to see you when you get here."

"Tell her not to speak to anyone until I arrive!" He sounded mad for some reason.

"She's not talking much, but she's in there with the doctor now."

"Fine." He sighed deeply. "Then please just tell her I'll be there as soon as I can."

Weird. Very weird.

After the doctor left—without telling me a thing—Anna and I sat in silence for about 20 minutes, occasionally interrupted by nurses checking Anna's vital signs and state of mind. The last time the door opened, though, it was Blake. He still had on his work clothes, a pristine white lab coat with "Lumen Labs" embroidered on the right breast pocket. He came in slowly, leaving the door cracked behind him.

One look at his face, and I knew that he and Anna needed privacy. "I'll come see you tomorrow, Anna. Feel better."

"Call before you come, please," Blake said, dropping his backpack on the window seat. "She might be resting."

He didn't wait for a reply, but instead made room on the bed to sit with his wife. They were already speaking in hushed tones as I walked out, unnoticed.

I headed back the same way I'd just come, but on the way through the entrance floor lobby, I ran into Allison.

"What are you doing here?" she asked. "Are your mom and dad okay?"

"Dad is just as ornery as ever and Mom is doing her best to keep him in line," she said. "So, yes—they are just fine. I'm here visiting a friend. You?"

"I'm fine, but it's Kevin…" she stopped talking and wiped away tears. "He was in an accident today." She wiped away even more tears.

I ran over to the registration table and grabbed some tissues. "Here. They aren't the softest in the world, but they'll get the job done."

"Thank you." She wiped her eyes and blew her nose. "I thought he'd rounded a corner. But I was wrong. I know he's been hanging out with some guy named, Niles—and I don't trust him. He's closer to my age than Kevin's, and I'm afraid Niles may have led my boy back down the rabbit hole."

When my brother was 18, he fell into a bad crowd and got addicted to drugs. I didn't want to tell her how it all ended up. *Addiction is no respecter of persons.*

"Is there anything I can do?"

"Just pray that we can get Kevin to agree to more treatment. It's been a long, long road." She wiped her nose. "I'm sorry about the way I acted at the shop earlier. I just don't know what to do."

"You don't owe me an apology, Alli. You're living in a nightmare right now. I'm sorry you're going through this." I reached out and gave her a side hug. "I can't fix it, but I can bring breakfast tomorrow. Would that help?"

"That would be wonderful. But are you sure you don't mind?"

"It's no trouble at all. I'll be here visiting Anna, anyway."

"Oh no! What happened?"

I didn't feel right about sharing Anna's information, but I also didn't want to lie. "I am not sure how much she wants to be shared, but I know she'd appreciate your prayers," I said.

"I totally understand that." Allison wiped away more tears. "Can your mama let the pastor know what's going on with Kevin?

"Absolutely. Do you want to add him to the prayer list?"

"At this point? Yes. Lots of folks already know that Kevin

has been struggling with drugs for the last year. Pride is a hard thing to put aside when we need help, but he needs all the help he can get."

My mom, Lana Mulligan, had been the secretary for the Craven Community Church since forever. She knew everyone and everything that happened around town, especially if they called to ask for prayer. And Mom was good about keeping confidential stuff confidential…mostly. She always confided in my dad, but he couldn't hear half the time, so mom always said it didn't count.

I hugged Allison goodbye and headed outside. As soon as I was finally alone, I called Jo, but she didn't pick up. So I texted her instead, giving her the lowdown. After a few minutes of typing, we started wrapping it up.

Me: My car is still at Anna's house. Can you come pick me up?

Jo: I'll send a ride to you shortly. Where will you be waiting?

Me: The entrance near the water garden. I don't know which one is driving, but tell the boys to be careful!

Jo: Someone will be there soon!

I had only ridden with the boys one time since they'd acquired their licenses. It had not ended in a wreck, but it wasn't an experience I would have chosen to repeat so soon. Still, I was thankful for a ride. I'd have to buy them a milkshake or something.

My stomach growled, reminding me that I'd not eaten much at all. "I'll get me a milkshake, too," I mumbled to myself. "This is officially another calorie-free day."

I called my mom while I waited outside.

She could tell instantly that something was wrong. "Are you okay, honey?"

I gave her the brief overview of Sebastian's murder.

"I knew you'd call and tell me sooner or later," mom said.

"You knew I'd found the body?"

"No…but I knew you were involved somehow. News

travels fast around here, but the details sometimes get lost in translation."

"Who told you?"

"The grapevine was all up in arms down at Fred's. Someone—I can't remember who—was listening on their police scanner; then they drove by the clinic. They saw you, Jo, and some handsome fella standing outside the Vet office. But I figured you were knee deep in interviews and writing a story for the Gazette."

"It's complicated," I said. I didn't have time to tell her about my lack of a job. That would have to wait until the next conversation. Instead, I explained about running into Allison at the hospital. "Kevin was in a car accident today and is in the hospital."

"Oh no! Is he okay?"

"Physically, yes. But the bigger problem is still hanging heavy on his shoulders. She said that I could ask you to put him on the church prayer list."

"Hang on." I heard feverish typing in the background. "Done."

I admired my mom's organization. There were many days that I wished I could just absorb a small fraction of it.

"I can smell the steaks your dad is grilling," mom said. "Wanna join us?"

"I'd love to, but it's been a super long day and I still have to go pick up my car. The boys are picking me up."

"Be careful…and stay away from any more dead bodies!"

I kept watch for the gray Honda van that the twins would be driving. Instead, a silver Chevy pick-up truck pulled up to the entrance. I recognized it right away. The passenger side window rolled down slowly, revealing the handsome driver on the other side.

"What are you doing here?" I asked. *This did not seem like a coincidence.*

"It's a long story, but at Hank's request, I gave Jo a ride home from work—and on the way there, she told me that you needed a ride, too."

"I assumed the boys were coming."

"She said to remind you that they were taking care of the dogs, then she warned me that you'd probably be upset with her for asking me to do this."

She looked back at the text Jo had sent. Yep, Jo had worded it perfectly—perfectly sneaky. They were going to have a long talk, soon.

"By the look on your face, I'm going to assume she was correct. But as my father would say, 'that horse is already out of the barn'."

"I can't argue with that." I felt myself smiling, suddenly not so mad at Jo or the situation. "But isn't this out of your way?"

"Nope. Jo told me the general area where Anna lives and I think that my apartment isn't too far from there. I can drop you off and head home. You'll have to act as GPS, though."

"I can do that!" *But we'd be taking a backway* "You'll have to let me treat you to a milkshake. It's what I was going to offer to get for the boys if they had been my chauffeurs."

"I'm always up for ice cream, it makes rough days better. And by the sounds of it, you've had one of those."

The trip to Anna's didn't seem quite as long as it had in the ambulance. I explained how I'd ended up at the hospital with Anna and the weird vibes I had picked up from Blake. "I think they are hiding something. There was just something off about the whole conversation."

"So you think she's guilty?"

"Of murder? No. But she's guilty of something."

I explained where the next few turns would be. "We aren't far from Anna's now."

He slowed down and pointed toward the green sign on my

side of the road. "My apartment is that way."

"You definitely won't have far to drive home," I said. I looked at my watch. It was way later than I thought it was. "Don't you still have boxes to unpack?"

"I do, but it's the kitchen and bathroom boxes—and I'm procrastinating as much as possible. So please don't remind me of what is waiting for me."

"I totally get it," I said. "I hate unpacking and organizing. But Jo? She's the queen of clean. She takes every opportunity she can to attack the dust bunny brigade at my house." *And the mountain of dirty dishes and clothes.*

"Sounds like my wife. She cleaned, cleaned, cleaned...until she couldn't. I wish she'd spent more time with us and less scrubbing toilets." He paused. "She passed away five years ago, but it feels like a lifetime." He looked straight ahead, a stoic look on his face. "I just wish she'd spent more time living and less time obsessing about the house. It wasn't nearly as important as she thought it was." He paused again. "I don't usually go around talking about my dead wife. As soon as I do, people start feeling sorry for me, then they try to set me up with their sister, best friend, or next door neighbor."

"You might want to let Jo know, or you could end up on a dating game show with Craven's most eligible bachelorettes."

"Hank told me the same thing. We talked about it. Jo said she understood and would be respectful of my privacy."

He must have talked to a different Jo.

The air was still filled with awkward energy, so I did what I usually did when things got weird—I got weirder.

For the next few minutes I gave the history of each house or farm that we passed. He received way more information than any human could be expected to remember...or care about.

"And where is our next turn?" He slowed down at Cordova Street, waiting on my direction.

"Oh yeah! Sorry. Take a left. There's a huge pothole once you turn, so be careful. We'll stay on here for just a bit longer."

"Our excursion and your explanations are just the things I needed to help me get to know the area a little bit better," he said. He had a gentle smile on his face. "I certainly need to know all I can if I'm going to be doing any house calls. I'd rather not be arrested for trespassing or sued for ending up at the wrong farm!"

"Ooooh! That reminds me—what happened with the lawyer?"

"It's a long story. I can tell you over supper tonight."

"Supper?" I felt my face turn red, so I was glad he had his eyes on the road and not on me.

"Supper with Jo and Hank? She said she'd already told you about it."

"Oh, yeah. She did mention that." I looked up from fidgeting with my watch just in time. "Turn right at the next road, Boone extension."

Half a mile later, I pointed to the giant sign on corner of the Mask property. "That's Luna's parent's farm out there," I said. "But she isn't exactly the farming type."

"I still haven't met her."

"Count it as a blessing."

"Huh?"

I explained about what had happened the morning of the murder. "Jo had to give Luna a bribe to get an appointment, even though there were no other customers in lobby."

Duncan sat up a little straighter, a storm briefly clouding his face. "I see a staff meeting in the near future."

We fell into a surprisingly comfortable silence as he took the final turn onto Anna's street.

"Her house is on the second on the right," I explained. "My truck is parked in the driveway."

He parallel parked in front of her house with no issue. But something didn't feel right.

"I feel like we need to make sure the house is still locked," I said. "I remember checking it before I left with Anna and the

EMTs, but maybe I'm wrong."

"I'm guessing that I can't convince you to stay here while I go see if it's locked?"

"Seriously?" I cocked my head to the side and raised one eyebrow.

"That's what I thought. Come on."

We made our way to the front door and stopped in our tracks. The glass front door was shattered and I could see a multi-colored brick just inside the threshold. The brick matched the other bricks in the flower garden under Anna's front window.

"Since it's busted, I'm guessing you definitely locked it behind you," Duncan said dryly. "Or whoever did this is a really dumb criminal and didn't care." Then he pulled out his phone and dialed 911.

Duncan and I were waiting in his truck watching the house like hawks when Hank and Florence arrived with Bishop, the K-9 member of their unit. Bishop had a good nose, but was getting on up there in age. Hank had mentioned that they were going to retire him soon. He'd need a new home, just like Holly.

"Don't go anywhere," Hank told us. "We'll be back."

While we waited, Duncan laid his head back on his head rest. Within seconds, he was lightly snoring.

How did he do that? Too many things were on my mind. First and foremost? Anna. We had never been close, but I trusted her. I just couldn't believe she killed Sebastian, but her overdose attempt made it look more like she was dealing with some pretty heavy stuff. *Was Sebastian's murder on that list?*

After another 10 minutes or so, Hank headed back out to the truck and knocked on Duncan's window. Duncan rolled it down and yawned.

"Catching a beauty nap?" Hank half-smiled. "You might want to sleep a little more."

"Thanks, man," he said, "but I'm afraid I'll be an ogre until the end of my days."

Seriously? Had he looked in mirror lately?

Hank's half-smile quickly disappeared when he took off his hat.

"That blood inside the door…please tell me that it's not yours." He stared at Duncan and me.

"Didn't touch a thing," Duncan said. "We barely even breathed on it."

"I just needed to know before we ran it through the system," Hank said. "I don't want any surprises."

"Then I should tell you that I think I saw a sketchy looking SUV when I found Anna. I think I saw it earlier today, too."

"Did you see who was in it?"

"No, but Jo and I saw Kevin crawl into a very similar SUV at the Book Nook today. And then Kevin ended up at the hospital not long after I got there with Anna this afternoon. He'd been in an accident."

"Hmmm…I'll stop by and see him this week," Hank said. "He and I need to have a chat, anyway."

That sounded ominous for Kevin. I hoped I hadn't just got him in more trouble.

"Looks like her whole place has been ransacked," Hank said, diverting his attention back to Anna's house. "Whoever did this was looking for something, or they were in a rage. Either way, I'd like to know who did it and why."

Florence walked out with Bishop and a bag of what looked like trash. "We found a pile of torn up letters and pictures," she said. "I'll take it down to the station for prints."

Out of the corner of my eye I saw a cat walking gingerly through the flower bed. Bishop was sitting still, but his eyes were following that cat.

I thought about Percy…then remembered that I had another house guest, as well. "I've got to go, Hank. The boys have been taking care of Holly and the puppies all day long!" I thanked

Duncan for the ride and climbed in my truck. Only after I was five minutes down the road did I remember that I owed Duncan a milkshake. *Maybe another day.*

I called Jo on the way home. "I know you planned for us to have supper tonight, but we probably need to put it off until tomorrow." I took the rest of the way home to tell her why her husband would be very, very late.

Fifteen minutes later, I whipped into my driveway, unbuckled, and ran around to the side entrance to the office, expecting the boys and the pups to be huddled, probably upset that I'd been gone all day.

I heard a voice answer back from the hallway, "In here!"

I stepped around the plastic pool, some dog toys, and the water bowl and made my way to the other side of the room. When I opened the door to the hallway, Booker and Grady were huddled together with the little hound family.

"Mom said you were probably not going to make it home in time to walk Holly," Booker said. "So we walked her, then bottle fed the babies like you asked."

Grady cleared his throat. "And Percy ate all of his food, but not without being tricked a little. He didn't seem interested until I pretended that I was going to eat it." His face twisted into a grossed out expression. "How does he eat that nastiness?"

"And I cleaned the litter box," Booker said, jumping in. "Is that okay?"

"It's more than okay." I wiped away unexpected tears. "You guys are awesome."

The boys took the puppies into the office and sat them down on the floor with Holly. Wobbling, they followed Holly to their make-shift bed, then snuggled with her. I smiled and told the boys to wait with them for one more minute.

"I'll be right back." I ran out to the truck and extracted the treats and dog bed I'd bought earlier that day. Grady helped me haul the goodies to the office. I put the "jacket" on her so the puppies couldn't try to nurse and they wouldn't need round the clock eyes on them. I was sure it wouldn't matter to Booker and Grady, though. They'd still want to help.

"Holly's not going to want to leave," Booker said. "She likes it here."

"I wish I could keep her," I said, "but Percy would not be a happy camper."

"About that," Booker said. "Dad might let us keep Thor." He pointed to the fattest puppy on the giant, new comfy dog bed. "He's kind of smitten with him."

"Um…what?"

"You don't like the name? We just thought—"

"No, I love it!" I waved my hand, stopping him mid-sentence. "That's not it." I took a deep breath and tried to word my next phrase carefully. "I am just trying to figure out how your dad thinks y'all can keep a dog when he's so allergic to them."

The twins gave each other a bewildered look, then back at me.

Booker was the first to speak. "Our grandpa is allergic to dogs and so is our uncle. But if Dad is, I've never heard anything about it."

Not allergic? I didn't say what was on my mind. But Jo would be hearing all about it—soon.

"Thank you both for your help today. I think you'll be wonderful vets!" I reached in my purse and pulled out some cash, but they stopped me.

"That's not why we're here," Booker said. "We didn't do it to be paid."

"I know. But I can't let you keep helping me if you won't let me at least pay you a little something."

"Fine," Booker said, shoving his hand through is hair. "But you can't pay us every time we come over."

"For once," Grady said, "I agree with him."

"You've got yourself a deal." I gave them both a hug.

They grabbed all of the stuff they'd brought with them and headed to their van. They'd only had their driver's licenses for a few months, so I was a little concerned anytime they were out on their own.

I waved and yelled through the night, "Call me when you get home!"

As I watched them drive down my long driveway, I wondered if Jo was ready for the long list of questions I had about Hank's "miraculous healing" from allergies.

After locking the outside office door and making sure that Holly and the puppies had plenty of water, I headed up to check on Percy and take a shower. Twenty minutes later, I was clean, in my favorite PJ's, and ready to snuggle under the covers. Percy joined me, purring a soft lullaby.

My brain was full of "what ifs" – but they didn't stop me from going to sleep within minutes of my head hitting the pillow.

When waking, it's hard to get good oxygen with a fat cat sprawled across your face. I shoved Percy off, then rolled out of bed.

After my shower, I got Percy settled and walked Holly. "I'll be back later, guys. The boys are on their way over and will make sure you all get fed." I left instructions for the twins on the kitchen counter, along with enough money for a couple of pizzas from the Pie Palace. It was the best and least expensive pizza place in town.

Fifteen minutes later, I swung by the café and picked up

some breakfast for Allison, just as I'd promised. Jo wasn't there yet, but I'd check in with her after I got back from the hospital. We had things to discuss.

I pulled into the parking lot about 8:30. If I had arrived an hour or so earlier, I might have seen Dad in the NICU. Several days a week, he volunteered to snuggle the preemies. *Yes, my gruff-on-the-outside dad had a squishy middle.*

By the time I got to the front desk, there was already a low hum of activity throughout the place. The extra-cheery front desk receptionist had the phone up to her ear and a coke in the other hand. Her extra-long sparkly nails shined in the morning light.

"I am here to visit Kevin Clark," I said. "His mother said I could drop by this morning."

"Give me just a second."

I wasn't sure how she did it with those nails, but she typed the name into the computer, then made a strange face.

"He isn't in his room right now, I'm sorry."

"Can you tell me why?"

She pulled her bright red-rimmed glasses down and stared at me. "You know I can't."

"Can you at least tell me where his mom might be? I've got breakfast for her."

"I can do that." She punched in a few more things on the computer. "Third floor. Family waiting room #207."

As I waited on the super-slow elevator, my phone rang.

"Hi Hank."

"Hi Tori. I'm almost to the hospital. Anna has some explaining to do."

"What do you mean?"

"I can't discuss the details, but I'll just say that your boss better have a good alibi for the night of the murder."

There was a lot of stuff going on in Anna's life, maybe even an affair. But murder? I couldn't believe it.

"I need to go," I said. "I've got some folks to visit."

"Remember what I said about not talking to Anna about the case?"

I made a weird, static-sounding noise. "Sorry, Hank. You're breaking up. Can't hear you—"

"Tori! I know you can hear me!"

"Sorry," I said. "Gotta go!"

I heard him sigh as I hung up.

Allison was not in the family room, so I decided to swing back by with her breakfast after I visited with Anna. As I turned to go to the elevator, a somber, familiar face caught eye contact with me.

"Luna?"

She looked different without her pale emo make-up. Matter of fact, she looked scared. Luna stared at her fingerless gloves and played with the frayed ends. She didn't speak, but she did sniffle.

"How's Kevin?"

Nothing. Just a sad stare.

I held out a box of tissues I'd picked up for Allison.

She took the box and immediately blew through four tissues, but didn't answer my question.

"It's obvious you care deeply for him," I continued, "or you wouldn't be here."

I saw a medallion hanging from a chain around her neck. I recognized it. My brother used to have one. *One year clean.*

"My brother was in AA, too," I said. "It helped him—at least for a while. Until he stopped talking to his sponsor and quit going to meetings."

She shoved the necklace back in her shirt, away from my prying eyes. It was clear she wasn't going to open up about anything.

She kept her response curt. "If you're looking for Allison, she'll be back a little later. Had to go talk to the doctors."

"I was looking for her, but I'll catch up with her later. Are you hungry?" I held out the bag of food I'd brought for Allison.

"Somebody's got to eat it while it's still hot. I'll grab her something for lunch."

She hesitated, then reached out for the bag. "Thanks."

"The folks downstairs said Kevin couldn't have visitors right now," I said. "Do you know when he can?"

"I don't know."

She didn't offer up why he couldn't have visitors and I didn't push. Allison could tell me when I talked to her again.

I sat beside her in silence for a while. I felt bad for Luna in many ways. She didn't seem nearly as surly now as when she wasn't hiding behind the desk at the vet clinic or getting her groceries knocked out of her hand. She seemed beaten down. I hated to leave her by herself, but I need to get to Anna before Hank got to the hospital.

"I better go," I said. "But I hope Kevin is better soon."

"Me, too," she mumbled. "I don't want him to wind up like Dr. Westminster."

I stopped in my tracks. *"What did you say?"*

"Nothing." She looked out the window, avoiding eye contact. *That was weird.*

I decided to tread carefully. "I didn't want to bring that situation up," I said, "but I do have a question. Did you ever get the camera footage to Dr. Westminster?"

"How…how do you know about that?"

"I was there when he mentioned it to you that morning. He said he wanted you to produce the footage by Friday night. I just wondered if you did."

"I don't like what you're implying."

"I'm not implying anything," I said. "You're going to be asked the same thing by Hank if he sees you. He's been talking to everyone who was at the clinic on the day of the murder."

"You talked to the police?" She stuffed the rest of the uneaten croissant in the bag, then held it out to me. "You can have this back. I don't eat snitches food."

"I am not snitching, Luna. I want to help. If you weren't

there that night, then tell Hank that. He can cross your name off the suspect list."

She was pretty upset for someone who hadn't even been questioned by the police yet. As far as I knew, Hank wasn't looking at Luna as a suspect at all. *Maybe he should be.*

"If it matters at all, I was with Kevin at an AA meeting." Luna pulled the hood of her blue jacket over her head. "Not that it's any of your business."

An AA meeting? Hmmm. The smell of marijuana wafting from her clothing made me question it. *Maybe it was second hand smoke.* And Kevin? I didn't believe for a minute that Kevin was at a meeting. *She was covering for him…and maybe herself.*

I didn't want to push her or bombard her with more questions…not that it would have mattered. I could tell she was done talking to me.

"I'll be back to see Allison later," I said. "I hope you get some rest while you wait."

She didn't respond. Instead, she turned herself completely away from me and stared out the window.

I left my name at the nurse's station and asked them to please let Allison know that I'd stopped by. I took the elevator to Anna's floor and hoped Hank hadn't already beat me there.

Surprisingly, Anna was by herself—no Blake. I gave her a gentle hug.

"How are you feeling? I mean, other than the obvious." She still had an IV and looked like she'd been hit by a mac truck.

"I don't know." She sat back and stared at the popcorn ceiling. "Everyone keeps asking me why I did what I did. I don't have an answer that they'll like."

"I can understand…at least some."

"What do you mean? Have you ever landed in the hospital with alcohol poisoning?" There was an edge to her voice, but I didn't blame her.

"No. I haven't. But my brother died of an overdose," I said. "The doctors said it was an accidental overdose, but that didn't make it any better for me or my parents. Then everyone wanted me to talk about it, except Jo. She didn't push me or force it."

"Wise woman," Anna said. "Words are sometimes overrated."

I just nodded in agreement.

I wasn't sure how long we sat in silence, but when Anna finally spoke, her voice was so soft that I had to lean in to hear her.

"I never meant for that to happen. I just…"

But before she could finish my sentence, Blake arrived.

"What are you doing here?" He stood in the doorway, a coffee in each hand. "You should have called first…Anna could have been resting."

I had never noticed how much he looked like an oversized Shih Tzu. He kind of acted like one, too.

"I'm glad she's here," Anna said, reaching for my hand. "She saved my life, remember?"

"Yes, of course." He sighed. then wiped his face with a small cloth. "I'm sorry. Tori. I'm just feeling very protective of my wife right now. She's been through a lot."

"It's okay," I replied. *Maybe his bark is worse than bite.* "You've both been under a lot of stress, I'm sure."

He handed one of the coffees to Anna, then sat down in the chair behind the door and immediately pulled his phone out of his pocket and started scrolling through social media.

I turned my attention back to my ex-boss. "Did you get any rest last night?"

"A little. The nurses kept coming in to check on me." She sat up a little straighter in her bed. "I know you didn't ask…but I want to tell you what really happened."

"Anna!" Suddenly, Blake was standing by the bed.

"Please." Anna touched her husband's hand in a soothing manner.

He was still visibly seething, but sat back down.

I scooted to the edge of my seat and got as close to the bed as I could.

Anna cleared her throat and reached out for my hand. "There's no getting around it," she said, looking straight at me. "The cameras…they're going to show that I was there."

"There? Where?" I didn't want to jump to conclusions, but I knew what my gut was telling me.

"I was at the office the night of the murder. But I didn't kill him," Anna continued. "I really didn't. He was mad and hurt, but alive when I left."

"What are you saying?" I leaned back in my seat, hoping I'd heard incorrectly. "You've got to back up, Anna. I'm really confused."

Anna blew her nose and wiped her eyes. By this time, Blake was pacing the floor with clenched fists.

"Remember the argument that Sebastian and I had in the lobby?" Anna asked. "Well, I came back right after closing. It was about 4:30. His Hummer was still there. I tried to reason with him about our earlier argument. I'd gone there to reason with him, but he wouldn't listen. Then, when I told him that I wasn't going to pay up anymore, he had me pinned on the desk. When I tried to pull away, he tore my shirt, so I grabbed what I could…and hit him with it. Then—I ran."

"That son of a…" Blake said, looking like he was about to punch the wall. "He deserved what he got."

I sat in silence with my friend, not wanting to make things worse than they already were. I wanted Blake to stop pacing, but he kept walking back and forth, back and forth. A fleeting thought ran through my mind to trip him, but I was raised better than that.

When she finally spoke again, it was between small sobs.

"Sebastian wasn't even knocked out. I thought he would be okay. He just seemed disoriented…and very, very angry." She paused again and tried to regain her composure.

"You need to explain this slower to me." I was trying to put the puzzle together, but didn't have all the pieces. "Why did you owe him money?"

"That doesn't matter!" Blake yelled, slamming his fist on the bed table. "What matters is that he was a self-indulgent, card-carrying narcissist who tried to hurt my wife. And her response was self-defense, plain and simple!"

Someone cleared their throat from the other side of the room. Hank was standing there with his arms folded.

"How long have you been there?" Blake demanded.

"Long enough to know that y'all have been holding back some important information," Hank replied. He walked to the end of Anna's bed and stopped.

Blake looked like he was about to explode.

"The guilt has been killing me," Anna said softly. She sounded relieved, but still scared. "How much did you hear?"

"Enough to know you probably want to retain a lawyer soon," Hank replied.

"But I don't need one! I didn't kill him!" The look in Anna's eyes was pure terror. "You've got to believe me. I defended myself against Sebastian, but he was alive when I left!"

"I wish there was a way to collaborate your story," Hank said, "because I've got fingerprints on the scene that we have linked to you. And you've just confessed to getting into an altercation with the deceased the night of his murder."

"The cameras!" Blake shouted. "Just look at the stupid cameras at the clinic. They'll show she's telling the truth!"

Hank leaned against the wall. "Unfortunately, those cameras are not in service."

Anna looked confused. "What do you mean?"

"There is no footage," he said. "According to Luna Hale, they have been out of service for a while."

Out of service? Then why didn't Luna tell Sebastian that on Friday when he asked about them? And why didn't she tell me that today? Something wasn't adding up. I needed to have another chat with the sunny bundle of joy.

"I didn't kill him, Hank," Anna said. "I'm not lying to you!"

"I didn't say you were, Anna. But setting that aside, let's go back to Tori's question that you never answered. Why were you paying Sebastian?"

"Leave her alone!" Blake hit the wall and filled the room with more cave-man grunts and expletives.

"Listen, Blake," Hank said calmly, "your wife can answer now, or she can come down to the station after she gets out of the hospital and answer then."

Anna held out her hand and reached for her husband's hand. "It's okay, honey. Please calm down."

He glowered for a moment, then plopped in the seat beside the bed.

"I'm glad to talk to you here, Hank," Anna said. She seemed to need a minute to wrap her head around what she was about to say. "He loaned me some money to get the paper up and running. I borrowed it right after Blake and I got married, but I didn't tell Blake about it. But Sebastian was charging me horrible interest, so I could never seem to catch up with the payments."

"I see." Hank jotted that down. "Why would you ask him to loan you money instead of going to a bank? Was there something more to your arrangement?"

"No!"

"So you weren't having an affair? Because we have reason to believe you were having an affair with Sebastian."

"How dare you!" Blake huffed. "You can't just make accusations like that!"

Hank ignored him and kept his attention on Anna. "I know this is hard, but I need you to be straight with me." He took off his hat and rolled it around in his hands. "Were you and Sebastian involved?"

"No!" Her eyes filled up with tears. "I mean…not anymore." Anna's spoke in the softest of whispers. "Blake and I went through a rough time before we got married. We even broke up for a bit. During that time, I made a mistake. A really dumb mistake." Tears flowed down Anna's face.

I hated to admit it, but Luna got one thing right.

"And did you know about the affair, Blake?" Hank's eyes were laser focused on him.

"I chose to forgive her." His jaw was clenched as were his fists.

Uh huh. Sure ya did, buddy.

"I see." Hank jotted down more notes. "Did Sebastian's wife find out about the affair?"

"I don't know," Anna said. "If she did know, Sebastian never said anything."

Hank scribbled in his notepad, then stood in silence rereading his notes. When he finally spoke, his tone had the same flat, serious tone that my undertaker grandfather used to have when he talked about work. "Anna, you said that you hit him, but what exactly did you use to defend yourself?"

"It's all a blur," she said, holding her head. "I think it was a paper weight."

"Yet you know for sure that he was alive when you left?"

She sat up straight and looked Hank straight in the face. "I might not remember what I had for breakfast yesterday or how much alcohol I drank last night, but I know that man was alive when I left. He was leaning against a wall in his office, yelling obscenities. I was worried that he was going to call you and have me arrested."

But Sebastian's body was found in a different room.

"Did you see anyone else when you arrived?"

"No."

"And when did you get back home?"

"Five-thirty? Maybe?"

Hank turned his attention to Blake, who was sulking in the

corner. "Where were you yesterday afternoon?"

"Me? I was at work. Got home around 6." He reached over and put his arm around Anna. They both looked uncomfortable. "Right honey?"

She took a deep breath, then smiled. "Yes. Of course."

"I'll need to verify when you left work," Hank said, his tone still flat. "Just procedure."

I could see Blake's face turning red again. I'd always thought he was easy-going; but his behavior over the last 24 hours had been anything but that.

"You'll just have to take my word for it. I was the only one working."

"You don't have key cards? You know, to track your time?"

"It's broken. We are all writing in our time manually."

"Uh-huh." Hank wrote something else down, then pushed his hat back a little and stared at Blake. He didn't speak, just stared.

The tension in the room felt like an over-full balloon that was on the verge of popping.

"Look," Blake said, his eyes bulging a bit. "I was angry when I found out what had happened. But I didn't kill him. I didn't have the chance,' he said, his hands clenching and unclenching. "Once I got home, I was with Anna all night. I wasn't about to leave her alone. I wanted to tear him limb from limb, but my darling wife wouldn't let me. I tried to get the day off of work, but I couldn't. She'd been drinking a little, but I thought she'd sleep it off. So this morning, I made her some breakfast and coffee, then I left. I had no idea she was going to keep drinking and end up here."

Anna gave him another weird look, but glanced away just as quickly. I wondered if Hank had noticed. Something wasn't right, but I couldn't put my finger on it.

Hank turned his attention back to Anna. "Do you remember anything else?"

"I have a fuzzy memory of hearing a weird noise down the

hallway, but when I left, there weren't any other cars out front except for Sebastian's and mine."

Hank tapped his cheek with his pen, then closed the notebook and put it in his pocket.

"I hit him in the head, Hank. I've admitted it. But I didn't kill him. You believe me, right?"

"I want to believe you, but it's my job to believe the evidence. And some of the evidence will be more clear once the autopsy is complete. Thankfully, our coroner is getting over his stomach flu a lot sooner than he thought he would. It should only be a day or two more before he's back in the office."

He reached out to shake Blake's hand, but Blake didn't reciprocate. He gave Hank a look that spoke the opposite of "bless your heart.""

Hank was unfazed, as usual, and tipped his hat toward Anna. "I hope you're feeling better soon. I'll need you to stay in town until this is all handled." Then Hank looked at me and motioned toward the door. "Can you walk outside with me? I have something that I need you to give Jo for me. I don't know when I'll be home tonight."

I patted Anna on the hand, nodded to Blake, then followed Hank out the door. There was nothing to say that would make the situation any better. I made a few mental notes about Blake and Anna's interaction. Something didn't add up.

Hank didn't say anything until we got to his car.

"Listen...I know you and Anna are friends, but you can't talk to her about the case. Whether you like it or not, she is a suspect."

"How can she be? She won't even let me put mouse traps in the newspaper office. They have to be live traps. I just can't believe that she killed Sebastian."

"She admitted to being there and hitting him."

"But why would she lie about not killing him if she knew there were cameras? That doesn't make sense!"

"Maybe she knew the cameras were broken, but is lying

about it." He leaned against his car. "And maybe, just maybe, her husband is, too. How do we know when Blake arrived home, other than the fact that Anna vouches for him?"

"He does seem to have a bit of a temper."

"Bingo. He never did like losing to anyone on the golf course. So maybe his wife's affair and Sebastian's loan shark tactics were enough to send him over the edge." Hank opened his truck door, pulled out an empty plastic food container, and handed it to me.

"Huh? What's this?"

"It's the made-up reason I asked you to come out here so I could debrief you a bit on the case. It used to have my lunch in it. However, Blake is now staring out the window of Anna's room, spying on us, I thought it best that I not look like a liar."

I didn't know Blake that well, so maybe he was always weird and overbearing. But how could I not have noticed?

"Do you really think Anna or Blake murdered Sebastian?"

"I don't know," Hank said. "But I'm sure they're hiding something, and I'm gonna find out what it is."

I waved as Hank pulled away and out of the parking lot. It was at that moment that I remembered I'd left my keys in Anna's room. When I got to her room, the door was closed. I knocked, opened the door slowly, and stuck my head inside.

"Sorry for barging in, but I forgot my keys."

Anna's eyes were even puffier than when I had left.

"Actually, your timing is perfect," Blake said. "I need to step out and make a few phone calls to work so I can take a couple of days off. Will you please stay with her until I get back?" He offered me his seat. "I won't be long."

"Absolutely. Anything to help."

Anna and I sat in uneasy silence. Anna spoke first. "I know what it looks like, but I wasn't trying to kill myself." She pointed to her purse and asked me to hand it to her. She reached in and pulled out a coin. "This is what I've worked for. Next month would be my 11th year sober." She turned it over and over in her hand, as if it were a long-lost treasure. "I made the choice to drink last night because I was scared and at my wit's end, I convinced myself that just a little liquid courage would be okay…then I went to see Sebastian. When he attacked me and I escaped – I went home and drank even more. But I didn't mean to drink that much and it was too much for my system. The mind of an addict doesn't make good choices."

I squeezed my friend's hand. "You don't have to talk about it if you don't want to."

"Actually, I do. It's part of the process that helps me heal," she said. "But if I can't prove that I didn't kill Sebastian, I'll be fighting for my own life behind bars."

"For the record, I don't believe you killed him," I said. "But you've now admitted to being at the crime scene around the time he was killed. So we've got to find a way to prove that you didn't do it."

"But how? The cameras aren't working. And we both know that Hank is not going to just take my word for it."

I stood up and walked over to the window. "You said you heard someone, but didn't see anyone. What if they were hiding somewhere in the building?"

"I really don't know," she said, 'but I've been thinking about his wife. What if she did know? Maybe she was jealous? He wasn't exactly happy being married to her. He said she spent money like it was water."

"That's definitely something you should have told Hank," I said.

"I wasn't thinking clearly…and I'm not sure I am now." She rubbed the AA coin one more time, then put it back in the purse.

"There is one thing I am clear about, though." Anna reached out and put her hand on mine. "I need to thank you."

"No, you don't."

"Yes, I do. They told me that you are the reason I'm alive. And though I feel like the bricks from a three story building fell on my head...at least I am here to feel it."

"I'm glad you are here, too."

"And if I can convince Hank of my innocence, maybe things can go back to normal again. I could reopen the paper since I don't owe Sebastian the money anymore." Then she paused. "Except that makes it seem like I have even more motive, doesn't it?" She sighed and plopped back in the bed. "I'm glad Hank didn't bring that up."

I didn't want to tell her that Hank had probably already thought of it. But he was savvy at police work and poker. I learned a long time ago not to bet against him.

A nurse came in the room to check Anna's pulse, and Blake followed quickly behind her.

"I better head out." I gave Anna a gentle squeeze. "You know where to find me if you need anything."

"Can I walk you to your car?" Blake's tone was overly polite, in huge contrast to his attitude yesterday.

"Um...no. I'll be okay, but thank you, anyway." I didn't think Anna had killed anyone, but I wasn't so sure about Blake. "Feel better, Anna. Talk to you both later."

When I looked at my watch, it was only 10am, but felt like noon. I could tell it was going to be a long, long day.

I got some gas, ran into Food Lion for some milk, then stopped by Mr. C's for a small basket of tater fries and large coke with pebbled ice. I didn't care that the line snaked around the building. Mr. C's food was worth it. I chomped on the tasty taters all the way home. When I pulled in the driveway around 1pm, Mom's jeep was in the driveway.

"Mom? Dad?" I yelled their names as I unlocked the outside office door.

"In the living room!" Dad shouted as I walked in the door.

My mom sat in one chair with a sleeping puppy in her lap, and an empty bottle on the table beside her. Dad had a puppy in his arms who was fighting hard to stay awake to drain the last bit of milk from his bottle.

"When we got here, the boys were just about the feed them," Mom said. "We offered to help and let them go home and have a break."

"They have been a huge help to me the last few days," I said.

"They told us all about it!" Mom said. "They also mentioned that their dad wants to adopt Thor. But I thought he was allergic?"

"That's a long story," I said. I didn't want to discuss it until after I'd talked to Jo. "So what are y'all up to today?"

Mom shrugged. "Nothing much."

Dad sighed. "Only because your mom wants it that way."

Mom and Dad had always bantered, and they had their share of real arguments. Most of them came about because they were complete opposites in most things. However, this little exchange seemed deeper than a simple misunderstanding.

I glanced from one parent to the other. "What's going on?"

"I want to adopt one of the puppies. The house is just so big and quiet."

"If we get a puppy, we can't travel. Why did we spend money on that monster of an RV if it's just going to sit in our yard?"

She shot him a look. "Tori doesn't want to hear about this, honey." She turned her gaze toward me. "I hope you've been staying away from dead bodies," Mom said, turning the attention away from the tension between her and Dad.

I glanced at Dad. He'd already laid his head back, closed his eyes, and was snoring—ever so slightly.

"No dead bodies," I said, holding up three fingers. "Scouts honor."

"I still can't believe he was murdered. It was the talk of choir practice last night." Mom recounted what she'd heard at the church about the whole thing. "Some folks think his wife did it. Others are saying his lover did it."

"Lover?"

"Don't play naïve, dear. We all know he was a playboy. And," she continued, "Mr. Langtree thinks Sebastian could have been targeted by a serial killer."

"Come on, now. That's a bit extreme."

"You know Mr. Langtree. He's got nothing better to do than to be in everybody's business." Mom snuggled the puppy under her chin. "Speaking of business—I'm guessing the rumor about the paper closing is true, too?"

She knew. "I was going to tell you about losing my job—I just haven't had time."

"No worries, sweetie. I know you've had a lot on you." She scratched Thor's belly. "So now you have time to open the B&B! Aunt Bert would be so proud!"

"But…"

"You aren't tied down to your weekly column, so you have time to invest in the Inn and getting it up to date. You could make a ton if you follow in Aunt Bert's footsteps."

She sounded so excited. I hate to be the one to burst her bubble.

"So when are you going to make it a go?"

"Probably never."

"Why not?" My mom sounded genuinely shocked. "It practically runs itself."

I had never run a Bed & Breakfast, but I knew instinctively that there was a lot more to running this place than just giving folks a place to sleep. I was good with numbers, but I didn't want to run this thing into the ground like Anna had done with the newspaper.

"I really don't think now is the time," I said. "Besides, I'm hoping Anna is going to be able to start the paper back up after she's recovered." There was, however, the pesky possibility of Anna being charged with a murder, but I didn't want to say that part out loud. It was too close to being a real thing.

"We haven't had a paper in almost a week," my dad said, his eyes still closed. "I'm missing your obituary column. I like to look every morning and make sure I'm still alive."

"Mmmm-hmmmm." Mom rolled her eyes. "If your father doesn't stop keeping me awake with his snoring, he might be in that column sooner than later."

"I heard that," he said, never lifting his head.

"Not to change the subject, but…" Mom pulled out a piece of paper from her purse. "I did what you asked and added Allison and Kevin to our prayer list. But I'd love to give an update. Is he home from the hospital? Can they have visitors? Ms. Sauerwein wanted to take by a casserole."

"Doing the Lord's work," Dad muttered. "Just make sure it's not her tuna casserole or he might end up in the hospital again. I avoid it like the plague that it is."

"George!" she exclaimed, trying to frown. "That's not nice!"

"Neither is her casserole."

Mom tried not to laugh, but couldn't help herself.

Dad chuckled a little, still not opening his eyes. I could tell he'd received the response he was looking for. I figured his early morning with the teeny-tiny babies at the hospital had worn him out. Even so, he wasn't too tired to tease mom.

The puppy snuffled in his lap and whimpered a little at the commotion. Holly immediately went over to check on him.

"I think they just want their mama for a little while. So let me get them all settled," I said, "then I'll tell you what I know about Kevin."

I took the puppies from my parents' laps, then ushered them all into the study. "Here you go, little mama." She was giving them a bath as I closed the door behind me.

Over the next few minutes, I shared what little information I had about Kevin and Allison's situation with my parents. "She gave me full permission to share with you. She's tired of keeping secrets."

Dad stirred in his seat a little, a pained look on his face.

"You okay?" I asked.

"Yeah. Just need to get some air."

And out the door he went.

Mom stared at the puppies and sighed. "I would love to take one of them off of your hands," she said. "But Dad is insisting that we travel now."

"You always wanted to do that. So what's the problem?"

"Do you think Anna was the other woman?"

Wow. She completely ignored my question. That made me even more suspicious.

"You think Anna is the other woman?" I wasn't going to gossip, but I also wasn't going to lie. "Where'd you hear that?"

"Word gets around, even when it's wrong," she said. Mom ran her hands through her long, silver-streaked hair. "I always liked her. I hope it's not true. I just can't see her trying to break up another woman's marriage or murdering a man because of it."

"I feel the same way." I meant it. Even though Anna admitted that she had been with Sebastian, something didn't add up. Something about her confession had just felt…off.

"If not her, then who?" Mom asked.

"I have no idea," I said. "But I do know that someone stuffed Sebastian in a closet, and I don't think that Anna has the strength to do that. She's no more than 125 pounds soaking wet. Sebastian was six-feet-tall, and at least 200 pounds."

"That's bizarre. Why would anyone stuff him in a closet? He was bound to be found at some point. If they wanted to get rid of the body, they could have just burned him in the incinerator."

"Mom! That's awful!"

"Oh, sorry dear! I've been watching your Dad's British TV murder mystery shows with him. I've gotten quite good at predicting what's coming."

My mom had always loved mysteries and tended to think there was one around every corner. When I was 10, she thought our new next door neighbor was a spy. And he was—sort of. He had worked for the FBI in his younger days, but then started his own private investigation company. He ended up being Aunt Bert's boss for five years.

"To answer your earlier question," Mom said, "Your father is keeping something from me, Victoria. And I don't know what it is yet…but I will."

Victoria? Yikes. She must really be upset.

"Want to talk about it?"

She crossed her arms and continued to stare out the window. My Dad was pacing in the side yard, while talking on the phone.

"He's smoking again," she said flatly. "He only does that when something is wrong. I just don't know what it is yet."

That explains some of the earlier tension.

"Have you asked him about it?"

"Yes. But he insists that it's nothing. At first I wondered if he was cheating on me."

"Mom! How could you think that?"

"He's been secretive and not talking very much. Then he suddenly wants to take me across country? I wondered if he was feeling guilty about something. But no…I think he's worried about something. This is how he acted after your brother died. He was grieving, but was also worried that I was going to lose my mind over the whole thing. But I didn't let him pull away then, and I won't let him do it now."

I recognized that steely resolve. Come hell or high water, my mama would get to the bottom of it.

"But enough of that," she said, walking away from the window. "Do you have any chocolate?"

"Duh—I am your daughter." I opened the fridge, got out the ice cream, and made us each a brownie sundae with some of Jo's mocha brownies. I didn't ask any more questions. When she didn't want to talk about something, there was nothing to do but move on.

Dad walked in just as we were finishing up our snack. There was one brownie left in the container.

"That's yours," my mom said, in the sweetest tone I'd heard since she got here. "I'll get you some milk."

As she poured the milk, Mom circled back to the paper. "Why did Anna have to shut it down to begin with?"

For the next 10 or so minutes, I explained what Anna had said the night she stopped by. "There's just not enough money to keep going," I said. "And yes, I think there's more to the story, but she's not sharing it with anybody. She's not one to share her personal business."

"Hope she's not a killer, then," my Dad interjects. "Or every paper in the state will be sharing it."

When Dad finished his brownie, mom washed the empty

container. "I know you aren't hungry right now," she said, "but we brought you one of Dad's steaks, a salad, and a bowl of homemade mac and cheese." She opened the refrigerator door and pointed to the colorful plastic containers taking up my shelf space. "I expect you to return those when you have emptied them. You've kept almost all of my good ones. I need them back so I can refill them for you."

"I promise." My mom had always shown love through feeding people. It was a family tradition. It didn't matter if you made the food to share or bought the food to share…it was the sharing part that mattered the most.

Dad pointed to a small bag near the microwave. "We also brought you some of my biscuits."

Mom never made biscuits. She didn't like for her hands to get sticky.

"It's a good thing I saved you some," Dad said. "We've been chowing down on them. They've almost all disappeared."

I knew exactly what I was having for supper.

"Speaking of disappearing…I was at the supply store today and heard some folks talking. A lot of the farmers have had equipment grow legs and walk away lately."

"Like what?"

"Mostly stuff that could be resold without too much suspicion. But Mr. Fisher had some vials of Moodini's medicine go missing."

"What kind of medicine?"

"Pain medication, I think. Moodini had surgery last month and they prescribed him enough to help him through the week. But before he could give it to him? Poof! Disappeared into thin air."

Maybe a chat with Mr. Fisher was in order.

When they finally headed home, it was close to 3. Dad left a $20 bill on the counter as he always did when he visited. I used to argue with him, but it did no good. I put it in a jar labeled "pet sitting". Grady and Booker would be on the receiving end of that Andrew Jackson.

The next few hours were spent catching up on laundry and email, while loving on the sweet canines and a fussy feline. The least fun part of my afternoon, however, was looking for jobs. I had received responses from the hospital and courthouse jobs, but after further investigation and contemplation, I turned down both offers. The jobs were not for me. I wasn't a nine-to-five kind of gal—never had been. I wasn't about to tell Jo that I'd turned them down, though. *Maybe after we finished proving that Anna didn't kill Sebastian.*

It was around 8 when I dug into the yummy food mom and Dad had left for me. It didn't take long for me to finish it off. As I washed my mama's now-empty containers, the puppies caught my attention. They'd been following Holly around and trying to run, but failing in the most adorable way. Their long, velvety ears were their constant nemesis. Holly nudged them to get up, but sometimes their legs just sprawled out from underneath them. My hardwood floors were just too slick.

Thor and Loki tripped over their ears and paws, then slid a couple of feet. *Looks like it's time to get the rugs out again.*

Aunt Bert used to have runners throughout the Nestled Inn. She said they kept her floors cleaner. But vacuuming the rugs was not something I'd wanted to do, so I'd rolled up the rugs and stored them in the hidden room under the giant staircase. Aunt Bert liked to call the weird closet-like area by the official name—the spandrel. Most spandrels were the size of broom closets or walk-in closets, but this one was big enough to house a lot of the extras that Aunt Bert hadn't wanted to store elsewhere.

The first floor of the Nestled Inn had three meeting rooms, a dining room, the sitting room, the living room, the kitchen, and the spandrel. But the spandrel hadn't been cleaned out since she'd died, and I'd been adding a few things to it here and there, including the runners. Usually I'd just open the door and shove stuff in an empty space near the door. But that had only resulted in more and more things that I would have to go through later.

I turned the glass door handle to the tiny room and the door creaked open, causing a draft and a fluttering of cobwebs. I pulled the long chain hanging from the light. It illuminated the stacks and stacks of stuff: vacuumed sealed bags of bedding, towels, a few chairs, and tons of other supplies that Aunt Bert had needed when the Nestled Inn was still up and running. There was even a disco ball hanging in the corner over a filing cabinet. I think she'd used that for a 1970's themed party when I was in my teens.

I spotted the rugs leaned up against the filing cabinet, right where I'd left them over a year ago. Unfortunately, as I bent over to the pick up the rugs, I toppled a tower of towels with my hip action, causing a domino effect with a few other piles of stuff.

Great. Just great. For the next hour or so, I rearranged and restacked the inventory and rethought my life's choices. At 48, my internal temperature seemed to hover around 300 degrees, so I was sweating like one of the twins' pigs, even though it was early December.

I was almost done when I decided to move the filing cabinet a little closer to the door. But I tipped it just the wrong way... and the bottom drawer slid out. Inside the drawer was a box labeled: *For Tori.*

Forgetting about the rugs for the moment, I hauled the box to the living room. I was almost afraid to open it. I wasn't afraid of creepy crawlies or mice. I was afraid this might be the last surprise I'd find from Aunt Bert.

At her will reading, the lawyer told me that she'd left little surprises for me throughout the Nestled Inn, but I thought I'd already found them all. I'd been through every room...except this one. The first day I was here, I found a picture of Aunt Bert and 5-year-old me. It was on the refrigerator with a note "My dear Tori" on the back. And when I finally got the gumption to move the piano to a different place in the biggest meeting room, named the Conservatory, I found a book of easy to play jazz tunes. And on the first page of the book was a longer note: "My dearest Tori, the piano sounds best when by the window, but put it wherever you want to…just don't forget to play. An unplayed piano is just over-priced firewood."

There were other things, some practical and some sentimental, but they all had one thing in common: a note with my name on them.

I slowly pulled off the lid to the box and looked inside. Immediately, I honed in on the leather bound ledger with the words "Our Guests" etched on the outside. The first entry was from January of 1976 and ran until Aunt Bert passed away two years ago. Under the ledger was another notebook. It had inventory needs for each month, special holidays, and the items she used for the monthly meetings of the Craven Historical Society. There was also a bank book and a flowery envelope with the words "Open me" on it.

Dearest Tori,

If you're reading this, then it means that I'm gone and you're living in the Nestled Inn, just as I'd hoped. Obviously I don't know if you decided to continue renting out the rooms, but I hope the answer is yes. And if you have, then the books in this box should turn out to be helpful to you. If you've not yet rented out the rooms…why the heck not? It would allow you to write in between rentals. And yes, I know you are still working on that book. Get on it, girl!

I found myself laughing and crying while reading it. I could hear it in her no-nonsense voice. She was one of the few people who had read a draft of my novel…and liked it. I wiped a few tears away so I could see the words, then kept reading.

You've got tons of stuff in here that can help you keep on top of things. The guest list is good if you want to start sending out a newsletter and drum up more business. We tend to have repeat customers. There is a folder with the names of all the rooms and their themes – but you should redecorate and rename them as you'd like. Add your own spin! You always had a unique, eclectic taste. Oh! And of most importance, I included the tax returns and the name of my tax guy.

I've also included my personal recipe book. But if I were you, I'd concentrate on running the Inn and let other people do the cooking. You can always order scrumptious eats from Jo's place or the Dairy Barn. Why reinvent the wheel? (But if you do make the sweet potato pies, please take Mr. Fisher one. That's his favorite. Better, yet, invite him over for supper. He gets quite lonely.)

I hope you've enjoyed finding my little surprises around the house. Most of all, I hope you're enjoying living here. And if you are still making up your mind about opening the Nestled Inn again, please know that I wouldn't have left it to you if I didn't think you'd do a great job. So don't let self-doubt talk you out of something you know you want to do and feel you are supposed to do. God has got you and will give you the strength to get it done and do it well.

I love you more,
Aunt Bert

P.S. One caveat: Don't you dare open up the Inn based on some misplaced sense of loyalty or guilt. Whatever you choose, don't let me—or anyone on this earth—write your story for you.

After calling Mom and Dad and leaving a message about what I'd found, I spent most of the night crying and slogging through the treasure trove of notebooks that Aunt Bert had left me. There was a lot to chew on, and no way I could digest it all in one night. I fell asleep around 3am on the couch.

I woke to the sound of Holly baying through the office door. I looked at my watch. 10am? She's probably about to bust. As I passed by the hallway mirror, I took a quick peek and laughed. I had the worst case of pillow face that I'd had in a while. I had probably drooled on the pillow, too.

I put the puppies in the high-sided box and grabbed Holly's leash, then we headed out the front door. I thought about calling Jo, but I wasn't ready to tell her about the box. I knew she'd immediately say it was another sign. And this time? I wasn't sure that I'd be able to disagree. So instead of calling her, I talked to Holly about my plans for the day.

"I need to talk to Mr. Fisher this morning," I said. "Actually, I'd like to talk to a lot of folks: Anna, Sophia, Kevin, Luna, and even the mysterious Niles."

Holly plodded along, listening as I listed the things I knew about the case and the things I didn't.

"Hank is not going to be happy that we're nosing around. You know that, right? But it's okay. It's for a good cause. Anna is not guilty. I can feel it in my bones."

I appreciated the fact that Holly was a good listener. I felt a little dumb, though, because I started waiting on her to respond. "If you ever do talk back," I said, "we're gonna make a lot of money...or I'm gonna need a doctor's visit!"

We walked for about 10 minutes down the long, lonesome driveway that lead from the farmhouse to the main road. When I got to the end, I turned around and headed back to the house. As we walked, I noticed that the fence posts on either side of the road were starting to look a little shabby. A good paint job in the spring would probably be in order. Aunt Bert had always kept it in tip-top shape. I wondered if she had a handyman's numbers in one of those notebooks, too.

As we neared the house, I made my way toward the front porch, but Holly had other ideas...and stopped in her tracks.

"Come on, girl," I coaxed. "I'll give you a double treat!"

But the hound dog was focused on something else… something I couldn't see.

And when we both heard glass breaking in the backyard, she yanked out of my grasp and ran as fast as she could, her giant, velvet ears flapping as she galloped. She disappeared as she rounded the side of the house, but her bay kept me in full awareness of where she was. I ran after her as fast as my plump legs would carry me, but I made a mistake by not looking down.

I hit the root of the giant oak tree that dwarfed all the other trees in the yard…and tripped. I scrambled back to my feet— first checking to make sure nothing was broken—and followed the continual barks and bays coming from my backyard. As I hobbled around the corner, I heard a scream, then saw a running figure disappear as they reached the well-worn path that led to the large wooded area between my property and the old Craven Community Cemetery.

I turned my attention back to Holly. She was in the fence, but the gate had been closed to keep her from chasing the trespasser. *Very clever.*

Holly was no longer paying attention to the intruder's scent, though. She had grown quiet and was sniffing near the fence.

"What ya got there?" I asked. I pulled her back before she decided to make a meal of the plate of food she'd found. "This is not for you, sweet girl. We don't know where it's been!"

I threw it over the fence, but when I turned around, I noticed an unsavory message spray painted on my fence. I was suddenly glad that my mama was not here to see this. She'd have clutched her pearls…then taken off after the intruder through the woods.

I dialed Hank's number; he was not going to be a happy camper.

"You can't stay out of trouble, can you? What is it with you this week?"

"It's not my fault. It seems to come looking for me!"

Hank had made it to my house in record time. He'd just got home from work, but Jo was still at the café.

"I'm beginning to wonder if you are a magnet for illegal activity. You might want to pace yourself."

I responded with a glare that yelled "bite me". We'd known each other a long time, so I was sure he knew exactly what I was thinking.

"So can you describe the intruder at all?" He had whipped out his notebook, ready for details. "Anything would be helpful."

"I never saw a face," I said, trying to remember everything I could. "But whoever it was had a dark colored hoodie and zero meat on their bones."

"You just described five people I saw walking downtown today," He said. "Got anything more distinctive?"

"Yes…something weird—but not about their appearance. I found a paper plate piled with freshly ground meat and threw it out over there." I showed him where I'd flung it. "I was worried it was poisoned or something. Maybe they wanted Holly to be drugged before they tried to bust into the Inn?"

He peeked over the fence. "I'll get it to forensics. Maybe we can find something that can help." He wrote up a few more notes. "So there's nothing else you can think of?"

Holly walked up, sat down at his feet, and plopped. When she did, I saw something hanging out of her mouth. It looked like a dark piece of cloth.

"Hank…" I said, pointing to it. "that might be the reason for the scream that I heard."

He carefully coaxed Holly into releasing it.

"Good girl," he said, carefully inspecting it. "There's not any blood, but that doesn't mean she didn't get them. I'll check the hospital for possible dog bite victims."

"Wait…will she be in trouble if she bit someone?"

"They were on your property and she was protecting it. So not for that reason. But has she had her rabies shot yet?"

"No…she's nursing. They didn't recommend it. Plus, she's a stray, remember? She might be up to date and we just don't know it."

"Then that might be a problem. Better call Duncan."

Within minutes, Hank had Duncan on the phone.

"So we've got a situation," Hank said. "Tori has attracted yet more criminal activity."

"Is that supposed to surprise me?"

"I can hear you!" I narrowed my eyes as if Duncan could see the look I was giving him.

"I should have mentioned that you are on speaker phone," Hank said, smiling. Then he gave Duncan the lowdown. Hearing him describe the situation made it sound like part of a mystery movie on the Hallmark channel. "As you can tell, we need you here as quickly as possible. We don't think Holly is a threat to anyone, but we have to make sure."

"I'm already on my way," he said. "I'll be there soon!"

Thirty minutes later, Duncan pulled up and had his veterinarian bag on his shoulder. As he checked Holly's pulse, eyes, heartbeat, and other things, she kept trying to lick his glasses.

"She seems okay," he said, "but keep an eye on her. She's been through an awful lot for a dog who's been here for barely a week."

"What about the biting issue?" Hank asked. "If she's taken a chunk out of someone…"

"I don't see any indication that she got flesh. Do you?"

"No, but if she did, doesn't the protocol include a 10-day quarantine?"

"Yes. *IF* she bit someone." Duncan leaned down and checked Holly's eyes one more time. "I can definitely put her in isolation if you want me to, but I feel confident saying that she does not have rabies."

"Are you willing to swear to that?" Hank asked. "Because if you can, then I can initial the paperwork and she is a free dog."

I hadn't said much in the last few minutes because I was trying to formulate my thoughts. If she was in quarantine, the house would be awfully quiet and lonely without her. I wasn't ready for that.

"My initial opinion is no rabies. BUT, I'm not willing to swear on it or fudge paperwork about it—because I could be wrong." He looked around and lowered his voice. "But I am willing to wait a few days to see if her owners contact us. By this point, I think your wife and Tori have placed about a million posters in and around Craven, so maybe they'll call soon. But without the previous owner's input, we have no way of knowing when she received her last shot. If we don't soon get that info, then she will have to go into a 10-day isolation."

"But—" I said, feeling my voice cracking a little. "Thor and Loki need their mama. Surely there is something you can do?"

"Give me just a minute. There might be a loophole."

Duncan walked away, but my eyes were still glued to him. He had the power to lock Holly up or give her freedom. *I knew which one I wanted him to choose.*

Hank touched me on my shoulder to get my attention. "Is that one of yours?" He pointed to a small clear bag hidden in the grass. It still had some leftover remnants of the meaty, fresh dog food that I'd thrown over the fence.

"Nope. Haven't been to Toasty's in about two weeks. And if I did, I certainly wouldn't throw the bag in my backyard now, would I?"

"I don't know," he teased. "You once chained yourself to a tree. Anything could happen."

Funny. Very funny.

"So do you think the recent break-ins have anything to do with Sebastian's murder?" I asked. "Mom and Dad heard some discussion about it today."

"Let me guess…at Fred's?"

"Yep. It's where all the hip farmers go."

"That's a truer statement than you realize. They know about some crimes before I do." He cleared his throat. "Speaking of crimes…I heard back from Sebastian's autopsy."

"And?"

"And I can't tell you what killed him."

"Then why even bring it up?" *Rude.*

"Because if you ask the right question, then maybe I can tell you what didn't kill him."

"Oh! I see." I thought about it for a moment to make sure I worded the next sentence as perfectly as possible. "Hypothetically, can a man be killed by a hand-sized paper weight?"

"Yes, but it's an improbable scenario." He pulled down his glasses and raised his eyebrows. "Especially if the hypothetical person holding the hypothetical rock is at a really weird hypothetical angle when striking the hypothetical blow."

"So she didn't kill him?"

"Not with a paperweight." He pushed his glasses back up. "But that doesn't mean she didn't kill him. It just means she didn't do it with the paperweight—hypothetically, of course."

"Of course."

As I pondered this new information, Duncan jogged back toward us.

"I've got it," he yelled. "According to NC law, she is supposed to be quarantined for 10 days at the clinic if she bites someone. But since there is no victim, then we don't technically have to do anything. If someone comes forward, then we can figure it out from there."

"But who is going to admit to being bit by a dog during the course of a crime?" I asked.

"That's kind of the point," Duncan said. "If they don't show up…Holly doesn't have to be locked up. Case closed."

"Glad you're on our side," Hank said.

I was, too.

The sun glimmered off something under the tree in the corner of the lot. "Hmmm…this might be of interest, too." I pointed to an almost empty can of spray paint.

"This is one of the sloppiest criminals I've ever seen," Hank said. "First the bag and then the can?"

"I guess they weren't expecting me back so soon."

"And how did they know you were gone? Your car was still here, right?"

Duncan had a point.

"So you think they were waiting for me to leave?"

"That's what we're going to find out," Hank said. "I can send it all off for fingerprints, including that broken glass, but I need to grab a pail from my truck. Can you get me a plastic bag? I'll need something to line it."

"Sure! Just be a minute!" When I stepped inside, I heard hungry, whining puppies. And so did Holly. I grabbed Holly's leash to keep her from bolting through the door "Can you call the boys, Hank? The puppies need to be fed, but I've got to clean this mess up."

"On it!"

Within minutes, the twins arrived.

"Y'all are life savers," I said. "Holly is probably hungry, too. You can put her in the study to eat while you feed the babies, but I don't think she'll give you any trouble."

She was almost dried up now, so I wasn't even sure she'd be able to nurse if she tried. It had been several days since she ate the chocolate, but the babies were used to the bottles now. As far as I could tell, Holly seemed perfectly happy with the arrangement, too. It was time to start feeding them solid food, anyway.

"Tori," Hank said, interrupting my dog-centered musings, "any idea who might be responsible?"

"Let me think about it," I said, knowing full well who immediately popped into my head. Luna was pretty upset with me at the hospital. But maybe, just maybe, she told Kevin that I was poking around.

"I'll take that as a maybe." Hank jingled his keys and took a moment before speaking again. "I have to get this information to the station, but I'm glad to come back and help clean up after I'm done."

"I'm available to help, too," Duncan said. "I'd rather do this than keep working at my place."

"That would be fantastic!" I had zero desire to paint my fence, but having company might make the task be less stressful.

"Feel like helping me replace the broken glass, too? If so, I think I have some extra panes under the house. My Aunt Bert never threw anything away."

"I know how to Youtube it," Duncan said. "We can figure it out."

With all the junk that Aunt Bert collected, she insisted she could have been a boy scout because she was always prepared for anything.

"I'll call Jo on the way back to the office," Hank said. "You know she's going to want to know why the boys aren't home doing school or cleaning their room…and why I'm not home grilling the tilapia she requested."

He knew my best friend very well.

After he left, Duncan and I gathered the panes from the basement, and there was some paint in the shed.

"Hank explained to me about the school situation. He said they really like working from home."

"Yeah, they get their work done a lot quicker, have time to pursue their hobbies, and even work some for Jo."

"Sounds like a win-win. Spending more time with family— if the family is a stable and good influence—can increase confidence, especially in teens."

"Heard that from your four-legged patients, have you?"

"Actually I have a master's degree in psychology, too; I had planned on being a therapist, but changed my mind."

"A therapist?" I tried not to look so surprised, but I couldn't help it.

"Yeah. Weird, huh? It didn't take me long to realize that animals are a lot easier to deal with than most humans, and usually nicer."

"Case in point," I said, gesturing to the words on my fence. "Not very nice."

"Exactly. But this wasn't just "not nice" or some high school prank. They brought meat, maybe tainted meat. What if it was the same folks who broke into Anna's house? Maybe they saw you and figured out who you are."

I held up my hands to stop him. "I have a hunch who did it,

but I'm not 100% sure."

"Care to share?"

"Only if you promise not to tell Hank."

"I can't make that promise."

"Then no. But I'll be curious to see if the meat was poisoned… or just spiked with pain meds."

"That's oddly specific," he said, sounding perplexed. "Are you sure you don't want to share?"

"Not yet. But I do want to get this fence painted!"

It took us about an hour and a half to get the first coat of "polar white" on the fence. While we let it dry, we worked on replacing the window panes. It wasn't terribly hard work; it was just tedious.

Two hours later, he handed me the last pane. I popped it into place, then replaced the supporting frame for the door. "Done!" I said, doing a little jig. "Bet this isn't how you thought you'd spend your afternoon, is it?

"Nope. But it's still better than unpacking."

We stood back and looked at the finished door. The panes needed to be cleaned, but that could wait until tomorrow.

"I'm proud of us," I said.

"And I'm hungry. Do you like BBQ?"

"Yes. But only from Big Bill's BBQ."

"Sounds good to me. What do you usually get?"

I listed off a handful of delicious entrees. "There isn't anything bad on that menu—except for the banana pudding. But I don't ever eat that."

"Me, either. But isn't that against the law around here? I've heard you can get your southern card revoked for crimes against food."

"Then I'm in big trouble; I don't like tea, either."

"I won't tattle if you won't." Duncan pulled out his credit card and handed it to me. "Since you know more about the good stuff than I do, do you mind calling? Order whatever you want—enough for you, Grady, Booker, and me. And while you're doing that, I'll start cleaning up. Deal?"

My arms were tired. My legs were tired. I was tired all over. "You've got a deal."

I ran inside and got the number from the list of restaurants that I kept on my fridge.

It rang seven times before Charlene Sharpe, the original owner's granddaughter and hostess extraordinaire, picked up the phone. She recognized my number. "Do you want your regular, sweetie?"

"Actually, I am going to make a few changes today. I've got a few folks to feed."

I ordered one pound of brisket, a dozen cheddar biscuits, slaw, pintos, hush puppies, and chocolate pie.

"That'll be $41.67," she said.

I gave her the name, number, and expiration date on Duncan's card.

"Um…Sugar? This ain't your card."

"No ma'am. But the person it belongs to is right here. Do you need to speak to him?"

"That won't be necessary," Charlene said with a giggle. "Your boyfriend's got good taste."

"No-no. Not my boyfriend. Just a friend."

"Whatever you say, sugar. Whatever you say."

Duncan touched up a few places on the fence while I kept a watch for the BBQ delivery. After a few more minutes, he took a break and came to sit on the front porch with me. The smell of new paint reminded me of all the Nestled Inn rooms that could use a little updating.

Booker stuck his head out the front door. "Mom said we should read Dr. Duncan's book. Where is it?"

"Top shelf in kitchen," I said, "Next to the book labeled, "Taking Care of your Elderly Cat.""

Duncan washed his splattered hands and chuckled. "So you know."

"Yeah. Jo and I have been meaning to talk to you about it. We found it at the Book Nook," I said. "Why didn't you tell us?"

"Immediately introducing myself as a best-selling author seems pretentious and feels awkward. Do you tell everyone you meet that you write the obituary column and a weekly murder mystery?"

"Number one: I don't do that anymore. Number two: Even if I did, I wouldn't have to tell anyone; everyone around here knows. As I was told earlier this week...not many secrets in a small town."

"Since we're on the topic of secrets," he said, looking up at me with his gorgeous gray eyes, "you never did finish telling me about the time Hank arrested you."

I felt my face grow warm, but it seemed only fair that he should know something about me that was a little awkward, too. Besides, telling the story definitely helped pass the time while we waited for the food.

"It had to do with the oldest tree in the city and city hall. They wanted to knock it down to build a park. Isn't that the dumbest thing you've ever heard?"

"I've heard worse," he said, "but it doesn't sound like the best marketing strategy."

I explained that I climbed to the middle of the tree and chained myself to it overnight, threatening legal action if anyone touched me.

"I thought I had a chance to force the city to see things my way" I said. "But by the time I realized that my plan was never going to work, Hank had talked me down from the tree, and somehow also talked the city out of pressing charges."

"Did the tree get cut down?"

"Yes. But I didn't go to jail. My mom and Dad were so happy about the outcome that they invited Hank to lunch with us at the café. Jo was a waitress there at the time. She accidentally spilled cheesecake in his lap when she delivered it to the table…and that was that. Love at first sight."

The food arrived as I was finishing up my story.

"Before we eat," Duncan said, "walk with me to the fence and let's check our work."

The spray painted graffiti was barely noticeable.

"I can come back tomorrow afternoon and add one more coat," he said.

"Maybe. Let's figure it out later. Right now, I'm ready for brisket!"

The boys were too hungry to say anything for the first few minutes. They just chowed down. Duncan was quiet, too, but after his first couple of bites, he let out a happy moan.

"I don't want to be a pig, but I can already tell that I'll be getting seconds."

"A pig?" Booker snorted, holding up a hushpuppy. "Pretty corny, sir."

"Good one," Duncan replied. "I think a pun war is in order."

After a few minutes of listening to their dad-jokes, I took my last bite, and the phone rang. I didn't recognize the number, so I let it go to voice mail. Then it rang again.

"Persistent, aren't they?" Duncan said.

"Yeah. Probably trying to contact me about my car's extended warranty."

The boys gave me a high five. "Good one!"

It rang one more time. "Fine. Let's see if I'm right!"

"Hello?"

"Tori? This is Blake."

Crap. When I'd called him at the hospital, I'd forgotten to add him to my contacts.

"Hi Blake," I said. "Sorry I couldn't answer. I was in the middle of a brisket biscuit. Is Anna okay?"

I put the phone on speaker, but gave Duncan, Booker, and Grady the "shush" sign. They got the hint.

"She's doing better," Blake said. "She's actually coming home today. That's why I'm calling. I was hoping you could help us out by keeping an eye on Anna tomorrow? I have to go back to work."

"I'm sure she's worn out. I can definitely keep her company. What time do I need to come over?"

"Actually, I need to bring her to you. We are having the front door repaired tomorrow—finally—and I want her to be able to rest."

"That makes sense." I made a face at the boys and Duncan. "What time will you be here?"

"Around 8:45am."

"Anything I need to know?"

"What kind of question is that?"

I wasn't sure why his tone was so caustic, but I didn't like it. By the looks on their faces, Duncan and the twins didn't like it, either.

"Well," I replied, keeping my voice calm, "does she have any medication she needs to take? Or anything I need to watch out for? She has been in the hospital for almost two days. I don't want her to end up there again."

"The doctor says she needs to stay hydrated and rest. That's all you need to worry about."

With that, he ended our call.

"He sounds like a lovely person," Duncan muttered.

"Until Anna landed in the hospital I had never talked to him much," I said. "He seemed a lot more likeable from afar."

Grady offered a small piece of BBQ to Holly. "Anna's not allergic to dogs, is she? If so, we could take Holly and the puppies to our house for the day."

"That's a great question and wonderful suggestion," I said. "And since your dad is totally not allergic, I'll take you up on your offer."

I could just imagine the look of horror on Jo's face when Holly and puppies pranced into her living room. *Maybe one of the boys could record it for me.*

"We probably need to get back to the house. We are supposed to be washing dishes. But…"

"Yeah. Your mom is not going to be happy if that sink isn't shining when she gets home."

"What time do you want us to come get the dogs tomorrow?"

"Hmmm…since Blake is bringing Anna over around 8:45, how about you come over around 8? We can get all their stuff together…then I'll feed you some breakfast. How's that?"

The boys shook Duncan's hand, then petted the dogs one more time. I noticed that they gave special attention to Thor.

They were going to be heartbroken if Jo didn't agree to keep the puppy.

I walked the boys to the door. "I wish I could see your mom's face when you bring the dogs in the door tomorrow."

"What if I record it for you," Booker said.

"Um, that sounds like a mission that might get you in big trouble."

"Eh. I've gotten in trouble for worse," he said. "Then again, I could get dad to do it."

"I'll think about it," I said, but immediately felt bad. What if this plan backfired? Jo had obviously been lying about Hank being allergic. But why? There was more to this story than met the eye.

When I returned to the kitchen, Duncan was already cleaning off the table.

"What do you want to do with the leftovers?" he asked. "I can pack it up if you tell me where the containers are."

"Hold that thought." I ran to the pantry and grabbed several plastic disposable containers, then ran back and stacked them on the table. "This should be enough."

The owners of Big Bill's BBQ believed in quality and quantity, so there was plenty to share. We filled up five lunch containers with brisket, BBQ, and a few sides.

"Here," I said, shoving three containers Duncan's way. "You have to take it home. I like BBQ, but I don't want to eat it for three days straight."

"Are you sure? You could share it with Anna tomorrow."

"I'm absolutely sure. And Anna is not a fan of BBQ. She's more of a fish and chips kind of gal."

The few times I'd brought BBQ to the paper to share with Anna, it had not gone well. She had explained to me that southern cuisine wasn't at all like the food she was used to in the UK. Then she insisted on bringing in some steak and kidney pie for me to try. It wasn't too bad…but it was definitely not my cup of tea.

"So what are your afternoon plans?" Duncan asked. "Besides watching paint dry, of course."

"I have an exciting afternoon of job searching ahead of me."

"Well…I've been thinking," he said. "You still owe me a milkshake, don't you?"

"Why yes. Yes, I do." I was surprised he remembered.

"Then how about we go for a jaunt to the metropolis of Craven? We can grab some ice cream, then maybe run by the feed supply store. It's about time for the puppies to start eating real food."

"That sounds like a good plan, except for one thing." I pointed to the small pack of pups in the corner. "I just sent the boys home. And I'm a little weary of leaving the dogs here by themselves after what just happened."

"Why don't we bring them with us? The puppies have only had one car ride, so they could use more exposure to other people and the world around them."

"The Dairy Barn does serve a small bowl of yogurt for dogs," I said.

"It's settled then. Let's get these puppies on the road!"

About halfway there, his phone rang. It was Hank.

"Uh huh…Yeah…okay." Then Duncan hung up and grunted.

"That would explain a lot."

"What are you talking about?"

"An anonymous tip was left on the police information line; someone has been stealing supplies from the office and reselling them on the black market."

"How?"

"I don't know enough about the inventory list or financial paperwork to know. I've got to figure out if the anonymous tip is real or just a stupid prank."

"You should get an accountant to look into it."

"Got someone in mind?"

I whipped out a business card from my wallet. "Dad and his associates do this sort of thing all the time."

"Really?"

"Minus the drugs, black market, and murder, of course. They have handled high-profile embezzlement cases, but mostly they do the boring work of reconciling financial books with inventory and such. I suggested that Anna use him for the paper, but she refused."

"Why?"

"She said the paper was beyond help…and she didn't believe in miracles."

"I'm the opposite. I am a big believer in miracles, even though sometimes my prayers aren't always answered in the way I'd like."

I liked the way he thought.

We drove around dead man's curve and my mind was taken back to the murder and missing meds.

"So how long has it been since the stuff started going missing?"

"I'm not sure, but I think it's been at least a month."

"Interesting. That's about when Jessica left and Luna took her job."

"Who's Jessica?"

"Jessica Fox—she was the front desk receptionist before

Luna. Left town about a month ago—then Luna was hired to take her place."

"That's very interesting."

"Isn't it?" I said. "I wonder how long Luna and Kevin have been dating?"

"Why?"

"Maybe there's a connection between the two of them and the missing supplies in the office. What do you think?"

"I think it would be a miracle if there wasn't a connection."

For a Friday afternoon, the road to town wasn't terrible. Holly and the puppies were in the floor of the backseat. Anytime they whined, she leaned over and gave them a motherly nudge or licked them.

"I really hope the puppies don't pee in your floorboard," I said. "Holly is fine...but they are definitely not house trained yet."

"This old truck has seen worse than that," he said. "I once agreed to transport a pot-bellied pig across three county lines for my wife."

"That sounds like an interesting ride. I bet the odor was just...lovely."

"If you like the smell of a barn, yes. We tried and tried, but the smell lingered, especially on hot days. I told her that if she agreed to never ask for another animal like that, then I agreed not to have pot-bellied bacon for supper after it's time on earth was done."

"Sounds like a solid deal," I said, laughing. "I'm sure the pig appreciated it the most."

"He's still alive and living it up with my daughter and her

roommate. I think it's trying to outlive me, just to spite me."

We pulled into the parking lot of the Dairy Barn, but there were about five sets of folks waiting for their turn at the window. The Dairy Barn wasn't a traditional ice cream store. It was more like a stationary food truck. They sold ice cream, pies, cakes, and other sweets. Customers parked, then walked up to one of the two windows. The owners always employed upbeat teens who started each conversation with cringe-worthy, but punny statements like, "Welcome to the Dairy Barn where we only have pies for you." Or my favorite, "Welcome to the Dairy Barn, where our customers are legen-dairy!"

The weird mottos were part of their shtick. They even had t-shirts with Dairy Barn-isms. Their desserts were dreamy and they had a huge fan base, so their marketing strategy worked.

We hopped out of the car with the dogs and made our way toward the line. I led Holly on her leash, and we each had a puppy.

"I'm relying on your expertise again," Duncan said. "Do they have anything with brownie in it?"

I pointed to the sign posted beside the first window. It had pictures and giant descriptions of each frozen concoction.

"Ahhh…which is your favorite?"

"The Brownie and Bacon shake."

"That's definitely in the running, but I'm leaning toward a Sir Brownie Sundae."

He hemmed and hawed for a few minutes while trying to make a decision. I was about to suggest that we go somewhere else when he grunted.

"Ugh! Too many choices! I'll stick with the Sir Brownie this time around. But I guess I'll have to come back again to try the others. I wouldn't want to insult the management." He paused, then squeezed the area around his waist. "So is there a YMCA around here? I'm gonna need it."

"Yes, but there are plenty of free places to run around here. We've got a greenway and tons of mountain bike trails. And you can always kayak at Helen's lake."

"I definitely want to hear more about that!"

After we ordered our food and a few small bowls for the dogs, we carefully balanced it all and walked around to the back of the shack to look for an empty table. There was only one table and it was already occupied.

"Tori?" Allison jumped up and wrapped me in a giant hug. "I'm so glad to see you!"

As I hugged her back, I glanced over her shoulder. Kevin was sitting in the Honda in the parking space nearby. His window was down so I knew he could hear us, but he didn't even look our way.

When we pulled back from the hug, Allison grabbed my hands. "It's nice to see a kind face. Please come sit with me." She smiled at Duncan with a quizzical look on her face. "I don't think we've met, but I feel like I've seen you before."

Duncan and I sat the puppies on the ground, then gave all three dogs their yogurt bowls. We had the puppies and Holly on leashes. They were doing great.

Duncan sat his food down, then reached out to shake Allison's hand.

"I'm Duncan Williams," he said. "New vet in town."

"Duncan Williams?" she cocked her head to the right, then narrowed her eyes for a second. "YES! I have seen you! I've sold several copies of your book at the store!" She seemed genuinely excited. "You should read it at our open mic night!"

"I appreciate the offer, but I'm not sure that a chapter on proper puppy hygiene or eating habits is the way to your customers' hearts."

"You should at least think about it," she said. "It would help bring in more customers and maybe get you a few new clients, as well.

"I'll let you know," he said with a smile.

"Do either of you have a plastic bag?" I asked. "I think I need to find a grassy spot for the dogs."

"I have some in the truck," Duncan said. He took two quick bites of his sundae, stood up, and handed me the leashes. "I'll be right back."

Allison watched him walk away, then looked at me. "He's a kind man. It must be nice having someone to lean on."

"We aren't…you know…" I said quickly. "I just met him last week."

"Oh! Sorry. I don't usually make assumptions like that. You just seemed so at ease with each other."

Had it really only been a week? It felt longer, but not in a weird or bad way.

Duncan returned quickly, ate a few more scoops of his sundae, then held out his hands for the leashes. "I'll take the pups for a walk. Enjoy your chat."

"Are you sure?" I asked.

"Absolutely. Be back in a bit."

"How are you?" I said to Allison, moving the conversation away from me. "And how is Kevin?"

"Honestly? Pretty awful."

I admired her candor. Most folks like to dance around the truth to make others feel less awkward.

"Kevin has one doctor's appointment this week, some therapy appointments, and lawyer meetings," she said.

"Lawyer? Why does he need a lawyer?"

"When the police got to the accident scene, they found that Kevin had some things in the back of the SUV that clearly didn't belong to him.

She paused, wiped away a few tears, then straightened her shoulders. "He's my son, and I love him. But right now, I don't like him very much. And to be fair, he probably feels the same about me."

I wondered if the items in the van resembled Mr. Fisher's

stolen property and the other missing goodies from local farmers. I handed Allison one of the napkins from the table, but didn't ask her about the questions in my head.

She blew her nose a few times, then continued. "This is a nightmare—one that feels like it will ever end. But if this is what it takes to wake him up…then so be it."

"Is there anything I can do to help you?" I really had no clue what that could be, but it seemed to be the natural thing to ask, even if the answer was no.

"My therapist said that I need to get out of the house to take care of my own mental health. I haven't had a date night with friends since my husband died. So once I get Kevin the help he needs, I was wondering if you and Jo would like to join me for supper?"

"I think I can say yes for both of us!"

Allison threw away her half-eaten bowl of ice cream. "My therapist says that I've isolated myself too much. But it's hard to talk to people when all my friends' kids are graduating, making plans for college, or getting jobs—and I'm just praying that mine makes it home alive."

"Loving someone who is determined to hurt themselves rips your heart out and stomps it into pieces, day after day after day."

"You sound like you've been in my shoes."

"That's a complicated story best suited for another time."

"I feel like a failure." Her voice was a whisper at this point. She looked up at the truck. Kevin had put on his headphones and laid his head back against the headrest.

"You're not a failure, Allison. You're a good mama and you're giving Kevin all the resources he needs to get better— but only he can make the decision to actually get better." *I knew this fact all too well.*

I didn't want to bring up Mr. Fisher and the stolen goods, but I needed to.

I quickly stood up and threw away my bowl, then slowly walked back to the table. "I hate to ask this, but have you found any odd drugs in your home? Maybe some that are in a vial with a Moodini's name on them?"

"No, but the day is still young." Allison sighed. "I am beyond surprised at this point in my parental journey."

I explained that some of the farmers had complained about missing items and medicine. I also told her that things were missing from the vet clinic, too.

"He and Niles have been out pretty late some nights the last month or so."

"I'd like to talk to Niles, but I don't even know what he looks like or how to get in touch with him."

"Kevin would be the one with that info."

"Do you mind if I talk to him for just a minute?"

"Feel free. I've grilled my son several times, but he's not talking. You're welcome to try again."

We made our way to her truck and tapped on the side of the door. He looked up at his mom and took off his headphones. "I'm ready to go."

"Tori and I were just chatting," Allison said. "There's been a spike in stolen property since you started hanging out with your new friend."

He put his headphones back on and tried to roll up the window. Allison put one hand on the window, and pushed his headphones onto his neck. "Pay attention."

He crossed his arms and stared straight ahead.

"Mr. Fisher and a few other farmers have had equipment go missing," I said. "But some medicine has disappeared, too. I wondered if you might know something about that?"

He uncrossed his arms and started biting is thumbnail. "I don't have any idea what you're talking about."

"Well, I happened to be at the police station a few days ago," I said. "They have some fingerprints from the break-ins. I expect all they'll need to do is compare any they find at Mr. Fisher's farm or any of the other farms who are missing items or drugs for their animals."

I didn't really know if there would be any fingerprints at Mr. Fisher's place, or anywhere else, but it was worth a shot. Maybe it would scare him into confessing.

He didn't respond, except to put his headphones back on his head.

"Listen to her!" This time, Allison removed the headphones completely and threw them on the ground. "If they happen to be your fingerprints, then I'd like to hear it from your lips, rather than get another surprise from the police. I am doing the best I can for you, honey. But you've got to help, too."

We stood there for a few minutes and waited, but he didn't speak. Just kept biting his nails.

Maybe I'd get a reaction if I asked about the clinic's stolen inventory. "A lot of things have gone missing at the vet clinic, too," I said. "Do you know anything about that?"

Kevin shot me a dirty look, but remained quiet.

"We know you are dating Luna," I said. "Maybe, just maybe, the two of you are working together. Maybe the two of you went to the clinic last Friday to steal more supplies. Maybe you both got caught by Sebastian and maybe things got ugly."

"Hold on!" he looked at me in horror. "I may be a thief, but I'm not a murderer!"

"So you admit to stealing from Mr. Fisher and others?"

His face went stony again. "You're not the police," Kevin said, "so I don't have to answer your questions."

"That's basically the same thing I heard from Luna," I said calmly.

I watched the blood drain from Allison's face, then a steel determination return in its place. "You'll answer our questions… and you'll do it now. Where were you last Friday night?"

I knew she meant business. Apparently so did Kevin. He took a deep breath and started mumbling. "I was with Niles. We got supper at the Irish bar."

"So you weren't with Luna?" I asked.

"No, um…she had to work or something. I don't remember."

"I see." Either Kevin was lying or Luna was. Maybe both. *But why?*

"Anything else you need to tell her?" Allison asked. "Like maybe where to find Niles?"

Kevin went back to biting his nails.

He'd put up a stone wall, just like Luna.

Allison walked around and climbed in the driver's side. "We have to get him to his appointment," she said. "But I'll see if I can get you more information and maybe a picture. I'll text later."

A few minutes later, Duncan, Holly, and the puppies pranced back over to the table.

"They didn't seem to mind the leashes," he said. "They even wanted to explore a little."

"Did they find anything?" I scratched Holly's back, causing her to lean into my legs.

"Yup. A decaying frog. Holly rolled in it."

"You're gonna need a bath, little mama!" I looked over at the puppies. Their tiny feet were covered in mud. "Guess you're both gonna need one, too."

Duncan finished his yogurt as we made our way back to the truck, but the puppies were clamoring for his attention. "They are getting hungry again."

I shook my head in disbelief. These puppies were already eating more than I'd thought possible. "I guess we need to mosey back to the house and get some bottles ready."

He reached in the backseat and whipped out two puppy bottles from a cooler he'd brought. "I fixed a couple, just in case."

"When did you do this?"

"While you were grabbing your coat and checking on Percy."

"The puppies are very impressed." *And so was I.*

"Glad someone is," he said. "What good is being an expert in the field if I don't have a chance to prove it?"

We sat in the parking lot and fed the puppies. "How was your chat with Allison?" Duncan said.

"Kevin is in a lot of trouble. But…"

"But what?"

"I think there's way more to this story than Allison knows. I think we need to make a trip to Fred's," I said. "He knows everyone and everything in this town. He's like the Chuck Norris of gossip."

We arrived at Fred's Feed and Seed Supply and parked as close as we could, thankful that Fred's place was hound dog-friendly. When the canine trio tired of sniffing every blade of grass and scratching at the cracks in the sidewalk, we made our way into the store.

Fred wasn't at the front desk. We looked up and down the first few aisles, then found him on the paint aisle.

"Hi Tori," Fred said, nodding toward us. "And welcome, Dr. Williams. It's a pleasure."

"Have we met?" Duncan's confused facial expression looked like mine when Jo first tried to talk me through posting an Instagram story.

"No, but I recommend your books to a lot of my customers. I'm the one who told Allison that she should stock them." He reached out to Duncan for a handshake. "You've got a lot of down-home wisdom. We need more of that in the world."

"Thanks." Duncan shook Fred's hand. "My granddad was a farmer and taught me a lot."

"Sounds like you chose the right profession." Fred reached down to pet Holly; she was all too happy to let him rub behind her velvety ears. The puppies whined and wiggled for attention, too. "So what can I do for you folks today?"

"It's a bit of a delicate situation," I said. "It involves Allison's son."

"Yeah. I know all about it. Allison's been down here to chat the last couple of days." He rearranged a few things on the shelves. "Kevin is in some big trouble. He needs to get his head on straight!"

"He's been running around with a new friend by the name of Niles."

"Niles Walters?" Fred picked up a leash from the floor and hung it back on the hook it had fallen from. "I let him start working here a few months ago, helping unload supplies and such. But didn't last long."

"I'm guessing you caught him helping himself to some merchandise?"

"Yep. Caught him red-handed."

"Your mystery corner column has come in handy," Duncan said, looking at me. "You're really good at this."

"She sure is," Fred said. "Remember last year when you suspected that Bubba Peterson had a dog-fighting ring going on? You were more on top of things than the guys on the case."

"Wait a minute," Duncan interrupted, "You broke up a dog fighting ring?"

"Yes!" Fred shook his head in a "I couldn't believe it either" kind of way. "She asked all the right questions and managed not to get herself killed by the dogs or by Bubba's crew."

"So you're a one-woman-crime-fighting-machine?" When Duncan smiled, his eyes crinkled on the sides. "I'm impressed, to say the least."

"I was doing a little sleuthing for a good cover story," I said. "It wasn't nearly as exciting as it sounds."

The dog-fighting ring consisted of two middle-aged brothers, Bubba and Willie Pressley (no kin to Elvis) who bragged about their operation, making it easy for me to track them down. When they got caught, they pretty much confessed to everything. At that point, they were more scared of their mama finding out than they were of going to jail. The Pressley's were not career or blood thirsty criminals; they were dumb criminals trying to make a quick buck. They spent a few months in prison before being let out on parole.

"Circling back," I said, trying to get us back on track, "do you know where I could find Niles?"

"Not sure. I don't know much about him other than he's been hanging out with Allison's boy lately. He said something about sofa surfing with friends."

"Do you know if he's got a girlfriend?" I asked.

"I saw him out one night with Hank's niece. It was a good while back."

Suri? I did not expect that. If Jo knew, she would have said something. I'd definitely need to have a chat with her.

"How do they know each other?" Duncan asked.

"I think he got a job as one of their kennel workers. But from what I heard, that didn't last long, either."

"That's interesting," I mumbled. "Do you happen to have a picture?"

"Actually…I do!" He ran to the front counter and came back with a store badge. "He was always losing it somewhere in the loading dock. I eventually just kept it up front in the lost and found box to see if he'd notice, but he never did. Need anything else?" Fred asked, obviously done with that line of inquiry. "I've got a lot of work today. Truck is coming in and I don't have any extra hands."

"I need someone to take one of Holly's puppies. Interested?" I was sure his answer would be no. We weren't exactly getting inundated with calls about the puppies.

"My German Shepherd passed away last month, and my cat, Penelope, still walks around looking for her. So yeah. I'm interested."

"Seriously?" I seemed to be saying that I lot lately.

"Have you ever known me to be anything but serious?"

He had a point. But if I was honest with myself, the offer to take her had been a hollow one. *I wasn't expecting a yes.*

"Wait a minute," Duncan said, "your cat misses your German Shepherd? I don't usually see that dynamic between my canine and feline patients."

"It wasn't always like that." Fred showed us a picture from his wallet. "But after about a year or so, they ended up sleeping in the same bed."

I thought about Percy and the havoc he and Holly caused in the B&B. That was not something I wanted to repeat. Percy would rather have three baths a day instead of having to live with a dog. *They'd never get along.*

A few other customers started trickling in. Some I recognized, some I didn't.

"I better get back to work," Fred said. "Tourist season is in full swing."

Most of the tourists came up to see the changing of the leaves, but if leaf-watching was their main goal for visiting, they should have come a few weeks ago. It was getting very, very cold now and most of the trees were almost naked.

"One more thing," I said, "did you hear any chatter about stolen goods from the clinic?"

"No. But if I do, I'll let you know."

"Thanks for your help, Fred," I said. "I'll let you know about the puppies. K?"

Duncan plopped a bag of puppy chow on the counter.

"It's on the house," Fred said. "If they like it, you can buy the next bag. Those are gonna be big dogs, so I know you'll be back a lot." Then he waved to us as we left. "And don't forget to keep me on the 'maybe list' for the pups!"

When we climbed back in Duncan's truck, he got a text. "Hm. This is kind of late notice."

"What do you mean?"

"It's from Luna. Listen to this." Then he read the text aloud. *"Sorry. Can't be at work tomorrow. I don't feel well."* He looked at me, then back at the text. "First day back since the murder and she's not going to be there?"

It was hard not to tell him what I thought. But if she happened to be nursing a dog bite, Holly would have to be quarantined.

"I really need to talk to her," I said, "and Niles, too. He and Kevin are as thick as thieves…pun intended."

"And how well do you know Luna?"

"Not very well at all. Why?"

"From what I've gathered from Suri and a couple of the other staff, most of the staff can't stand her. Suri is the only one who had anything nice to say about her."

"What did Suri say?"

"Luna is abrupt, mean, and downright nasty on occasion… but she's also the only one who can figure out how to fix the computers anytime they go down."

"And that explains her conversation with Sebastian the day of the murder." Suddenly, something clicked in my brain. "I completely forgot to tell Hank about their conversation! Luna was supposed to drop by and give Sebastian a copy of the camera recordings the night of the murder. But Hank said she told him there was no footage."

"And I assume you think she's lying?"

"I definitely think she's covering something up."

We were almost home when I got a call from Jo.

"Can I come by later?" she asked. "I've got some information, and Hank can't know! If I tell him, he might have more fuel to arrest Anna."

"What is it?"

"Suri came for lunch at the café. She told me about an argument she'd overheard the morning of Sebastian's death.

She didn't want to gossip, but thought maybe it was important to share with Hank."

"Oh no!"

"Exactly! I didn't want to discourage Suri from talking to Hank, but told her she could come to the house after her shift was over. That gives us some time to discuss!"

"When can you be here?"

"In about 30 minutes," Jo said. "I don't want to text this. A paper trail is not always a good thing."

When I hung up, Duncan looked at me and grimaced.

"You heard what she said, didn't you?"

"Unfortunately, yes. But I can forget it if you need me to."

"I definitely want you to forget it."

"Forget what?" he said with a shrug. "Last thing I remember is talking about the rude front desk help."

When we pulled into the driveway, Jo drove in right behind us, hopped out, barely waiting for us to get out of the truck.

"I don't mean to be rude, Duncan, but I need you to leave," she said. "I don't want you to be stuck between a rock and a hard place. You need to be able to say that you know nothing about what I'm about to tell Tori."

"Understood, but can I at least help take the dogs in…and grab the leftovers Tori put in the fridge for me? I was really looking forward to the brisket for supper."

Jo looked at me, then at him, then back to me again. "By all means," she said, a smile at the corner of her lips. "Leftovers are important business."

That was it. No mention that he overheard part of our conversation in the car. I wanted to hug him, but I didn't want to give Jo a reason to start matchmaking again. She was already giving me a side smile. *Subtlety was not her strong suit.*

"Thanks again for the leftovers and ice cream," Duncan said, grabbing his stuff from the fridge. "I'll be joining the Y next week or I won't be able to fit into my work scrubs. They aren't nearly as stretchy as you'd think."

"It's crowded before 7," I said. "But if you head over between 1 and 3, there are plenty of free lanes in the pool."

Jo didn't say a word, but I could tell she was about the bust at the seams.

He waved at both of us as he headed toward the front door, then pointed at Jo. "Tell Hank that I'll call him tomorrow. He'll know what I'm talking about."

"If it has something to do with the murder," I said, "the rest of us would like to know."

"It has zero to do with the murder," he responded with a sly smile, "but you'll know soon enough."

As soon as the door shut, Jo turned toward me with her mouth wide open. "What is going on? You had lunch with Duncan? And ice cream? Why haven't I heard about this?"

"Your boys were here for lunch with us. But yes, Duncan and I just got back from getting ice cream."

"We usually tell each other everything."

"Yeah, we do." It slid out of my mouth in a much more sassafras way than I intended.

"What does that mean?" She stuffed a chip in her mouth and furrowed her brow. "You okay?"

"Never mind. I'm just tired," I said, hoping she moved on. "What did you need to tell me about Anna?"

"You're going to need to sit down for this!"

Holly followed me to the living room and curled up beside me on the red sofa. Jo chose the other end, kicked off her shoes, then grabbed a blanket and got comfy. The puppies were out like a light on the small rug by the fireplace.

"It's all very interesting," Jo said, her eyes lighting up. "The morning of the murder, Suri overheard more of the argument between Sebastian and Anna. The door was cracked and she heard Sebastian threatening Anna. He said, "I want the money next week…or our little secret is no longer a secret. It's sold to the highest bidder."

"What is the little secret he's talking about?"

"I don't know, but then he said that he'd get his "pound of flesh" one way or another."

"There are some words swirling in my brain right now to describe Sebastian," I said. "My mama would not be pleased."

"She wouldn't be pleased with me, either—but I think she'd understand."

"Did she hear anything else?"

"No. Sebastian and Anna must have realized someone was listening, because they shut the door and started whispering."

I was still trying to process everything when my cell phone rang. It was Fred.

"Hi! Did my special order come in?"

"No, not yet. The dog jacket should be here soon, though. Maybe three more days?"

"Great!"

"But I didn't call about the jacket," Fred continued. "I just got an announcement about the dog beds you bought—there has been a recall due to a manufacturing defect. The beds are falling apart when washed. If you bring them in, you can get a refund or exchange for any other beds in the store."

I was just about to hang up when Jo pulled a stack of flyers from her oversized pocketbook. She waved them in the air with one hand, then pointed to the phone with the other. "Ask him!"

"When I come over, could I bring by a lost and found poster?" I said. "We desperately need to find Holly's owner."

"You can. But I've been thinking…how'd you find her?"

"Actually, she found me." I explained her origin story and how she came to be at my house. "We just really need to know where she belongs."

"I know I said that I could take a puppy," he replied, "but I'll take Holly, too. She sounds like a good family dog."

My stomach dropped a little. "Um, okay. I'll keep that in

mind. We've had several folks interested in her, but I'll add you to a waiting list and keep you up to date. Thanks! Goodbye!"

Jo stuffed the flyers back in her bag. "Several folks are interested in Holly? Really?"

"Okay, maybe not. But I can't just give her away to anybody."

"Uh-huh." She clicked her tongue, then narrowed her eyes. "I thought you wanted to get her out of your house as soon as possible?"

"I do, but she still has puppies. And they aren't ready to be away from their mama quite yet. I can always call Fred later."

"Uh huh," she said again. "I see."

I could smell Jo's brain working overtime. She didn't believe that I wanted to find Holly a new home; I had to prove her wrong.

"But if you're up for it," I said, "we can make the trip to Fred's tomorrow to put up flyers after Blake swings by to pick up Anna."

"Hold your horses—Anna's coming here?"

"Yup. Bright and early." I explained the phone call from Blake. "I was surprised he reached out. When he first got to the hospital, I got the distinct impression that he didn't want me to talk to her. He was like a little watchdog. But the last time I saw him, he seemed overly friendly."

"Maybe he was just worried about Anna?"

"I dunno, Jo. I didn't get that feeling. It felt more like he was worried about himself. And if Suri overheard their conversation correctly, then Blake definitely has a reason to be worried about himself...and Anna."

"We really need to talk to Hank about all this," Jo said. "Why don't we just go to Fred's now? We can return the beds to the supply store and pick up new ones."

"Think the boys will want to come back over and dog sit a bit more?"

"Do Sasquatches pee in the woods?"

"I really don't know the answer to that," I said laughing. "But if the answer is yes, I hope they aren't peeing in my woods."

While Jo was calling the boys, I went upstairs to check on Percy. He wasn't in the window or laying in a sunbeam in the corner. Nope, he was in the place I least expected to find him—the bathtub.

"Are you trying to tell me something?" I asked. "The puppies will get a sudsy bath later. You can take one with them!"

He immediately jumped out and hid under the bed.

"I was just kidding! Besides, tomorrow is your day to roam the house. The dogs will be at Jo's!"

Percy stuck his head out from under the bed and meowed.

Sometimes I was sure that cat understood everything I said. I got on my knees and gave him a quick kiss…and a handful of treats.

When the boys arrived, Booker had Duncan's book in his hand. "This is great! Have you read it yet?"

"Not much. I think I will need you to give me the cliff notes version."

They took off their coats and made a beeline for Holly and the puppies.

"We're pros at this now," Grady said. "And I'm pretty sure we're their favorites."

"Don't get too attached," Jo said. "You know the rules."

"But Dad and Tori said—"

I quickly interrupted. "We said that the boys are doing a GREAT job."

It wasn't a lie. We did say that. But I knew that wasn't what he was about to say. He took the hint and stopped talking, but I could feel Jo's eyes boring a hole in my skull for a few seconds. Then she let it go and hugged the twins. "Be good," she said. "And keep the door locked."

As we approached town, Jo went straight for the question I knew she'd been dying to ask. "So…what happened when you two went to get ice cream?"

"I already told you."

"No. You attempted to circumvent my question by disregarding my inquiries and redirecting the conversation."

"Those are some mighty big words for a random Thursday afternoon, Jo," I said. "You should save some of them for our next scrabble game."

"Quit trying to avoid the question again," she said. "What in the world did y'all talk about?"

"We actually didn't talk much. We ran into Allison and Kevin."

"How's Kevin feeling?"

"Kevin stayed in the truck. He barely looked our way. But then…Allison let me ask him some questions."

I told her all about the conversation and how he'd seemed shifty about everything I asked him about. I also told her that his alibi did not include Luna.

"You thought she was lying the whole time," Jo said. "So he

proved you right."

"Yeah, but I think Kevin is lying, too. I need to find Niles," I said. "You think your husband would be able to help us?"

"That's a very good question." We pulled up to the front of the supply store. "But first? Fred's!"

Fred was behind the counter helping another customer with a bird cage. He looked our way and tipped his hat. "Tori! Long time, no see! Just leave the bed over there." He pointed to a small pile of returned beds beside the front counter. "Do you want a refund or are you here to exchange?"

"I need to exchange."

"Go ahead and get whichever one you'd like. The ones that are left are all cheaper than the one you bought, so be sure and bring it up here. I'll owe you some cash."

As we walked toward the beds, Jo smirked. "You can put your refund toward those jackets. You know…the jackets for the dogs you're not getting attached to."

"You're one to talk," I said. "You're in love with Holly and the puppies but are too stubborn to admit it."

"I am not!"

"Your boys are. They've already named one. His name is Thor."

"Don't do this." Jo crossed her arms and glared at me. "You know we can't have dogs because of Hank's allergies."

"That's what you keep saying," I mumbled.

I expected a smart-butt reply, but her attention was glued to the person coming through the front door.

"What in the world is Sophia doing here?"

"I don't know, but I want to ask her where she was Friday night."

"Wait!" Jo whispered, whipping out her phone and feverishly texting.

"Why? What are you doing?"

"Hank has been trying to get in touch with her for days, but she's not returned his calls. I figured he'd want to know that she's only a few doors down from the station!"

After Jo hit send, she received an immediate reply.

"Uh-oh," she said. "He's not at the station, but he's heading back from another call."

"How far away is he?" I asked. "Maybe we can keep her occupied until he gets here."

"He's about 10 minutes away, but I think she's going to leave before he has a chance to get here."

Sophia walked up to the counter and talked to Fred for a moment. If she could have moved the muscles in her forehead, I am sure she would have been frowning.

"Looks like she's about to leave," I said. "I wonder what she's talking to Fred about."

"We need to stop her! Ooh! What if we wait until she leaves, then follow her, and let Hank know where to track her down!"

"Or," I said, my voice as quiet as possible, "we could just stall her here and avoid being accused of stalking."

"That works, too, I guess. But my idea sounds more fun."

"Follow my lead!" I made my way toward the super-fashionista.

"Sophia?" I tapped her gently on the shoulder. "I'm so sorry about Sebastian."

"Excuse you! This jacket is Italian leather!" She gave me a disdain-filled once over. "Do I know you?"

"We met two years ago at the 200th Founder's Day celebration and auction." I held out my hand to shake hers. "I'm Tori Mulligan. This is my best friend, Jo Parker."

"I hated that event. Boring people. Boring town." Then she turned and started click-clacking her way toward the front door in her ridiculously high heeled boots.

I had to think of something.

"Wait!" I ran to catch up. "I've seen you since then. Most

recently, the day of Sebastian's, um, passing. You were at the vet's office—with papers for him to sign."

She froze in her tracks and turned her head toward me slowly, like an owl focusing in on its prey.

"You must be thinking of someone else. Now if you'll excuse me…"

"Actually," I said, making three other customers turn and stare, "there were several of us who saw you waving the papers around."

The dogs were my witnesses, but I left that bit of info out of the conversation.

Sophia stopped in her tracks and turned back toward us, arms crossed. "What is this all about?"

"I was just wondering if the papers you needed him to sign were also the reason for your argument."

"They were nothing."

"Are you sure they weren't divorce papers?" It was the most logical question. Maybe he was having an affair. Maybe she found out. *Maybe she killed him.*

"I'm absolutely positive," Sophia said, "but even if they were, it would be none of your business."

She turned to leave again, but Hank had finally arrived. He was waiting at the door.

"I'm Lt. Hank Parker…and you are one hard woman to track down, Mrs. Westminster."

Sophia looked him up and down, a slow smile spreading across her face. Then she sauntered up to Hank and put her gloved hand on his forearm. "If I had known you were the one looking for me, I would have come in right away."

I felt Jo stiffen and lock her eyes on the not-so-grieving widow in front of us.

Jo was tiny, but mighty—especially when it came to her man.

Hank extracted his arm from Sophia's grip. "I have some questions for you regarding your husband's murder. Would you like to do it here or at the station?"

"Right here is fine," she said, still exuding a flirty vibe. She threw her shoulders back and batted her eyes at Hank. "I have nothing to hide."

She was worse than a cat in heat.

"Witnesses said you seemed upset with your husband on the day of his murder," Hank said. "You had some papers for him to sign, correct? Did the papers have anything to do with the argument?"

"Seriously?" Sophia pointed toward me. "Nancy Drew over there has already asked me that question. But the answer is still the same. Your witness misheard our conversation."

"I see." He jotted down a few notes. "And where were you between 3 and 6pm that day?"

"I was meeting with my attorney."

"Care to share what the meeting was about?"

"And why would I tell you that?"

"To eliminate you as a suspect."

She crossed her arms and remained silent.

"I'm just following procedures, ma'am," he said, "but if you'd like to do this interview on a more formal level, we can."

She uncrossed her arms and patted Hank's. There's no need for that!" Sophia pulled a card from her purse and handed it to him. "Client privilege is still a thing, but since I'm the client…I give you permission to talk to my lawyer. He'll back up my alibi."

I tried to see his name, but it was too blurry. *I really needed to start wearing my glasses.*

"Give him a call," Sophia said, "He will tell you that I was with him all night."

Hank raised his eyebrows. "All night?"

"We were working—mostly." She shrugged. "He's known for his—thoroughness."

"And how did your husband feel about your, um, working relationship with your lawyer?"

"Oh I see. You think I killed my spouse because I had a

lover? The spouse is always the first to be accused, right?"

"I haven't accused you of anything, Mrs. Westminster… yet." Hank's voice was as calm as I'd ever heard it—and it was a little scary.

At Hanks reply, Sophia laughed, but it was as shallow as her smile.

"I can assure you," she said, "I did not murder my husband over an affair; I had no reason to. We had an open marriage. He knew where I was and who I was with. But as long as I came home to him, he couldn't care less."

"Interesting arrangement," Hank said, judgment dripping from his voice.

"You should try it sometime." Sophia slipped both of her hands over his. "You might like it."

Hank quickly extracted his hand from her grasp and moved back a few steps, an obvious declination of her offer. I wondered if she'd ever been turned down before.

"Thanks for the info," he said, waving the lawyer's card in the air. "I'll give him a call tomorrow."

"Please call me if you need anything else," Sophia said. "I'll definitely answer from now on."

"One of our team will be in touch," he said. "Thank you for your cooperation."

When Sophia looked our way, she must have recognized the warning glare that Jo was shooting her way. Without another word, Sophia turned and sashayed out the door.

Hank was still looking at the lawyer's card when Jo punched him lightly on the arm. "You could have at least told her that she wasn't your type!"

"I've only got one type," he said, "and I'm looking at her."

"What he's trying to say," I interjected, "is that most men can only handle one crazy woman at a time…and he made his choice a long time ago."

"Hey now!" Jo said, feigning outrage. "I resemble that remark!"

Fred headed down our aisle, stopping long enough to rearrange a few small bags of dog food. "Have you found the replacement beds you want Tori? If not, we have a few more in the back."

"Not yet," I said, "We got a little side-tracked."

"I noticed," Fred replied. "I think the whole store noticed."

The cuckoo clock at the front of Fred's store struck 8pm.

"As much as I'd love to stay and chat," Hank said, "This murder isn't going to solve itself." He tipped his hat to me and shook Fred's hand. Then he kissed Jo on the cheek. "I'll see you later—I hope!"

When the door creaked shut behind Hank, Fred lost no time in letting us know that it was only 30 minutes until closing. "Want me to pull a few of the beds from the back? Or would you rather come back tomorrow?"

"Got any that you recommend over the others?" I asked. "I'm not exactly an expert on picking out dog-related supplies."

He pulled a few to show us. "These are the top three sellers, but I prefer the rectangular shape for bigger dogs. They need a little more leg room."

"Then I'll take one of those, and two smaller sizes for the puppies."

"You probably don't need beds for them yet."

"Sucker," Jo muttered. "You're wrapped around their little paws."

"No, I'm not." *I totally was.* "I guess I'll just take the big one, then."

"Sounds good," Fred said. "Let's go ring you up."

After we got the transaction finished and Holly's new bed in a giant bag, he walked us to the door.

"Thank you for your help," I said. "I am learning a lot about dogs through this process."

"It's always a pleasure. Not all my customers are as easy to please."

We all knew who he was referring to.

"I was surprised to see Sophia here," I said, saying what was on everyone's mind. "Was she returning a dog bed, too?"

"I don't think she's exactly a dog person," he said. "I'm not sure she's a people person, to be honest."

"Then what was the problem?"

"She was looking for more of her favorite pumpkin spiced candles and wanted to add them to Sebastian's tab. I told her that she'd have to start her own tab now—she wasn't pleased with me."

"I don't think she's pleased with anyone," I said.

"Well, what would please me," said Jo, while pulling the posters of Holly from her purse, "is to hang some of these up. Where do you want 'em?"

By 8:25, we were done and on the way back to my house.

"I'm glad the boys have already taken care of the dogs," I said. "Because when I get home, it's going to be time for bed… for all of us. Anna's coming bright and early."

"I forgot all about that. Can I bring y'all lunch?"

"Yes, please!" And for the rest of the way home we discussed which southern cuisine we could introduce to Anna's very British palate.

The next morning, a hard knock and the buzzer on my front door woke me up. I shot up out of the bed, completely frazzled. I squinted my tired morning eyes, wondering why my alarm hadn't gone off. I squinted at my watch again. *7am? They were supposed to come at 8!*

Percy purred next to me, completely disinterested in my early-morning dilemma.

I jumped out of bed and wrapped myself in my tie-dyed housecoat and hurried down the stairs. Blake was knocking the door like he'd lost his mind.

"I'm coming!" I yelled, hoping it didn't wake the dogs up too soon. I reached the door just as Blake buzzed my front door bell again. I took a deep breath and opened the door.

My mouth dropped open. It was not Blake.

"Mr. Fisher?"

"I'm so sorry, Tori. It's Moodini. He's out again! The last time I saw him was when he shot across the road and back around your place and toward the woods."

"I appreciate that you checked with me first, but you know I don't care if you chase him down. My woods are your woods."

As many times as Moodini had escaped, Mr. Fisher probably knew my land better than I did.

"I appreciate your trust in me, Tori, but I've got a problem." He lifted his pants leg to show a knee wrap.

"Give me just a minute. I need to don something a little more appropriate for hunting a bull." The day was already weird, and it had barely started.

"If you have a red cape, that might work," he said with a smile.

"You're kidding, right?"

"You know I am! Everyone thinks he's a fighter because he's so huge and looks the part. But really? He's just a big ol' baby."

Mr. Fisher had a point, but his big ol' baby had interrupted my last hour of sleep. I rubbed my eyes, then held up my open hand. "I'll be back in five minutes. Tops!" Then I ran upstairs to get changed.

For years, Mr. Fisher had a crush on my aunt, and I remembered him helping her with odd jobs around the property. But since her passing and my inheritance of the Inn, he hadn't stepped foot in the house. He always stayed on the porch or waved from the yard.

I had no idea where Moodini was, but we had to find him quick. I was dressed and running down the stairs faster than Mr. Fisher could say, "Abracadabra."

When I passed by my study, I heard scratching at the door and peeked in. Holly had snuck away from her sleeping pups. I moved the puppies in the high sided crate I kept for emergencies. Holly had to pee, and I had to track down a bull.

And that gave me an idea.

"Come on, girl," I whispered, grabbing her leash. The puppies were still out like a light, so I shut the door behind us and led her to the front door.

Mr. Fisher was still waiting on the porch when Holly and I made our way out the front door. "She's a beauty," he said. "But can she win a game of hide-and-seek with a stubbornly evasive bovine?"

"We're going to give it a shot." *Holly had already found a dead body. So a live bull should be no problem.*

We had barely made it to backyard when Holly started baying and pulling hard on the leash. "Woah!" I said. "Calm down!"

"That's not how that works," Mr. Fisher said. "Once they've got a scent, it's the only thing they are focused on. Best to let her run, then follow her voice. She'll let us know exactly where she is."

"Are you sure?"

"Absolutely. I used to have a few Redbone coonhounds. They were the same way." He patted my arm gently. "It's hard to let 'em go the first time."

"But what if she runs off? What if Moodini gets scared and hurts her? What if she gets scared and hurts him? What if—" Before I could finish my sentence, Holly jerked the leash out of my hand and tore off toward the woods.

For a big dog, she sure could boogie—much faster than my 48 year-old legs could carry me. But 85-year-old Mr. Fisher? Even with the knee wrap, he was a few steps ahead of me. I was glad no one else was here to see me being whooped by an octogenarian.

"Come on, Tori!"

"If I walk much faster, Hank's gonna have another dead body on his hands!"

We followed the sound of her bay to a less-traveled trail that led through a grove of aging oak trees. A few minutes later, we turned a sharp curve. In the middle of the grove we found—Moodini.

I knew she could do it!

"I have no clue how you got out this time, boy," Mr. Fisher said as we got closer, "but adventure time is over. It's time to go home."

Mr. Fisher slipped the lead rope over Moodini's head and tried to make him move, but he wouldn't budge. His giant, beautiful eyes were focused on the foggy, ongoing trail. Holly had disappeared.

"Holly?" I called her name a few more times, but she didn't come.

"Do you hear that?"

There was a distinct whimpering coming from further down the trail.

Mr. Fisher quickly tied Moodini to a thick, solid tree branch. "I think she went that way," he said, pointing down the trail.

If I remembered correctly, the trail he pointed to would eventually lead to the gated fence that butted up against the sprawling graveyard of the Craven Community church. I hoped Holly didn't run that far.

We hurried down the trail, and found her about 30 feet away from a small bend in the trail that led to the graveyard.

Holly was frozen in place.

"Easy girl. It's okay…" As I moved in slowly, it was clear that Holly was guarding something, but the combination of fog and morning darkness made it hard to see what it was.

As I inched a little closer, I felt the hair on my arms stand up. Holly's hackles were at attention and she emitted a low, fearless growl.

Mr. Fisher edged closer to her as well.

"What's she got?" he whispered.

"I don't know, the fog is too thick," I said. "But she's not letting it out of her sight."

Then she bayed, and her intense hound dog refrain echoed through the forest like some sort of warning.

"She's caught the scent of something else," Mr. Fisher said.

"Maybe a bear? I was hoping they'd steer clear of my land this year!"

He laughed softly. "If your Aunt Bert was here, she'd swear it was the Squatch."

Suddenly, the hefty hound took off through the woods.

"Holly! No!" I yelled. But she didn't even pause. She took

off down the trail, leaving us in the dust.

But then, as if on cue, the morning sun cut through the fog, revealing what Holly had been guarding.

I stifled a scream and pointed.

Then Mr. Fisher gasped. "What in blue blazes…"

Slumped against a fallen, gnarled tree was the crumpled body of Niles Walters.

66 H e's lucky to be alive," Florence said, patting the back of the ambulance as it sped out of my backyard. "It's a good thing you found him when you did."

It had taken the paramedics and police less than 15 minutes to arrive and find our location in the woods, but getting Niles on the gurney and back to the ambulance was a feat. He was breathing, but never opened his eyes.

Mr. Fisher shook his head in a "this ain't right" kind of way. "I thought he was deader than a doornail. But then he moaned and Tori called 911!"

"I felt for a pulse, but it was too faint. I thought he was a goner, too."

"Holly should get the lion's share of the credit," Mr. Fisher said. "That dog is something."

"Yeah. She was guarding him until we got there."

"What do you mean?" Florence whipped out her handy dandy notepad.

I explained how Holly had acted before she took off through the woods. "She had the scent of something—or someone." I sighed. "And she's still not back."

Mr. Fisher looked my way, then patted my arm.

"And you didn't see or hear anyone else?" Florence asked, pushing her sunglasses back up on her nose.

"Only Moodini," Mr. Fisher replied.

"He's not going to be much of a witness," Florence said, "but it seems pretty obvious that someone else was involved in Niles' accident." Then she paused and pointed toward the trail where Holly had disappeared. "Where does that lead?"

I explained the lay of my land and how it connected to the church graveyard.

"And who knows about the connection between the graveyard and your property?"

"Most everyone in town," I said. "Aunt Bert used to let the Civic club use her property for their haunted trail each year. They raised money to help build the new elementary school."

"I remember that trail," Florence said. "I only went on it once; it terrified me! Too many places for folks to hide and then scare your pants off!" She put her pen behind her ear. "I think I've got all I need for now, but Hank will be here soon to talk to y'all. He was in the middle of a meeting with the Captain and couldn't get out of it."

Hank hated that part of being a high ranking officer. He made no bones about the fact that he'd rather chew his arm off than deal with politics...but he also had no choice if he wanted to move up the ranks.

Moodini bellowed from across the yard. He'd been tied there until Mr. Fisher had finished giving his statement.

"Were there any...puncture marks?" Mr. Fisher's question was even heavier than Moodini. "I can't imagine him hurting anyone."

"I am absolutely sure that Moo-dini didn't do this." Florence gently placed her hand on Mr. Fisher's shoulder. "Niles had minor lacerations, not gaping wounds. They looked to be caused by thorns...not horns."

"I hope I don't sound uncaring, but that sure does make me feel a lot better," Mr. Fisher said. "Moodini is not a bad fella—just lonely."

Moodini and Mr. Fisher had a lot in common.

"Anyone who has known Moodini for more than a minute also knows that there's not a single drop of violence in him," I said.

Florence nodded her head in agreement. "But whoever did this to Niles didn't exhibit the same moral code." Her walkie-talkie hissed a low announcement. "Shouldn't be long now. Hank is on his way."

He arrived two minutes later with more of his team. The other officers hadn't wasted any time—they'd already roped off the area for the police photographer.

Hank took off his hat, played with it for a minute, then asked me to sit down on the tailgate of his truck.

"What have you gotten yourself into?"

"What do you mean?"

"First a murder. Then the targeted message on your fence. And now this?"

I felt like I was getting a "talking to" by my dad instead of being questioned by the police.

"You know as much as I do!"

"I don't believe you…and I don't believe Jo."

My eyes about popped out of my head. "What do you mean?" I tried to sound surprised.

"You and I both know that Jo is holding something back. She promised me banana pudding for dessert tonight."

"Huh?"

"She always cooks my favorites when she's feeling guilty about something."

I didn't say a word. I wasn't about to throw her under the bus. Maybe he would interpret my silence as ignorance.

"You can keep your mouth shut," he said, putting his hat back on his head, "but your face is telling a different story. This is a murder investigation, Tori. I can't find the killer if I don't have all the information. And I really don't want to have to put you and my wife in jail for obstruction of justice."

I thought he was joking, but his serious tone made me question my interpretation.

Then he turned to Mr. Fisher. "Did you hear anything, Horace? I know this was a shock, but I need you to give me any details, even if they seem unimportant."

"Not a thing. I was too busy trying to keep my knee from cracking under all the pressure. But if I remember anything, I know where to reach ya."

"Thank you, sir." Hank put his notepad back in his pocket. "I need to get back to the team. We are gonna be here a while."

"Can I take Moodini home?" Mr. Fisher asked.

"Of course." Hank smiled. "I think he's going to need a nap."

"That makes two of us." Mr. Fisher yawned. "See you later."

As Mr. Fisher led the gentle beast away, Hank crossed his arms and looked at me. "Come on, Tori. What do you know?"

"Nothing for sure. It's all gossip."

"Sometimes there's more truth in the rumors than we want to admit. I'd love to hear any information you've been privy to."

My phone rang, and I was glad…until I saw who was calling. "Oh no! I forgot all about Blake and Anna! I've got to go! Can I catch up with you more later?"

He narrowed his eyes. "Doesn't seem like I have much of a choice."

I answered the phone as I powerwalked back into the house at 8:30.

"Hi Blake! I'm here! I'm so sorry."

"Where else would you be? You promised to watch Anna for me."

"Yes, it's just that…"

"No need to explain," he said, interrupting me, "because it doesn't matter. There's obviously been a delay, so I won't be at your house until closer to 11."

I sighed in relief. "That's fine. Hopefully the police will be gone by then."

"Police?"

"There was an emergency," I said. "It's complicated, but it won't interfere with me being able to watch Anna for the day. I'm looking forward to introducing her to some of Jo's southern food."

"What kind of emergency?"

"I can't go into it, but someone was found hurt—very badly—in the woods on my property. They might not make it."

Blake didn't speak for so long that I thought the line had gone dead.

"Hello? Blake? Are you still there?"

"Yes." He cleared his throat. "But I don't want to add more stress to Anna's already heavy load. I will find other arrangements for her."

"But I…"

"You seem to have a nose for trouble, Tori…and I'd rather keep my wife away from it."

I wasn't sure if I was more insulted that he'd said what he'd said…or that what he'd said was right. I did seem to have a nose for trouble these days. But apparently, so did Holly. *I hoped she found her way back home…soon.*

I texted Jo and asked her to tell the boys that I didn't need them to dog-sit. A few minutes later, Jo was in my kitchen. "Hank told me to stay home, but you know how well that went over." She sat herself down at the table and opened the plastic containers of food she'd brought with her. They were filled with breakfast croissants, air-dried sausage, fried eggs, and goat cheese. She constructed two sandwiches while I poured us two glasses of orange juice.

"What in the world happened?" she asked. "The gossip train is already flying down the tracks."

In between bites, I explained all about the visit from Mr. Fisher and our quest to find Moodini. When I got to the part about Niles, she gasped just like Mr. Fisher had. "How did he end up in your woods?"

"That's a great question. But whoever was in the woods with him got away—at least for now."

"You saw someone?"

"No, but I'm sure that Holly did."

"Then maybe Hank can use her to help track the culprit down! She did a great job of finding Moodini and Niles!"

"That's the thing," I said, "Holly seems to already be hot on their trail—but we've lost hers." I explained the rest of the story about her disappearance. "Mr. Fisher said that she'll find her way back and that I shouldn't worry." *Too late.*

"I've got a better idea." She picked up the phone and called the boys. "Change of plans, sweeties. We need you over right now."

"What are you doing?"

"Calling for backup. They can feed the puppies while we go look for Holly. Maybe she's just scared with all the people on your property right now."

The boys walked in the door just as I heard puppy cries from the other room. "Perfect timing," I said. "They are probably starving. You know where the food is." We could work on feeding them puppy chow tonight. Maybe Duncan would be willing to help.

We stepped onto the trail, staring into the woods. Police tape blocked off the trail, and there was probably way more tape and investigators where we found Moodini and Niles. "We can't explore the trail until they've moved the tape."

"But what if she's lost in the woods somewhere?" Jo's voice broke with emotion. "Her leg is not completely healed."

"I don't think she's going to get lost. She survived with the puppies for at least 3 weeks in the woods…all alone."

"But what if she finds the person who hurt Niles? They probably won't have any qualms about hurting a dog, too!"

I turned to stare at my best friend. She was wiping away

tears.

"For someone who doesn't like dogs and can't have one, you sure do seem upset," I said quietly. "Wanna talk about it?"

"Just stop it." More tears rolled down her cheeks. "You aren't very subtle with me. I know that you know about Hank's allergies."

"You mean his lack of them?"

"Yes. But for the record, I thought he was allergic to all pet dander, then he told me that it was just cats. But by the time I found out that I was wrong, I'd already told everyone he was allergic."

"So? Why not fix the mistake?"

"Because I didn't want to get attached to a dog again." She reached in her bag for a tissue.

"You had a dog?"

"Yeah. My mama was afraid of dogs and swore she'd never own one. So my Grandma got Ruby. She stayed at Grandma's house, but I went over every day to feed her, give her baths, and walk her as often as I could."

"I didn't know that!"

"Grandma got her for me in 2nd grade, but you and I didn't become friends until 4th grade. Right before I met you, Ruby passed away. She ran out in a storm and got lost…then hit by a car."

"You never told me!"

"There wasn't anything to talk about. My grandma passed away, too, and my mom refused to let me have any animals at all." She smiled, her eyes still filled with a few tears. "And yes, I know I'm being dramatic about something that happened a long, long time ago."

I reached over and squeezed her hand. I didn't want to say anything because I was still feeling a bit salty about her lack of transparency, but I also didn't want to say something that would hurt her. So I kept my mouth shut, instead.

"I know you're upset," she said. "Your eyes say it all. I feel awful for lying to you. And yes, I should have told you the truth right away. But when the dogs showed up at your house, I was afraid the twins would fall in love with them and have a similar experience that I did. I wanted to protect them…and myself. I should have just told you the truth. Forgive me?"

"Yes. And do you forgive me for not just coming out and asking about it?"

We hugged, cried, then hugged again.

"So now that the cat—or in this case, dog—is outta the bag," she said, "where do we go from here?"

"What do you mean?"

"My husband and sons are in love with Thor…and I can't say that I'm not. That chunky monkey has a swing on his back porch. It makes me smile every time!"

"Then he's yours. Now I only have two dogs to give away."

"Two? Don't you mean one?"

"No. I mean two. I can't keep Holly. I'm not a dog person, plus…she can't stay here. There's not room."

"You've got a giant farmhouse and 20 acres, right?" Jo squeezed my hand this time. "Who's not being honest now?"

I heard a beep in front of the house, saving me from answering Jo's question.

We walked around the house into the front yard.

"Why is your mom here?" Jo asked. "I thought she'd be at work."

Mom climbed out of her jeep, followed by a furry, familiar red friend.

"Holly!"

Holly looked none the worse for wear, but she had a few briars stuck to her underbelly. I carefully picked them off while mom told us what happened.

"When Holly showed up at the church office door, I was a bit baffled," Mom said. "But then I thought that maybe my daughter and this sweet baby had come to surprise me with anniversary cake."

"But that's still two-months away, right?" My mom was usually as sharp as a tack. "50 years for you and Dad?"

"I'm talking about my work anniversary as church secretary—twenty-five years."

"I thought that was last week?" Jo said.

"It was." She flashed a smile that only moms have.

What was I missing? I stared at her for a moment, then it all flooded back.

"Oh no! I was going to bring you a slice of Jo's 14-layer chocolate cake." It was my mom's favorite. Had been for years.

"Don't feel bad. I was impatient and sent your dad to get me one last week."

"I remember," Jo said. "But he got you a whole cake!"

"Yup. We've already eaten most of it." Mom patted her hips. "It was worth every bite!"

We walked Holly into my study with the puppies. I lifted them out of the crate, but they were so excited they almost jumped out of my arms. I sat them on the floor and they crawled all around her legs, following her back to the new bed I'd bought for them.

Mom leaned down and petted the puppies, a small smile forming over her face. "These really are some of the sweetest pups I've ever seen."

I felt awful about forgetting her anniversary at the church. She never forgot birthdays, anniversaries, or even those obscure holidays like "National Peanut Butter and Jelly" day. Mom was our human calendar.

"I'm so sorry, Mom. With the murder and everything…"

"No worries, sweetie. You've had a ton on your mind. I'm just glad that Holly is okay and back where she belongs; those puppies sure are glad to see her."

I was, too.

Mom sighed, then cleared her throat. Then she sighed again, like she wanted to say something, but shouldn't.

"You okay, Mom?"

"Yeah. It's just—I don't like to gossip, but—"

"But…" Jo leaned in for more info. "Go on…"

"Okay, okay," Mom said, sighing one more time for good measure. "I heard that Sophia Westminster is having an affair with her lawyer, but I don't think it's true."

"It's not a rumor," I said. "It's a fact."

"Are you sure?" Mom made a face. "I think your intel might be wrong."

Intel? She was definitely watching too many of those mystery shows.

"Trust me," I said, "She admitted to having an affair."

"Hmph." Mom shrugged. "Then maybe she and the lawyer aren't exclusive."

"Why do you say that?" Jo asked.

"Because I saw Sophia with that Niles fella last week. And it seems that Sophia might know him in a biblical sense…if you get my drift."

My mouth dropped open. "The same Niles we just found in the woods?"

"Yep. I saw him and Sophia the evening of the murder behind the Book Nook."

"This doesn't make sense," I said. "Sophia told Hank she was working with her lawyer all night—mostly. And Kevin said he was with Niles at a pub."

"Hmmmm," Mom said, pulling her glasses down her nose and looking over the rim, "that sounds like a lot of bull-malarkey to me."

"Are you absolutely sure it was Niles?"

"Yup, unless he's got a doppelganger running around town locking lips with married women."

Why would Sophia lie about having an affair with her lawyer in order to cover up having an affair with Niles? A follow-up conversation with the doctor's widow was in order.

Mom insisted on giving Holly another treat before she left, then hugged Jo and me.

"Come by tomorrow and get some cake; Dad and I are gonna be in a sugar coma if you don't finish it off. And when you come, bring this sweetie and her puppies. I've almost convinced your dad to let us adopt one of them."

Jo and I high-fived each other.

"Don't start dancing yet," Mom said. "You know he's stubborn."

"His stubborn streak doesn't hold a candle to yours," Jo said. "And I mean that in the kindest of ways."

"Thank you, my dear." Mom smiled, showing off her dimples.

I recognized the devious sound to her voice and the mischievous look in her eyes.

"You already have a name picked out, don't you?"

"Maybe," she said. "I like to be prepared."

She didn't act like she was upset with dad anymore, so I didn't bring it up. Maybe they'd worked it all out. Then again, my mom kept things close to her chest, too, so maybe I'd ask dad next time I saw him.

Mom headed back to work and Jo had to go home to get ready for her shift, but the boys stuck around to help me a bit with the pooches. I gave Holly a bath, then let the boys give the puppies one, too. The puppies had never been in a tub, but seemed to enjoy the whole affair. Holly, on the other hand, was ready to get out of the tub as soon as her claws hit the porcelain bottom. It took me less than 10 minutes to get her suds up and rinsed off. "I'm glad Percy isn't here to taunt you," I said. "My house would be in shambles!"

Percy was in the guest room at the end of the hall, taking full advantage of his solitude, the sunbeams shining through the windows, and the catnip I'd promised him.

"So," I said, as I toweled her off, "I wonder if your former owners are still looking for you? The flyers are up everywhere."

By the time I got her out, we were both ready for a snack and a nap. I sent the boys home for a bit. "I'll probably need you a little later this afternoon," I said, "but I'm gonna get some shut eye. It's already been a long day…and it's barely started."

I woke up to the sound of my phone ringing.

Duncan?

"Hello?"

"I'm heading out to Asheville and Jo said you might need to get out of dodge for a while. Wanna join me?"

"Join you for…?" I didn't want to jump to conclusions. But it sounded like Jo was matchmaking again.

"Sorry!" he said. "I need to back up. I've got an appointment with Sophia's snake of a lawyer this afternoon. I was hoping you wouldn't mind being a witness, just in case he tries to pull anything."

"What time? I could go for a drive." *A day without hurt or dead bodies actually sounded nice.* "I mean, if you're sure?"

"I'll be there in about an hour."

I had time to eat, brush my hair, and make sure Percy was fed and happy. I thought I heard Duncan pull up just as I was about the check on the dogs. I looked out the window to make sure it was him and not another visit from Mr. Fisher or Moodini.

"Come on in before your beard freezes off," I said. "I was just about to feed Holly and the pups."

"I brought her a little something." He pulled out a treat from his backpack. "I found these at Fred's. He said they are one of his best sellers."

He followed me to the study. Holly immediately moseyed over, but she bypassed me and went straight to Duncan. She sat at his feet as if she already knew he had something for her.

"Keep bringing her those and you'll have her eating out of your hand."

"I've been told I have a way with the ladies," he said with a smile, "but only the furry ones!"

I chose not to mention that I'd not shaved my legs in a month.

"You are such a good mama, Holly." He leaned down and gave her the treat he'd brought. "Whoever put you out didn't deserve you."

"I can't understand why someone hasn't claimed her." I reached down and scratched behind her ears. "We've put up flyers all over town, but no one has called."

"That's just it. Hound dogs are an investment – and they are not cheap to keep. If she got loose, and the owner loved her, then he or she would be looking for Holly."

"But I read in your book that some dogs can travel up to 100 miles away from home if they are hot on a trail."

"That's true, but it's rare. I think someone brought Holly here from another county and put her out. That's how folks used to do when they didn't want a dog anymore. Just drop them off in the country and let 'em fend for themselves."

"That's awful!" I tried not to imagine how heartbroken she must have been when her owner dropped her off, then drove away.

"There wasn't a chip, either," he said. "Some hunters don't chip the dogs if they don't plan on keeping them past hunting season." His watch beeped. "If we don't leave now, we're gonna be late."

As we drove, our conversation veered away from Holly and back to the financial issues at work. "We are struggling to keep up with clients right now. Sebastian was right about the merchandise growing legs. We are missing a lot of it. And according to the paperwork I found in Sebastian's office, it's been happening off and on for the last few months."

"That's not good."

"It's definitely not. From what I can tell, Sebastian had the cameras installed one weekend two months ago. The only people who knew were the folks who installed it and Sebastian."

"Interesting. So no one at the clinic knew they were being recorded?"

"Nope. But they are all pretty upset about the thoughts of it now. In addition to that, Luna has called in sick again. And some of the other techs told me there's a curse on the clinic."

"Huh?"

"Somebody said they first heard it at Fred's a long time ago. Told them that the clinic was built on sacred burial ground."

I felt the laughter bubbling up in me. "They are just yanking your chain," I said. "Fred used to tell tourists that to keep 'em interested. They want a glimpse of something weird. Something different. Something they can't explain. For some reason, they think they'll find it here. They're also willing to pay good money to have a guide."

"Ahhh…like sasquatch?"

"Exactly. We might be a small country community, but we know how to use our reputation to our advantage."

"And then Fred sales tons of Sasquatch memorabilia, right? I guess his gnarled, old guy persona is also greedy."

"Not really. He actually puts a lot of that money back into the community. You just have to get to know him. He's a loveable curmudgeon. And his store is the epicenter of town gossip. It usually starts on the seed aisle, or with the local folks who sit and chat in the rocking chairs on store's front porch."

"So, what's the 411 on the murder investigation so far? Learn anything since the last time we chatted?"

"Sophia and her lawyer are having an affair—or so she says. Sophia had no problem telling us all about it. She also had no problems flirting with anything else with pants on." I told him about the way she'd acted toward Hank and what mom had said about seeing Sophia and Niles. "So she lied about her whereabouts on the night of the murder. But if she's telling the truth about her marriage, then it has nothing to do with the murder at all."

"So…Sebastian knew that Sophia was cheating on him and didn't care?"

"Right. According to Sophia, they have an "open marriage."

"Then why would she lie about being with her lawyer if she was with Niles the night of the murder?" He raised an eyebrow. "What does that mean?"

"I don't know why she'd lie about Niles. But if what she's saying is true…then Sebastian's affair with Anna was probably only a problem for one person—and that person has a nasty little temper."

"Blake?"

Nailed it. "I've had a horrible feeling about him since he came to the hospital to see Anna."

"Hank told me that he hated playing golf with him; he was

a sore loser." Duncan took the last turn into town. "He saw him attack the golf cart of one of this golfing buddies."

"Why did he do that?"

"Blake thought that the other guy cheated."

"So if he acted that way about a dumb game of golf, then how would he react if he thought his wife was cheating on him with Sebastian?"

"Number one, ouch. Don't knock golfing until you've tried it. Number two, I think you're onto something. Blake is a piece of work."

"And if he is the murderer, then Anna might be too afraid of him to tell the police."

"That's a very, very good point."

We pulled off the interstate and into the outer limits of Asheville. The lawyer's office was a mile outside of town in a stand-alone building. The sidewalk was pristine and the mirrored front door was as clean as a whistle. The inside was as boring as I imagined a lawyer's office to be.

We approached the receptionists window and a 30-something year old secretary looked at us with a raised eyebrow. "You aren't on the appointment log," she said. "And Mr. Shatley has a full calendar."

Duncan showed the receptionist the text. "I guess he forgot to tell you about it."

She huffed and picked up her phone. "Give me a moment, please."

She spoke in a tense whisper, as if we were in a library…or morgue. The chill in her stare made me think it could have been the latter. "You can come back now," she said. "He's waiting for you. First door on the right."

We'd barely spoken a word since we'd arrived, but our facial expressions had done all the talking. I expected interesting conversation on the way home.

The office door was open and Todd Shatley waved us inside. "Come on in! I'm glad you could be here!"

He shook our hands, then wiped his hand on a small tissue he pulled from his pocket. "I hate that you had to ride all the way out here, but this needed to be taken care of as quickly as possible."

"What's this all about?" Duncan asked.

"I'll just cut to the chase," Todd said. "Sophia Westminster wants to buy the vet practice from you."

Duncan laughed. "This is why you brought me all the way over here? I could have told you no over the phone."

"She's willing to pay a pretty penny, Dr. Williams."

He wrote down a number, turned it upside down, and passed it across the table like they do in the movies. Duncan turned it over and showed it to me. I had to stop myself from gasping.

The half-balding lawyer continued his explanation. "Mr. Westminster failed to tell his wife about the sale of the clinic before his untimely demise. She deserved to have a say in this decision and that was taken from her. She'd like to settle this quickly so she can…move on."

"Has he even had a funeral?" Duncan asked.

"No. His body will be donated to science," Todd said flatly. "So my client is doing what she can to distract herself from the pain of losing her life partner."

"She sounds more like a gold digger than a grieving widow," Duncan said. He crossed his arms and sat back in his chair.

"People grieve in different ways," Todd said flatly. Then without missing a beat he handed Duncan a pen and moved some papers toward him. "You can sign on the dotted lines with the x beside them."

"I didn't move across the state for the fun of it," Duncan said. "I moved here in good faith and uprooted my life to make a change…to make a difference."

"I am authorized to offer you twice the original offering."

Was Sophia made of money?

"The answer is still no," Duncan said as he stood up. "We're gonna head out. I have a business to run."

"Before we go," I said, holding on to the door frame to stop Todd from shutting it, "I do have one question for you."

He crossed his arms and stared. It looked like his bright blue eyes were going to bulge out of his head. "Please hurry. I have actual clients waiting."

"Where were you the night of Sebastian's Westminster's murder?"

"I'd have to check my calendar, but I think I was at home with a cold."

"Really? Because Sophia said you were together—all night."

"Oh…she's right." His face turned as red as his tie. "I was thinking of the wrong Friday night."

"Then it's good that you both have each other as an alibi," Duncan said. "Otherwise, that would be awkward."

Todd cleared his throat, then brushed something invisible off his jacket, composing himself. "I hope you'll reconsider my client's offer or we will be forced to consider contesting the sale of Sebastian's practice in court. Now if you'll excuse me…"

He practically shoved us out the door, then slammed the door behind us.

"He's lying," I whispered. "Did you see the way he shifted his weight when I brought up the affair? And he blinked several times when he said they were together. Definitely lying."

"That's something we learned in psychology, too. Where'd you learn it?"

"Aunt Bert! She worked for a private investigator before she opened up the B&B. She used to tell me and my cousins all about her previous work. We all wanted to be super spies."

We made our way to the car, but my stomach realized how late in the day it was.

"Care to grab a bite to eat on the way home? I know an Irish Pub with the best Shepherd's pie around. They also offer the same thing as Fred's store—gossip galore."

"I'm more of a bangers and mash kind of guy," he said. "But I'm game. Which way?"

"It's on the outskirts of Craven. Maybe we can ask around about Kevin's alibi…and grab something good to eat, of course."

"I like the way you think."

Half an hour later, we were almost there. "It's right up here, two streets down from Petesie's Pizza."

"I'm fond of pizza, too," he said. "Unless you try to mess it up with pineapple."

"I don't think we can be friends anymore," I said. "Those are fighting words."

"Hold on just a second. Did I hear you correctly?" He gave me a side glance. "We're friends?"

I shrugged, trying to act nonchalant. "I guess."

"Thanks a lot."

"I mean, I don't share my brisket with just anybody and you made the cut, so…"

"Well that seals it then. I guess I can let the pineapple on your pizza slide, then."

A giant grin spread across his face.

"Touché!" I couldn't stop the smile spreading on mine.

"Speaking of food," Duncan continued, "has Jo told you about supper tonight?"

"Oh…we're trying to do this again? I don't think we're ever going to make it happen."

"Oh ye of little faith!" He pulled into the parking lot. "That's what Hank and I have been working on together."

"Keep working," I said, "but I ain't gonna hold my breath."

Our meal was enjoyed mostly in silence; we were both starving. Surprisingly, the quiet between us wasn't awkward. Just the comfortable passing of time between friends.

"Dessert?" he asked. "They have a chocolate bourbon volcano cake."

"It is delicious, but it doesn't hold a candle to Jo's hot fudge volcano cakes."

"Suit yourself," he said. "I'll have one here, then tomorrow at the café. Life is short, so I eat all the dessert I want."

I liked his way of thinking.

Our waitress, Wendy, was doing her best to keep all her customers happy. The food was great, but the service was a bit on the slow side. We ordered our dessert, stopping her long enough to ask her a quick question.

"We're looking for information," I said. "I was hoping you could help us."

"I can sure try, sweetie!" She chewed her gum with a smile and flipped her gray hair out of her sun-kissed face. The twang in her accent was strong; there was no doubt she was a native member of our southern community.

"A friend of ours said he was here with a guy named Niles last Friday night."

"You're gonna have to be more specific. What's your friend's name? Also, I know three guys named Niles. One is a baby and one is the best gardener in town. He won the Garden Gnome award each year for the last three years in the 80 to 85-year-old age group."

"And the third Niles?" I held up a picture that Allison had sent to me for reference. It was clearer than the badge Fred had showed us. "This is Niles we're looking for."

"Oh yeah! I know him. And is that other guy your friend? They are both kind of messed up." She sighed. "But to be fair, your friend seems a bit more stable than Niles."

"Were they here last Friday night?" I asked.

"Wait a minute," she said, staring at us both with narrowed

eyes. "What's this all about? I know you!"

I couldn't tell if she was talking to me or Duncan. Duncan didn't move, probably afraid he'd get smacked upside the head with the loaf of soda bread in her hand.

"You are that reporter for the Craven Mountain Gazette! I love your mystery column!" She slapped her leg and a giant grin spread across her face. "When are you going to finish the last one? I am dying to see if the back-stabbing, gold-digging wife gets caught for Craig's murder!"

Duncan broke into a huge smile, barely hiding a chuckle.

"Oh, um…thank you very much. And I'm not sure. We are… still working out the details."

"Are you trying to figure out a real life case? Cause those two fellas are trouble. Plain and simple. I wouldn't be surprised if they knocked off a liquor store or something."

Duncan and I gave each other a knowing look.

"I don't mind talking to you, but don't use my name. Just in case they wanna know who ratted 'em out."

"Of course not," I said. "Besides, this is unofficial business. We are just, um, scoping out a story. Not sure where it will lead if anywhere."

"Niles comes in here a few times a week. Always seems to have the munchies. He loves our fries. Your friend is in here once in a while, but usually with Niles. But come to think of it, I haven't seen them together in a week or so."

"So they've not been in?"

"Like I said…not together. I saw Niles in here two days ago with some woman."

"You didn't recognize her?"

"No. But if it helps, I do remember her earrings. They were big enough for a Squatch to use as a hoola hoop."

She'd just described the earrings worn by about half the females in town.

"Any other distinguishing features?"

"No. Sorry, hon. She was whispering and stopped talking

every time I walked over," she said. "Wait! There was one thing. They didn't seem to move in the same circles, if you know what I mean. And she had a wedding ring on, if that helps. It was bigger than my triple wide trailer!"

It had to be Sophia.

"Thank you," I said. "You've been a big help."

She patted me on the shoulder and winked.

"Yes, thank you for the information," Duncan said, looking at his watch. "We probably need to get back if you still want to make it to Jo's."

He was right. I started gathering my things, but accidentally knocked my empty glass off the table.

Duncan caught it mid-tumble.

"You are quick on the draw," she said winking at Duncan. "And I have to say…you make the cutest couple!"

"We aren't a couple," he said quickly, handing her the glass. "Just friends."

Just friends. I was about to utter the same words, so I don't know why it gave me a little jolt in my gut. *Why did I even care?* I shook myself out of my mini-funk and reached in my purse for cash, but Wendy patted me on the hand. "He's already paid, darling. Tip and everything!"

Oh…he'd slipped her the money when he'd handed her the glass. Wendy was right…he was quick on the draw.

"You can get it next time," he said. "But we're getting pizza with no pineapple."

"You are a smart man." Wendy winked at him and slapped him gently on the shoulder with the cloth she'd been carrying around. "Y'all better come back and see me!"

On the way to Duncan's truck, I felt him giving me an odd look.

"I didn't mean to make things weird back there," he said. "I just don't like for people to make assumptions. It's not good for anyone."

"We are friends," I said, my mouth dry. "You were just

saying what I was already thinking."

"Okay. Then good. We're in agreement."

"Yup. Totally."

We climbed in the truck and he drove toward the Inn but the comfortable silence we'd had over dinner had disappeared. I was only able to stand it for about five minutes, then I turned on the radio. I hummed, then let loose and joined in with the oldie-but-goodies blasting from the speakers. Before long, he did, too. His voice was a nice baritone and fit in well with my middle-of-the-road alto voice.

"Not too shabby," he said. "Who knew we could pull off Dolly Parton and Kenny Rogers."

"I wouldn't buy our tickets to Nashville just yet!"

"Still want to swing by Jo's on the way home?"

"Yeah. If it's not too crowded."

We drove past the front of Jo's café; it was packed. Duncan drove around the lot three times before we found a spot near the back door. I sent Jo a quick text.

Me: Is now a bad time to talk?

Jo: Yeah, but I need a break, anyway. I saw you pull around. Be there in a sec!

She came out with a red cooking smock on and a big bag in her right hand. She climbed in the back seat.

"I hope y'all are ready for something good," she said. "This bag contains four pieces of pie, two pieces of cake, and a batch of my cheddar biscuits with a jar of plum jelly."

"I gained five pounds just listening to that menu," Duncan said. "But it's worth it. I am looking forward to my midnight snack tonight!"

I could smell the biscuits. They reminded me of weekends at Aunt Bert's during the summer.

We gave her the lowdown on what happened at the lawyer's

office.

"That's odd," Jo said. "Why doesn't Sophia just take you to court instead of threatening to take you to court?"

"I think I know the answer to this," Duncan said. "If she takes me to court, it could be bad publicity for the clinic…and that could mean loss of revenue. Plus, court costs could drag out for a long, long time. So it's easier, and probably cheaper, for her to buy me out. "And from what I've seen with my colleagues, lawyer fees tend to multiply faster than fleas."

"That makes sense," I said. "But is the woman made of money? How can she afford to pay double?"

"I heard she was a widower before she married Sebastian—and her first husband was older than Mr. Fisher." She nodded toward the restaurant. "People talk."

"How did he die?" Duncan asked.

"According to Mr. Porter, Sophia's first husband was undergoing plastic surgery to, ya know, help him keep up with his much younger wife. But he died on the surgery table. It was just too much on his heart."

"And Sophia lived happily ever after…with all his money?"

"Well, she lived—but I don't know if she knows how to be happy!" Jo looked at her watch. "I've got to get back inside. See you later!"

Driving down my long driveway seemed like it took twice as long as usual, but I didn't mind. I was thinking heavily on our meeting with Sophia's lawyer and all the other aspects of the case that still weren't lining up in my brain.

"Thanks for going with me," he said quietly. "Would you be interested in helping me work through more of the inventory? I am heading over tomorrow after I finish putting together my guest bed."

"Maybe, but I'll let you know for sure in the morning. I want to go over everything we've figured out so far."

"No worries. Just let me know when you know."

He parked in front of the porch and I opened my door.

"Thanks again," he said. "I have a feeling Hank is going to be telling you the same thing before the case is over. He might even owe you a consultant's fee."

"I'll just be glad if he doesn't throw me in jail. He's usually an easy-going guy, but he's very much a by-the-book kind of guy. He's not too keen on interference in official police business."

"I can see that," Duncan said, "but even by-the-book people know when to bend."

I waved goodbye then locked the door behind me, more thoughts swirling in my brain. I needed to talk to Anna again. She would have to be honest with me, or I'd take my suspicions to Hank. I was certain she was covering up for someone, and the best possibility? Her angry, Shih-Tzu inspired husband. I yawned and stretched. The day was catching up with me; the conversation with Anna would have to wait until morning. I was too worn out to do anything else.

The next morning, I had a weird vibe before I my feet hit the floor. Everything felt off. Nothing was right about this case. Sophia, Niles, Kevin, and Luna's alibis were not lining up.

Maybe Kevin, Luna, and Niles all killed Sebastian? Maybe Kevin and Luna tried to take out Niles so he wouldn't rat them out? And what about Sophia's man-eating ways? Was it all just a ruse? Maybe she killed her husband. But why would she do that? And then there was Anna and Blake. Did Blake have something to do with Sebastian's murder? He seemed overly protective of Anna, so maybe there was more to his alibi than met the eye.

My phone buzzed. It was Hank.

"I can't talk but a minute. I'm sitting in my car outside the station. There's a few things that don't add up in this Sebastian's case and Nile's attack."

"A few?"

"Remember how I told you that Sebastian didn't die from a head injury?"

"Yes."

"I heard back from the coroner. He and Niles were both injected with the same substance. Niles just didn't have as much in his body. I can't tell you the name of the medicine, but I can tell you that anyone who worked at the clinic had access to it."

"I thought you couldn't give me details? What changed your mind?"

"Jo and I had a big discussion last night. She convinced me that I should be happy that you are working for me, not against me," he said. "And if we put our heads together, maybe we can get to the truth sooner than later."

I owed Jo a triple batch of cheese straws. "Got anything else?"

"Yes. We found one ticket to the Bahamas in Sebastian's office. But on his bank account, we discovered he'd been charged for two tickets. We are still following up on that lead, but it takes time. Unfortunately, the Chief is pushing for me to close this case soon. He's looking for a quick resolution before his retirement. And if I mess this up, well, let's just say I might end up as a busboy at Jo's café."

"I'll keep digging to see what I can find."

"Thanks," he said. "I gotta go. Give me a call if you find anything…but be careful. Someone dangerous is on the loose and I'd rather you not be their next target."

"Thanks. We're in agreement about that."

After we hung up, I added his info to my notes. It still didn't make any sense. I took a break and tried calling Anna, but she didn't pick up. So I bounced more ideas off of Holly. "What do you think about Jessica's quick departure? What does it have to do with Sebastian's murder? Maybe she snuck back in and killed him, then snuck back out into the night?"

Holly looked up at me with droopy eyes.

"Anything at all?" I asked. "There is something hinky there; I can feel it in my bones. What do you think, girl?"

The furry mama was zero help.

No matter how I jotted down the clues, they all added up to one thing: people were lying and the murderer was still out there.

Between washing my mountain of dirty clothes, mopping my floors, vacuuming up dog hair, looking through Aunt Bert's books again, and trying to figure out who killed Sebastian, the day flew by. Before I knew it, suppertime was upon me. After scarfing down a bowl of cereal, I took Holly and the puppies for a walk to clear my head. When I got back, I didn't feel any better. Matter of fact, I felt like I knew even less than before.

It didn't matter that it was 7pm—I was ready to throw on my jammies and call it a day.

As I was snuggling up on the couch with my trusty computer, my phone rang. *Anna!*

"Hi there!" I said. "I'm glad you called me back. I was hoping we could chat a little more about—"

"Tori," she said, interrupting me, "did you mean it when you said you'd help in whatever way you could?"

"Yes, but…"

"Then please come get me. I don't have much time." Her voice was calm, but there was an urgency to it. "I promise to explain later."

"You don't have much time? What do you mean?"

"Just please come pick me up from my house, as soon as you can. I need to get out of here. And don't call the police."

I called Jo on my way out the door.

"Can't explain now, but if you've not heard from me in a couple of hours, please have the boys check on my furry guests. I'll be home as soon as I can."

"We'll take care of Percy, then we'll bring the dogs to our house," she said. "Have fun!"

I had a feeling it wasn't going to be that kind of evening.

I didn't remember making all the correct curves and turns to get to Anna's house. All I remembered was trying to decide whether or not I should call the police. By the time I got there, I'd made the decision to wait to call them. Anna was usually reasonable and sober-minded, so if she didn't want the police, then I could grant her that desire…at least for now.

It was after 8 when I arrived at her house. I parked and ran up the driveway, I instantly regretted my decision not to give Hank a head's up. I heard shouting and crying—and it was not from some loud TV show.

The front door was shattered and glass was everywhere, just as it had been the night I found Anna unconscious. I opened it slowly and tiptoed around the dangerous shards. I couldn't see anyone, but I could hear them. They sounded like they were in the kitchen. I stepped over several luggage bags.

"You will do as I say," he growled. "Let's go!"

"I'm not going anywhere with you!" Anna's voice was pained and afraid…but I could tell she was not budging. "I'm done, Blake. We're done."

"You've forgotten your wedding vows. To love and obey…

'til death do us part." His voice was calm, but menacing. The vows—once loving—were now threats.

As I got closer, I could see that Blake had Anna cornered, her back against the sink. I inched my way closer. Blake didn't hear me, but Anna did; her eyes tracked my entrance.

Blake whipped around. "Still showing up unannounced, I see?"

He looked like a man with nothing to lose.

"Hi Anna. Hi Blake." I didn't want to make the situation worse and certainly didn't want him to know that Anna had called me. "I was just in the neighborhood and um…" I had never been good at lying, especially under pressure. "I needed to ask Anna about my last paycheck. And my phone is dead, so ya know…"

"The phone you're carrying in your hand?" He sounded more than irritated. He sounded on the precipice of crazy. "You need to leave. This discussion is between my wife and me."

Anna's eyes were telling a different story than Blake's narrative.

"I asked her to come," Anna said.

"Then you can ask her to leave." There was no arguing in his tone. "Now."

Anna shook her head no, but stayed silent.

"That's how it is? Then I guess I'll escort her out." He pointed a menacing finger at his wife. "Don't move."

"She doesn't want me to leave," I said. "I'm not going anywhere."

"Wanna bet?" Blake grabbed me by the arm.

"Let go of me!" I yelled, squirming to get loose.

But he didn't.

Blake never said another word, just dragged me as I yelled, then opened the fractured front door, shoved me out, and slammed the door behind me.

I immediately called Hank. "You've got to get down here. I'm at Anna's." I quickly explained what happened. "Blake is on the verge of a breakdown."

"We will be there in five minutes. Don't do anything heroic!"

I heard a loud crash coming from the house and Blake's voice, even louder than before.

I wasn't about to wait on Hank.

I looked around the yard, then grabbed a brick from under the window. I wasn't exactly sure what I was going to do with it, but it was better than nothing.

As soon as I opened the door, I heard Anna sobbing. "You're hurting me!"

"I'm going to do more than that," he said. "You shouldn't have tried to leave me!"

I had the brick in my hand and barreled toward their voices, ready to use it in whatever way was necessary. But before I got to the kitchen, I heard a groan, a loud thud, and—

silence.

I found Anna, her back still against the sink. She had a swollen lip, red marks on her neck, and blood running from her nose. Tears ran down her face as she pointed to the floor. My eyes followed hers to see Blake, sprawled on the linoleum, with a knife sticking out of his chest.

"He attacked me..." Anna's voice was barely audible and she couldn't stop staring at Blake. She dropped to her knees and felt for a pulse, then looked up at me with horror. "What have I done?"

Heavy footsteps and loud voices filled the house, including Hank's.

"Step away from the body, Anna," Hank said gently. "And put the brick on the counter, Tori. Then both of you back away slowly."

Twelve hours later, I was still at the police station. It hadn't taken them long to figure out that I'd not killed him, but the whole process of giving a statement for this incident took longer than it had for Sebastian's murder. The majority of my time was spent waiting.

"Anna is going to need a good lawyer," Florence said, handing me a few last documents to sign. "She's here on a green card, right? She never officially became a US citizen, did she?"

"I really don't know," I had no doubt that Anna had acted in self-defense. But the chips were stacked against her now, more than ever. "How did you get there so fast?"

"We were only five minutes away. We were supposed to be meeting with her about Sebastian's case. The autopsy revealed that Sebastian died about an hour after she claims she went home…but there is no one and nothing that collaborates her story. She had threatened him in view of witnesses, she had motive, and she had access to the drugs that killed him."

"Drugs?" I pretended I didn't know what she was talking about, just in case Hank hadn't told her that I knew. And maybe she'd let something slip.

"He was given a fatal injection of gabapentin and phenobarbital."

I acted nonchalant. "Sounds like an awful way to die."

"Yeah, it is. And since Anna still had a key to the office, she could have grabbed some at any point and had it ready for their confrontation when they met in his office that night."

That couldn't be right. "But she admitted to hitting him… and that's not what did it."

"Everyone lies, Tori. And in this case, the Chief believes she lied about the murder. All roads lead to your British boss. And now that she's killed again…"

"There is no "again"; the two murders are completely different! And you see how she's acting now. If she had killed Sebastian, she wouldn't have been able to handle it. She'd have turned herself in!"

"She almost killed herself the day after Sebastian died," Florence said. "Sounds like remorse to me."

"But she didn't even know Sebastian was dead until I told her. She is not a killer!"

"Oh really?" Florence raised an eyebrow. "There's a knife in her dead husband's chest that proves otherwise."

"You have a point…*pun NOT intended.* But this is a different situation, and you know it. Anna was truly fearful that he would kill her last night. And by the sounds of his voice and threats, she had reason to feel that way!"

I closed my eyes and put myself in her shoes. It was the second time someone had busted through Anna's glass front door. We thought it was the intruders the first time, but now I wasn't so sure.

"Can I see her before I go?" I asked.

"She's under arrest, Tori."

"I won't stay long. I just want to check on her and make sure she's okay. She has no one else. Her mom is still in England and her sister is in Germany."

"Hang on a second." She picked up the phone and called Hank. He was still in a meeting. "Anna is the only one in lock-up. I can give you 5 minutes."

Anna sat on the bench in her cell, looking more frail than she had in the hospital. "I'm sorry I dragged you into this."

"I'm afraid I made things worse."

"We both know that if you hadn't come over, I'd be the one in the morgue." She spoke in a monotone voice, as if she was telling someone else's story. "I don't even remember picking up the knife. I just remember him coming at me the last time and then—well, you know the rest."

"Why did he break the glass? Didn't he have a key?"

"This time, yes. But I'd jimmied the lock so his wouldn't work."

"This time?"

"The first time he broke in was the day you found me drowning in alcohol."

"Back up…I think I'm missing something. I thought Kevin and Niles broke into your house? Hank suspects they've been casing and robbing homes in Craven—I assumed yours was one of them."

"No. Blake just let you think that. He was good at misdirection," she said. "The week before Sebastian's murder, Blake had left for a business trip to Vegas. But I had already been making plans of my own—secret plans. The day he left, I had the front door lock changed. I opened a new bank account under my name, and only my name. On the day of the murder, he called to talk, but I told him not to come home—we were over. I'd already filed divorce papers."

"But he said that he was with you the night of the murder."

"He lied. He told me that it was to protect me because he thought the police were going to arrest me."

Blake was dead now, so he couldn't exactly collaborate her story.

"But if you didn't kill Sebastian, then you didn't need an alibi," I said, trying to figure out how everything fit together. "So that doesn't make sense!"

"You don't believe me?" Dejected, she flopped on the bench. "You can just go, Tori. I don't have it in me to defend myself."

"That's not what I meant, Anna. I don't think you killed Sebastian. I'm just trying to figure out Blake's motivation for giving you an alibi. What if he killed Sebastian out of jealousy? And needed you to be *his* alibi?"

"I guess it's possible." She closed her eyes and breathed in and out, as if trying not to have a panic attack. "If he claimed to be my alibi, then he could control the narrative and try to control me, too."

I reached through the bars and put my hand on hers. "You've got to give it to me straight. If you've been protecting him…you don't have to do it anymore. You've got to stand up for yourself now."

Tears streamed down her face and she took in several deep breaths. When she finally spoke, her voice was barely above a whisper. "He watched my every move. He had very specific ideas about what I should do as a wife and as a person. That's why I couldn't cover as many stories for the paper as I wanted to." She wiped away more tears. "But I never reported anything, so Hank isn't going to believe anything I have to say now."

"But I was there. I know you killed Blake in self-defense. Your bruises and my testimony should be enough to back up your story."

Hank was wrong about Anna, but so was Jo. Anna hadn't run the paper in to the ground by her absence, she was just trying to stay alive. There was a lot more to her story, but I was running out of time.

"What can I do to help?" I asked.

"I'm scared, Tori. Florence told me they are building a case against me for Sebastian's murder, too." Anna's petite hands were wrapped around the bars. "I killed my husband, but I didn't kill Sebastian. You've got to help me prove it."

"That's what I've been trying to do, Anna, but—"

Florence stuck her head in and motioned for me to leave. "Visiting time is up. Hank's orders."

I was sure there was more to Anna's story, but I didn't have time to dig deeper.

As I left, I got a text from Jo: *The boys and I are at your house. I've put supper in your crockpot and they've brought Holly and the puppies to our house until you get some rest. All you have to do is come home and sleep. Call me when you wake up. I'll bring over some Hot Russian Tea.*

The drive home felt like it would never end as I went through different scenarios in my head. I had to help Anna. She killed her crazy husband, yes. But no part of me believed she killed Sebastian and stuffed him in a closet. How long had her abuse been going on? I wish I had seen the signs. If I had, maybe we could have prevented Blake's death and Anna's arrest.

I pulled in the driveway, unlocked the door, and went straight upstairs to plop on my bed. Percy greeted me with a soft meow, then snuggled up behind my head on my pillow. His rhythmic purr was like a strange, soothing lullaby.

An alarm was going off somewhere in the house. I looked at my watch. Two o'clock? I'd been asleep for almost 6 hours. I rolled over to see Percy staring at me, no longer purring. He head-butted me and put a soft paw on my face.

"Hungry?" For a moment, I wished he could grow some thumbs and feed himself. "Give me a minute to wake up, sir."

I stretched, washed-up, then attended to His Hungry Highness. With his face in the bowl, I heard the purr machine start up again, so I headed downstairs. The warm, spicy aroma from the crockpot wafted throughout the house. It reminded me of rainy days here at the Inn with Aunt Bert. I was ready to stick my face in a bowl like Percy, but I didn't want to eat alone. I called Jo.

"I'll pack up the tea and be on my way," she said. "I've got a surprise, too."

I had time to take a quick shower before she made it over. I put on my most comfortable pair of pants and the softest oversized t-shirt I could find. *It was one of those days.*

Jo came in and gave me a much needed hug. "When life

hands you lemons, what do you do?"

"Throw them back and aim for the forehead?"

"No…you make lemon meringue pie!" She pulled a pie box from the bag she'd placed on the counter.

"That's a much better solution than mine," I said. "Can we dig in?"

"It needs to set a little more, so go get comfy. I'll get our main dish. You can tell me all about everything when you're ready."

I didn't argue. I was too tired.

We were almost done with our first bowls of soup before I started describing what had happened at Anna's. When I'd finished explaining the whole ordeal, she sat in stunned silence. It was one of the few times I'd ever seen her speechless.

"It's a lot to take in, I know." I stood up to get another bowl of chicken gnocchi soup. It was exactly what I wanted, but didn't know I did.

"I hate that Anna had to do what she did," Jo said. "But I can't say that I blame her."

"You and me both…but Florence isn't convinced it was self-defense. And the Chief has told them to charge her with Sebastian's murder as well. But I know—deep in my deepest knower—that she didn't do it."

Jo nodded in agreement. "So what can we do?"

"The same thing we've been doing…trying to find the real killer."

"Sounds like you've got a plan, and I bet it's not one that my husband should be privy to."

"Probably not."

I told her the information we'd gleaned from Wendy the waitress. "We tried to verify Kevin's alibi, but it didn't wash. He and Niles were not at the pub last Friday night. However, it seems that Sophia and Niles were there the day before Niles showed up in my woods."

Jo almost choked on her coffee. "Sophia?"

"Yup. Mom saw them together the night of the murder, too."

"How many guys is she with at once? I'm barely able to keep up with one!" Jo stood up to get more soup, too. "And what in the world could Niles see in her?"

"Dollar signs, maybe? I don't know. But we need to find out."

While she was up, Jo checked on the pie. It gave me a minute to figure out how to address the issue about Hank's niece and Niles. I decided to just rip the band aid off.

"There's another thing—it has to do with Suri."

As I explained the gossip I'd heard, Jo narrowed her eyes and plopped the pie in front of me.

"There's got to be another explanation," she said. "That girl has got a better head on her shoulders than to go out with him."

"We all make mistakes," I said. "Remember Ryker Craven? You thought he could be 'the one' until he drove you out to Lookout Point and tried to get you drunk and, ya know…"

"I kicked him so hard that I think he couldn't walk for a day or two. Still," she said, "Suri is smarter than we both were at her age. Shoot, she's probably smarter now than I was at 30!"

"We definitely need to get to the bottom of this," I said, "but maybe it would be best if you asked her and let me know what she says? She might feel more comfortable talking to you about it."

"I'll make a call later. Right now, I'm ready to eat. You?"

"Yeah," I said. "I was about to start drooling."

By the time we finished eating, talking, and cleaning up, two more hours had passed. I didn't feel like going anywhere and Jo needed to get home and feed the boys. "I have been thawing some chicken and need to get it in the fryer," she said. "Want to start fresh tomorrow? I have the day off."

"Actually yeah. But what about Holly and the puppies? I don't want the boys to feel taken advantage of."

"They are completely in their happy place. They can bring them back tomorrow when you're more awake. You look a bit like a zombie." She poured me another mug of tea. "They've been reading Duncan's book, but had some questions. He offered to come over tomorrow and show the twins how to mix up solid puppy food for them."

"I need to tell him what happened today, too. I think he's convinced of Anna's innocence, too. I'm not sure who killed Sebastian yet or who attacked Niles…but the two incidents have to be related."

"Tomorrow," Jo said. "It's a new day and maybe, just maybe, you'll have a revelation during the night about the case."

I pitter pattered around the house a bit, then watched some TV downstairs. After that, I dove back into the journals and books from Aunt Bert. Snuggled in my bed with Percy, I perused each of the pages of the guestbook. It was full of names that I recognized from around town, but also some from the last three decades of TV and movies. It didn't take me long to see she was way more of a legend than I ever knew.

Around 8pm, I heard a knock at the door. It was Mom and Dad. I could tell by the way they were holding hands that something was off.

"Your father has something to tell you," Mom said.

"What's wrong?"

"I'm sorry," he said. "We don't mean to be dramatic about it. It just might come as a shock…but your mom was right."

"Hey!" She hit him playfully on the arm, but she still had a serious look in her eyes.

"Right about what?"

"I have been keeping something from her. I've been in pain for a few months but didn't want to tell her.

"He was worried it was cancer," mom said. "His dad died of that."

Cancer?

"And I was right," Dad said, "sort of. But also wrong." He paused, then took a deep breath, and paused again.

"Dad…please just tell me." I readied myself to hear the bad news.

"I do have cancer, but it's in the earliest stage and it's treatable. Matter of fact, I've already talked to the doctor who is going to do the surgery and I'm going to be just fine."

I broke into tears, but they were happy ones. "Then why all this secrecy?"

"I've been waiting on the test results. I didn't want to worry your mama needlessly."

"Big fail," she said. "I know you were keeping something from me!"

"I know. And it was dumb. I was scared and wanted to protect your mom from being scared, too." He reached over and kissed her on the cheek. "We've worked it all out," he said, "but I have to travel across the country to have the procedure done. There is a specialist in New Mexico that will be handling everything. But we will need to be there for about a month."

"I'm glad you're going to be okay," I said. "But mom? What about your job?"

"They told me to take all the time we needed, but Dad says we should be back for New Year's"

"We have to be—it's when we'll be picking up our new puppy," he said.

"You've lost me," I said. "I thought you didn't want one? And isn't that going to be a bit much with everything you've got going on?"

"Actually, a few months ago, I made arrangements to get her one for Christmas. I was going to surprise her, but then she started talking about adopting one of yours. I had to talk her out of it. You know how stubborn she is! Then I got my diagnosis. It was just bad timing all the way around."

It was midnight before they left, but 2am before I was able to get to sleep. It was scary, but at least he already had good news.

That was something to be thankful for.

It was almost 9am when I woke up. "I guess I really did need more sleep," I said to Percy. As usual, he didn't care what I did, as long as I fed him, gave him treats, and snuggled—but only when it was his idea.

I took another quick shower to wake up, dried my hair, and got dressed for the day. I'd rested enough; there was work to be done. When I got out, I had a text from Duncan.

Duncan: Want to join me for some breakfast? We can chat about the inventory issue if you're up for it.

Me: Sounds good!

Duncan: See you in a bit!

I was putting on my boots when Duncan pulled up.

"Good morning!" He sounded way cheerier than I felt. "How are you feeling? I heard that you've slept more in the last 36 hours than you have in years."

"I'm gonna make a wild guess and say you talked to Jo."

"I stopped by the café and she caught me up on stuff." He held up a bag for me to inspect. "Also, breakfast. She picked out stuff you liked. Doughnuts, Bear Claws, and Plum Jelly Pop Tarts."

Food—my love language. The deliciousness in the bag smelled like my childhood summers at my grandma's house mixed with fall evenings at the county fair.

"So," he said, "want to eat out here or inside?"

"Inside. I cleaned up yesterday,; somebody needs to see it besides me!"

We chatted about the food as we chowed down. By the time we were done, we'd decided which of the goodies we would eat every day of our lives if we had to choose only one. After much debate, I chose the doughnut. He chose the pop tart.

"The one thing Anna had ever liked from Jo's bakery was the

bear claw; it reminded her of her mom's," I said. "And if Hank will let me, I'll take her one when I go back to visit."

"How was she?" he asked. "I mean, other than the obvious."

"She's scared. But I don't blame her. Yes, she killed her husband in self-defense, but I believe now, more than ever, that she is innocent of Sebastian's murder."

"You believed that before. Why are you so worked up about it now?"

"Because they are going to charge her with his murder soon, unless we are able to provide an alternate suspect," I said. "Ya know, like someone at the clinic."

"Whoa…you think someone there did it?"

"Yeah. I mean, it could have been you," I said with a giant smile, "but you didn't have a motive that I can think of. You were already owner of the place and didn't have any reason to take him out."

"Gee, thanks for the vote of confidence," he said with a smirk. Then he grabbed another doughnut. "And just for the record, Hank already checked all my alibis and made sure I was telling the truth. Just in case you had any real doubts, feel free to ask him."

"Good to know." I had never really thought of him as a suspect, but it was nice to know Hank had eliminated him from the get go. "But I never worried."

"That's good to know, too." His smile showed off a dimple under his eyes. "So…are you still up for working on the books for a while? I know that it's not exactly the most fun thing to do on a Saturday."

I had an idea, but it was on the risky side. "What if we looked through the books, but also searched the office for clues?"

"Um…Hank specifically told me not to touch anything in there," he said. "I'm not sure that's a great idea."

"But he didn't tell ME not to touch anything. And if we wore gloves then…"

"Then I'd start to worry that you are way too good at this."

Hank had practically given me permission to run my own investigation. I was okay with digging in a bit.

"Give me just a minute," I said. "I need to grab my shoes and give Jo a quick call."

I ran upstairs and dialed my best friend's number. "Hey! Can the poochies stay with you for a few more hours?"

"Are you okay? You sound out of breath."

"Yeah, Duncan's here."

"What are y'all doing to make you breathe so heavy?"

I could hear the laughter in her voice.

"Jo! That's not what I meant!" I felt my face get hot. "I just ran up the stairs to grab my jacket. Duncan and I are heading to the clinic."

"If you're doing anything that you don't want Hank to know, then don't tell me."

I agreed, but we both knew I'd tell her eventually, especially if I found something that proved Anna was innocent of Sebastian's murder. And if I could prove Anna's innocence, Hank would know soon, too.

Our trip to the clinic seemed faster than usual, probably because I was going through all the reasons someone might want to kill Sebastian.

"He cheated on his wife," I said. "Maybe she killed him."

"But she knew and didn't care."

"That's true, but Blake cared." Then I explained my theory about Blake using Anna as a false alibi for himself. "But Anna doesn't think Blake killed Sebastian."

"She also just killed her abusive husband, so maybe she's not the best judge of character."

"And what about Niles? He was seen the night of the murder with Sophia. What if he wanted her all to himself?"

"To each his own, I guess." Duncan took a turn into the clinic's parking lot. "Um...isn't that her?"

As we pulled in, Sophia was pulling out. She stopped and rolled down her window.

"I was just about to call you, Duncan." She seemed a bit flushed. "My lawyer needs some financial records, so I need to get into Sebastian and Luna's computer to download them. Can you give me their access codes?"

"Did you already try to access my financial files?" Duncan asked, calmly. "I thought your lawyer would have warned you against that."

"Of course I wouldn't do that! I just stopped by in hopes that you were here. And well…my wish came true!"

"I'm not accessing the files unless your lawyer speaks to my lawyer about it. Or we could call Hank?"

"No, that won't be necessary. I'll have Todd contact your lawyer."

Duncan didn't say anything.

"I'm just trying to get my business taken care of," she said. "I hope there's no bad blood between us? I mean, if I am able to talk you into letting me buy the property—or the courts award it to me—I sure wouldn't mind being your boss," she said with a wink. "Want to discuss it all over a bottle of chardonnay? I can be very persuasive."

"I'm not much of a Chardonnay man," he said. His voice was dry and there was no smile on his lips.

"Too bad," she said. "It would have been a lot more fun than having my lawyer talk to your lawyer."

"But that's probably the wisest way to handle this situation, don't you think?"

"I suppose." She caught my eye and raised an eyebrow. "You must have something special, honey. Cause not many people say no to me."

And with that, she spun off, leaving both of us speechless for just a moment.

"I wonder what's on those computers that she wants so badly?" I asked, breaking the awkward silence. "You reckon it's the missing footage that Luna was supposed to give Sebastian?"

"No. Hank has already looked through her computer. Those

files aren't there. And we know she didn't give them to Sebastian, so they wouldn't be on his computer, either."

"What if Hank didn't know what he was looking for?" I said. "Maybe we should have another chat with Luna?"

"Sounds like a plan…but where is she?"

"I know who will know." I dialed Allison's number. She picked up right away.

"Hi Allison," I said. "We need to ask Luna a few more questions regarding the night of Sebastian's murder. Do you know where she is?"

"Yes. She's staying a few days with Kevin and me. Come on by. She and Kevin needed to talk to you, anyway."

When we arrived at Allison's double-wide trailer, Kevin was in the corner of the living room, sipping on a water bottle. He didn't look our way. Luna was snuggled down on the couch, cover pulled up to her chin, eyes closed.

Allison put her hand on Luna's shoulder and gently woke her. "You and Kevin have got company," she said. "And whatever they want to know, you better tell them the truth. Both of you." Allison's tone was gentle, but firm. I could tell she wasn't going to let Kevin or Luna get by with anything but the truth this time. And I had a feeling that Luna was gaining a mama figure whether she wanted it or not.

There was a lot of ground to cover, so I started at the beginning. "Were either of you at the clinic after closing the night of Sebastian's murder?"

"No!" They both said it at the same time. Their body language spoke volumes. If they'd been on a lie detector, I have no doubt it would have shown "no deception".

"Then tell her what you were doing that night," Allison said. She sounded like she already knew.

Kevin took a deep breath, then stood up and walked over and

sat beside Luna. "We were riding around together."

Luna sighed. "But he didn't tell me why until after we were already in Anna's neighborhood."

They were waltzing around their elbows to get to their thumbs.

"And when we rode by Anna's house, there was a car in the driveway, so I didn't stop to, um, check anything out."

"Stop trying to sugar coat it," Allison said. "You were casing the neighborhood last Friday night, just like you've been doing for weeks."

Nothing like a mom's bluntness.

"But Luna didn't want to go. I begged her. Niles was usually with me, but he said he had a date with Suri that night."

"Are you sure that's what he said?" I asked. "Because Suri was on a date with someone else that night…and there are witnesses."

"I thought he was lying," Kevin said. "She kicked him to the curb a long time ago."

"Back up," Duncan interjected. "You only saw one car in her driveway the night of the murder? What time?"

"Yeah. A gray Mercedes. Like I said, the first time was around 5:30 or 6. But the second time we rode by was after 10."

"Why did you drive by twice?"

"She drove a Mercedes. We figured the contents of her house were worth checking out, but that car was still there the second time."

One car. Only one car. She was there when she said she was. *Kevin and Luna could prove that Anna was telling the truth.*

I had other questions. Luna's bandaged hand gave me part of the answer. "What happened?"

"Oh…nothing," she said. "I accidentally cut it on a fence last week."

"Can I see it?" Duncan held out his hand. "I'm just a vet, but I can still recognize if a cut is infected…and you might need stitches."

"No," she said, her face turning an even paler shade of white, "I'm okay."

Allison stepped in, her arms crossed. "Luna…"

She sat up slowly, then held out her hand to Duncan. "Please be careful. It hurts bad."

He nodded and took his time removing the gauze. When he finally got to the wound, he looked at me and raised his eyebrows. "You really, really need to have this looked at. Dog bites are nothing to play with."

I knew it!

"So the spray painted message on my fence? That was you, wasn't it?" I tried not to sound mad, but I'm sure it came across much less gently than I'd hoped.

"I just wanted to scare you off," Luna said. "That was all."

"Scare me off from what?"

"From investigating. You ask too many questions. I was sure you would figure out that Niles and Kevin were stealing things from folks…and from the clinic."

"But then Holly bit you," Duncan interjected. "And that wasn't in the plan."

"Yeah. If I went to the doctor, then I figured you'd put two and two together," she whispered. "So I tried to lay low for a while. Do I need a lawyer?"

"I'm not the police," I said. "I'm just trying to figure out what happened to Sebastian." I paused, then added one more name to the list. "And also…Jessica."

Her face turned pale and she looked like she was going to be sick. Kevin jumped up and gently moved her hair out of her eyes.

"I really don't feel well," she said. "Maybe we can talk about this later."

"No. I really need to know now. An innocent woman is in jail and if you don't tell us the truth, she could end up there permanently."

"We need to tell her," Kevin said. "Or they might come for

you, too."

"They?" I asked.

"Somebody texted both of us today, but I haven't told Hank yet. They said if we went to the police with the camera footage, then we'd end up like Niles."

I'd seen him mad and high…but never scared. This was a first.

"Take a breath and slow down," I said. "You are both talking in circles. Luna – you first."

"After Jessica left and I got the front desk job, I used my key to get into the clinic after hours once a week. I turned off the alarm and Kevin and Niles…they took some stuff."

"A lot of stuff, apparently," Allison said.

"And what about the cameras?"

"I didn't know there were any until Dr. Westminster started hounding me about them. He'd had them installed not too long after the first burglary, but didn't tell anyone until a week before his murder. So when he started asking me for the footage, I knew we'd be caught. So I took the memory cards until I had a chance to doctor them a bit…and just kept stalling him."

"Why didn't you just delete them?"

"He would be suspicious if I didn't have any footage at all. I had planned to go through and just delete any footage of the break-ins. But then Dr. Westminster got killed and I panicked. I told Hank that the cameras were broken and hadn't worked at all."

"But then I told him what you'd said the afternoon of the murder…"

"Exactly. I didn't know what to do."

"Do you still have the footage?" I asked?

"Yes." She pointed to her backpack. "But I hid it in plain sight. It's in my desk at work."

"I'll need to know exactly where it is."

"It one of those cute mini flash drives that looks like a dog bone. I hid it in a clear bag of real mini dog bone treats in my desk at work, but I don't remember which drawer I put it in."

"Clever," Duncan mumbled, still looking at her hand.

"Ouch!" She reached in her bra with her healthy hand, then pulled out a key. "I'm guessing you're going to want this, too?"

Duncan was rewrapping her wound, so Luna dropped the key in my hand. I put it in my pocket and made a mental note to give it to Duncan when we got back in the truck.

"Now," I said, turning my attention to Kevin. "Who is threatening you two?"

"I wish I could tell you. All I know is this: the night before you found Niles in the woods, he told me he had some good stuff, but was worried he'd made a deal with the devil."

"Drugs?"

Kevin nodded, starring at his black-painted fingernails. "We'd been selling the goods we'd been stealing to buy...stuff."

"Did he give you a name?" I asked. "Or was it a new dealer?"

"No. But he said he was meeting someone the next morning, bright and early."

"You've got to tell Hank about this," I said. "And Luna–you need to see get some antibiotics."

Kevin and Luna gave each other a glance, but didn't say anything.

"Yes, they will," Allison said. "I'm calling the Doctor and Hank as soon as you leave. These kids have some major adulting to do."

"One more question," I said. "You never told me what happened to Jessica."

"She was there one day...then gone the next," Luna said. "I heard rumors that she and Dr. Westminster were, ya know—a thing."

She'd been right about Anna and Sebastian, so maybe she was right about him and Jessica, too.

As soon as we got in Duncan's truck, he started it up, but

didn't go anywhere. "I've been thinking," he said. "I wonder if something has happened to Jessica. Bad things keep happening to everyone who is close to Sebastian."

"Niles wasn't close to Sebastian," I said.

"But he was close to Kevin and Luna. And Luna worked for Sebastian."

"That does at least connect them."

My phone rang. It was Hank. "Tori—I need you to come to the station asap."

The clinic would have to wait.

C C **A** nna is asking for you," Hank said, leading me to her cell. "And she's refusing to talk to a lawyer until she's had a chance to talk to you."

"But isn't this against procedure or something?"

Hank wasn't one to give into blackmail or pressure.

"It is highly unusual, but not against procedure. It is, however, in Anna's best interest to talk to you. I want her to talk to her lawyer and get some help or she's going to be railroaded. The Chief wants to end his career with a solved case load."

"But we have witnesses that can testify that Anna was home around 5:30 or so, and then again at 10."

"Got the names of these witnesses?"

"You should be hearing soon. I expect within the next couple of hours."

Anna's cell was still stark, but she looked more cozy than the last time I saw her. Matter of fact, I thought I recognized the sweater she was wearing.

"I was freezing," she said, "Jo insisted that Hank bring me some of her clothes."

For a man who was by-the-book, Hank must have been feeling pretty bad about the way things were going down for Anna.

"Hank said you aren't talking to your lawyer yet?"

"I wanted to talk to you first," she said. "I didn't get to finish telling you everything about Sebastian's murder—and I don't want you to learn it in court or through the Asheville times."

I knew there was more to the story.

"I know I told you I borrowed money...but it wasn't for the paper."

"I'm listening…"

"Blake had a gambling problem. He'd had it for a long, long time. We were on the brink of ruin. Sebastian was the only option. Blake was too proud to ask his family and we didn't have enough collateral to borrow from the bank."

I sat back and considered her story. "When was the affair, Anna? You said it was years ago."

"I lied about that. The affair was about a year ago. Blake was focused on work...a lot. I was lonely. And one day I interviewed Sebastian for a write-up in the paper. Then one thing led to another. But it was a stupid mistake. It only lasted 2 months. Then he hired Jessica...and that was that."

Huh. Very interesting.

"Did Blake know about your affair?"

"Not at the time. I had no desire to add fuel to the fire. He was gambling...and losing bad. That never ended well for me." She showed me a nasty looking bruise on the inside of her arm. "This is what he did when he was mad at himself for losing— and mad at me for telling him to get help or saying that I was going to leave."

I wanted to punch Blake in his dead face.

As Anna continued talking, she paced the floor. "The day of the murder, I told Sebastian that I was leaving Blake. And

I told him that the loan was Blake's debt, not mine. But then Sebastian pulled out some pictures from his desk drawer that I didn't know about. Pictures that Sebastian took without my consent or knowledge. Pictures that Blake never needed to know about." She stopped pacing for a moment, sighing deeply. "He said he had contacts…people who liked that sort of thing. Then he threatened to sell the pictures to recover the money Blake owed him."

"Did you really think he'd go through with his threat?"

"I don't know. But I wasn't willing to take a chance." She took a deep breath and continued. "Sebastian put them in his desk and said that the decision was up to me. He laughed and bragged that he'd get his pound of flesh…one way or the other."

Suri was right!

"I begged him to give me the pictures, but he refused."

"That's a lot of motive, Anna. It sounds like you had reason to come back and kill him."

"I know. But if I really killed him, do you think I'd be telling you all this? It would just make me look worse!"

She had a point. Blake and Sebastian were both gone. She never had to divulge any of that information if she didn't want to. "Did you get the pictures?"

"Yes." She pushed her hair out of her eyes and continued. "It was after closing, around 4:15. His Hummer was gone, so I thought no one would be there until Monday. I still had the spare key that he'd given me when we were having an affair. We used to meet at the clinic when his wife was otherwise occupied."

I knew what that mean. So did half the men in town, apparently.

She stood up and walked around, then stopped at the tiny, barred window. "Sebastian found me rummaging through his desk drawers for the pictures. He'd apparently stepped out for food, because he dropped his bag of Tacos, then pinned me to the table when I tried to leave. He said he would call the cops. I tried to break out of his grip, but he was stronger than me and ripped my shirt. That's when I grabbed the paper weight and hit him as hard as I could. While he was holding his head, screaming like a banshee, and trying not to completely fall over, I grabbed the pictures and ran."

Anna wiped away tears and grabbed the bars. "But he really was alive when I left—that part of my story has never changed."

"Anything else?"

"The next morning, I called you. I needed to talk to someone about what had happened. I figured Sebastian was going to report me to the police for what happened. But I had the pictures, so I could prove that he tried to blackmail me. Then you said Sebastian was dead. I lost it. I started drinking." She took a deep breath. "But then I got a call from Blake. Said he was coming home and knew about the pictures, too. Sebastian had called and threatened to go to the police. I lied and told him that I'd destroyed them. Blake didn't believe me. He said I better let him in when he got home—or he'd burn the place down with me in it." She looked like she was about to cry. "But then you came by before he did."

"I assume he tore up the house looking for the pictures?"

"Yeah. And when he found out Sebastian was dead…then he decided to refocus on our 'relationship' and make sure I didn't stray again."

"So all that lovey-dove stuff at the hospital?"

"All make-believe to keep him happy. When he was happy, I was safe."

"If you'd just told me sooner. Or maybe Hank…he could have helped."

"Don't you think I wanted to? Do you think I liked living like a prisoner in my own home?"

She was right. I'd never been abused. How did I have a right to question her about any of this? "I'm sorry, my friend. You were in a situation no one should be in."

"I'm going to tell my lawyer, too, and Hank. But I wanted you to know first. You've been in my corner this whole time. So if anyone should know the whole truth, it was you."

"I have some news for you, too," I said, hardly containing the news. "Someone has admitted to seeing your car at home during the time of the murder!"

I told her about our conversation with Luna and Kevin. "They are not holding anything back," I said. "But they are also scared. Someone is threatening to hurt them like Niles got hurt."

"I wonder if that's what happened with Jessica? Maybe someone was threatening her?"

"Wait a minute…you know her?"

"No. But I knew she and Sebastian were seeing each other. Everyone knew. But from what I heard, it was more than that. For all of his faults, Sebastian seemed to truly care about her."

The two tickets to the Bahamas suddenly made sense.

Duncan and Hank were waiting at the door. Hank took off his hat and played with the rim. He looked at Duncan. "I might need your expertise tonight," he said. "I just got a call from Allison. But you probably already know the rest of the story."

"About the dog bite?"

"Yeah. That one. And we know which dog it is," he said. "So we are going to have to talk about the rabies issue."

I had a sinking place open up and swallow my heart. I pushed it down. I could cry when I got home…but that was going to be a while.

"One more thing," I said, "I have a hunch that I know where to find Jessica Fox."

"Actually, I just got a fax from an inquiry I made two days ago. Jessica is in—

"The Bahamas."

"Exactly."

"I'm the only one who didn't see that coming," Duncan said. "I was worried she'd been knocked off, too!"

I had another hunch about the case, but I wasn't going to share it yet. I needed more proof.

"Listen, Tori, in my official capacity as a policeman, I'm telling you that investigating a murder is dangerous business." He lowered his voice. "So in my official capacity as your friend, I'm asking you to be super careful. There's a killer out there—and they could have their eyes on you."

"I'll be careful," I said. "Promise."

"Good. Because if you get hurt, Jo will murder me."

"So...home?" Duncan asked, buckling his seatbelt. "We can do the inventory tomorrow."

He pulled out of the driveway and toward the direction of my house.

But I really wanted to find that footage...and get it to Hank as soon as possible.

"What if we went to the clinic instead?" I suggested. "We could find the thumb drive...then "not-search" the office for other clues."

Before he could agree to my fabulous plan, he got a call from Mr. Fisher. Duncan put him on speaker phone, and he just kept driving.

"I know it's late," Mr. Fisher said, "But I really need some help with Moodini. He's not feeling well at all and I can't get him to stand up."

"What's going on with him?"

Mr. Fisher described his bull's condition in detail, with a few rabbit trails thrown in for good measure. To his credit, Duncan seemed to follow along with the conversation just fine. He nodded and said "uh-huh" in all the right places.

"I'll be there as soon as I can," Duncan said. Then he gave Mr. Fisher some instructions on what to do for Moodini until he got there. When he finally ended the call, we were almost to my house.

"I'm so sorry, Tori. We can search for the footage tomorrow."

"I can always go to the clinic on my own while you help Mr. Fisher. I'm a big girl. I can handle being there by myself." For good or bad, my stubborn streak had kicked in.

"I don't have a good feeling about that," he said, driving up to the house. "But like I said, we can definitely go tomorrow."

"I understand. It's just…" I shoved my hand in my purse for my keys…then remembered the other key I'd come into possession of. But I didn't remind Duncan. "It's okay," I said quickly. "Go help Mr. Fisher. I'm good!"

"Are you sure?"

I started to bite my nails, but stopped myself. "I'm sure."

The lie felt smooth coming out of my mouth, but my stomach was in knots.

I told myself that it was for a good cause. And argued with my conscience that means justified the end.

My stomach still hurt.

I waved goodbye, then ran inside to check my fur-people. Jo and the boys had checked on them for me throughout the day, so they were all good. It took about ten minutes to give the dogs some belly rubs with promises to give more when I got home. Percy, on the other hand, shunned my kisses and hid under the bed.

I locked the house door behind me, then climbed in my truck and drove back to town. I pulled into the vet clinic's parking lot about half an hour later, then changed my mind. *No need to announce my presence.* I parked a block down and walked the rest of the way. Since the clinic's alarm was still unarmed (per Luna and Kevin's last conversation with us), I was safe to just unlock the door and slip in. I was the only one at clinic, but it felt weird…like an old school does at night.

After locking the door behind me, I made my way over to Luna's desk, using the light on my phone to look through her desk. She'd described the flash drive very clearly, but I had to find the right drawer.

The top two drawers were full of the stuff you'd find in any office drawer. By the time I got to the fifth drawer, I found five clear bags of small dog treats; exactly as Luna had described. *YES! The drive has got to be in here!*

I dumped out the treat bags one at a time. I went through four bags before I found what I was looking for. Luna had hidden the drive well. If I hadn't known where to search, it would have stayed hidden.

I put the thumb drive in my pocket. I needed to get it to Hank now. If this had enough clues, then no other snooping would be necessary. Duncan was probably going to be upset that I came without him, but I hoped he'd forgive me—

Anna's life was on the line.

I locked the clinic door behind me and made my way down the street to my truck.

As I climbed in, I suddenly had a weird feeling in the pit of my stomach. Something wasn't right. I heard a rustling in the back seat—then felt something cold, sharp, and metallic on my neck.

"I'm going to need you to drive back to the Inn, Tori. And don't draw any attention to us."

I recognized the male voice right away.

It was dark, and he had on a hoodie, but the streetlight illuminated the car just enough that I could see Kevin's sullen face in the rearview mirror.

I really should have got that lock fixed.

"What are you doing this, Kevin?"

"I don't have a choice. And if you make any trouble for me, she will kill Luna." His voice was shaky. "Please just drive. She's waiting on us."

"I'm assuming that "she" is Sophia?"

"She said you probably already knew."

She was right.

I mentally kicked myself for not listening to Duncan's advice.

"How did you get to the clinic?" I asked, trying to distract him so I could figure out a plan. "I didn't see a vehicle when I left. And how did you know where I was?"

"She stopped by the house tonight. Mom wasn't home because she'd gone to get us some supper. When I opened the door, Sophia shoved her way in and demanded that Luna give her the thumb drive. Luna told her she didn't have it...but that you probably did by now."

"That still doesn't answer my question. How did you get here?"

"She forced us into her car and made me drive. Sophia was in the backseat with Luna, and Sophia threatened to kill her if I didn't do precisely as she said. We were on our way to your house when she saw you pulling out of your driveway. She told me to do a U-turn…and we followed you. We waited until you were in the clinic, then she dropped me off. I was supposed to break in your car, but it was already unlocked. So I crawled in, waited for you, and—"

"Here we are? Why didn't you just go to the police?"

"I told you! She's got Luna! She's going to kill her if I don't bring you back."

Sophia was taking some pretty big chances. *Maybe she thinks she has nothing to lose.*

As we passed by the police station, I hoped Hank would miraculously know something was wrong and run out to follow us.

He didn't.

My mind raced as I drove slowly out of town, waiting patiently at the stoplight, as if we hadn't just entered Crazy-Town at full warp speed.

My heart raced; if I was going to die, I wanted to know why. *And if Kevin was doing this under true duress, I might be able to talk him into doing the right thing.*

"Why does she want the thumb drive so badly, Kevin? You weren't completely honest with me, were you?"

"I've already said too much."

"I assume she's going to have you kill me, so can't you at least let me die with closure?"

He was quiet for about a minute, then he sighed. "About a week before Sebastian's murder, Sophia caught us breaking into the clinic. She made us a deal."

"What kind of deal?"

"She said she'd help us if we'd help her."

"And how were you supposed to do that?"

"She wanted us to kill her husband."

My eyes felt like they were about to bulge out of my head. "You killed Sebastian?"

"NO! I didn't! I told her that I didn't want anything to do with it. Drugs and stealing was one thing…but I wasn't about to add murder to my resume," he said. "She said she'd give us a week to think about it."

"But a day or so later, Sebastian informed Luna that the whole office was being recorded and he needed her to download all the footage.

"We freaked out. Our break-ins had been caught on tape."

"But so had the conversation with Sophia!" I said. "You could use that as leverage."

"Right. And when Niles realized that, he told us to not worry about it. He had a plan."

"What do you mean?"

"I didn't find out what his plan was until the day after the murder. He called and said he'd made a deal with the devil. He told us that he had helped her kill Sebastian and promised we would destroy the tapes…but only if she agreed to pay us $250,000."

"And she agreed to his terms?"

"Yeah. At least that's what he thought. So after he helped her kill him, she agreed to meet him and give him the money. But then…"

"Then she tried to kill him to shut him up. And that's how he ended up in my woods."

"Yes. And if I don't do what she wants, Luna is going to die, too."

He sounded terrified, and I understood why. Sophia had gone from being a plasticized man-eater to a bonafide man-killer.

"Why didn't you just get rid of the footage?"

"We couldn't get back in the building to get it. And even if we could have, mom had me on lockdown. She's not let me out of her sight until tonight. She thought that she could go get us some food…and it would all be okay."

He didn't say anything else for a while, and I didn't speak again until we were riding down the Inn's long, lonely driveway. I parked in my usual spot and turned off the car.

"Now what?"

"Now we get out." He opened my door and looked at me with true remorse. "I'm so sorry. I really am."

I exited the car, started up the steps, and saw that Sophia and Luna were sitting on the porch swing. Sophia's gun was pointed at Luna's temple.

"The guest of honor is finally here!" Sophia said, in a sing-song voice. "Now be a good girl and get your dog, then let's all go for a walk." She held out her hand to Kevin. "And you won't be needing that knife anymore, sir. Hand it over."

When he hesitated, Sophia pulled the hammer on the gun. "Don't try me."

I watched Kevin's face as he went through emotion after emotion. But his feelings for Luna made the decision for him. He placed the knife in Sophia's hand. She motioned for me to unlock the door.

I did as she wanted, but had no desire to go anywhere with her. The farther away we were from civilization, the more likely I was to end up as fungus food. And as much as I liked mushrooms, I didn't want to be part of their world. There had to be a way to get out of this. What would Hank do in this situation? He'd probably already have her down on the ground in some fancy police hold. I didn't have those skills…but I could talk my way out of a paper bag. And Sophia? I got the feeling that she liked to be heard. She also seemed to like to be the smartest one in the room. *Maybe I could play on that.*

"Why are you kidnapping us?" I asked. "Wouldn't it be

easier to just kill us here?"

Kevin and Luna whipped their heads to look at me, horror on both of their faces. I ignored them, hoping they'd understand what I was doing.

"Kidnapping you?" She laughed, but it sounded as hollow as I imagined her soul looked. "That's not what's happening here. No, my dear, you're going to take your dog for a walk. But then, sadly, you're going to be attacked by intruders on your property. The same intruders who spray painted your fence the first time. The same intruders who have been breaking into the clinic and other properties around town." She continued pointing the gun at Luna, but watched every move we all made. "If the police find your bodies, then they'll surmise that you were shot first in the shoulder, but able to fight your attackers. You somehow grabbed their gun, then shot them both in self-defense. However, all three of you will have succumbed to the injuries inflicted on you before your demise."

Kevin's eyes flashed with anger. "But you said you'd let us go!"

"I tried to make a deal with you to help me kill my husband... and you trusted me not to kill you?" she shook her head and chuckled. "You and Niles are cut from the same cloth."

"So you were the one who tried to kill Niles?"

"See? I knew you'd catch up, Nancy Drew!" She laughed. "Niles got greedy. He thought he could blackmail me. And these two got scared and dropped out of sight for a few days, so I had to track them down."

"Wow," I said. "You've got this all planned out. How are the authorities going to know where to look for us?"

"They won't. But as smart as that handsome Hank is, I'm sure he'll send someone out there to look for you sooner or later. But by then, I'll be long gone."

My phone rang and buzzed in my pocket at that moment. My ringer was not on high volume so I hoped she didn't hear it.

She did.

"Hand me your phone and don't try anything," she said calmly, "or I will kill you where you stand. Got it?"

I handed it over; Sophia read the text silently, then cleared her throat. "Seems that the handsome doctor wants to stop by and see you, Tori. Listen to this: *I'm almost done at Mr. Fisher's. He gave me a surprise for you and made me promise to bring it by tonight. You still up?*"

"He will come by if I don't respond," I said.

"Then you better give him a call and tell him that you are too tired and it will have to wait until tomorrow. And you know better than to try and use any stupid code words to get him to come out here."

She handed the phone back to me. "Put it on speaker phone." She pointed to Kevin and Luna. "You two better stay quiet."

Duncan picked up right away and I tried to sound as tired as possible.

"Hi Duncan. I am already in bed. It's been a long day."

"But it's chocolate zucchini bread. I can just hand it to you through the door and leave."

"Really. I'm tired. I don't want any company."

"But I made a promise…and I don't want to be a liar. I can't just leave the bread on your porch. It will attract every bear in your woods!"

"Didn't you hear me?" I said, sounding as mean as I could make myself. "I am not in the mood for Mr. Fisher's nasty bread!"

"I see." His voice was quiet and dejected. "Sleep well, Ms. Mulligan."

"Awww!" Sophia said, snatching the phone from my hand. "That was beautifully done! You won't have to worry about him calling on you again…for many reasons. Now get the dog."

The puppies were asleep and so was Holly. I called her to me and she came right away. Surprisingly, the puppies didn't stir, and Holly didn't bark or snarl; maybe she could sense this was not the time or place. Or maybe she was scared. I couldn't blame her…I was, too. I saw her glance at the people behind me in the room, but I rubbed her ears and told her it would be okay. She probably knew I was just trying to make us both feel better. As I put her harness and leash on her, I prayed for a miracle.

"Let's go." Sophia said. She pointed the gun at us…and we all filed out the study door into the yard.

I could hear Luna softly crying and Kevin trying to comfort her. Sophia wanted none of that.

"That's enough whining," Sophia said. "You brought this on yourselves. If you'd just done what I asked, you wouldn't be in this mess—you'd already be dead."

"I'm sure that makes them feel a lot better," I said. "You really know how to give a pep talk."

"Shut it, Sherlock," she said, "Or I'll shut it for you."

We walked in silence, even though I had tons of questions. Holly still didn't growl, but the longer we walked, the more side-eye she gave me. I knew she knew.

We came to a fork in the road and she stopped. "I will find satisfaction in feeding you to the bears, Tori. But first, the thumb drive."

"Thumb drive?"

"Stop playing dumb. I know you have it."

"I really don't—"

"Do it now, or the puppies will end up just like you and their mama are going to."

I pulled the thumb drive out of my pocket and slapped it in her outstretched hand. "You're a psychopath."

She stood for a moment, then shined her flashlight to the right. "That way," she said.

I knew these woods like the back of my hand. She didn't. I picked up my pace a little. The dirt path was full of rock gardens, roots, and natural pot holes; maybe she'd trip and break her face.

"Stop where you are and don't move!" She stopped walking, then pulled my phone out of her pocket. "Looks like your best friend wants to come by and chat."

"I'd rather talk to her husband."

"Funny girl!" She texted something, then put it back in her pocket. "If she still comes by after that text, I'll be long gone… and so will you. Now move."

I turned, but somehow got tripped up in Holly's leash and fell flat on my face. The pain running through my right cheek felt like fire. *Great.*

"Help her up!" she yelled to Kevin and Luna. When they put their hands on me, I felt Holly tense, then turn. Sophia followed suit, shining her flashlight down the path.

We all froze.

At that moment, I wish Aunt Bert had been right about the Sasquatch.

About 30 feet away stood the biggest black bear I'd ever seen. He had to be at least 300 pounds. I was glad he wasn't any closer; Holly on the other hand, didn't feel the same.

She bayed, pulling hard at my leash. When the Bear ran, Holly did, too. I lost my grip and stared in horror as she disappeared in the darkness.

I felt the gun in my back. "Show's over. Move."

We walked a little until we reached the first cluster of Aunt Bert's old buildings. The first one was where the boys had buried the puppies.

"Choose one," she said. "It's your funeral, so you should at least get to pick where you drop dead."

"How kind." I remembered what they'd placed on their grave...and had an idea. "The first barn. I used to play in here as a kid."

"It's the circle of life," she said, laughing. "Come on, love birds. In you go."

Kevin and Luna were still being as quiet as church mice. They shuffled forward obediently, just as they had been doing the entire journey.

Sophia herded us in and had us stand opposite of each other. Then she stood beside Kevin and pointed the gun at me. To the right of us, I saw a small mound with several medium to large rocks on the top.

"Where would you like to be shot? Arm? Leg? Shoulder?" she asked. "You're going to bleed out in here, so pick a spot that won't take long."

"Wait…" I said, not quite ready for that conversation. "Can you at least answer some questions before you kill me?"

"You're stalling."

"Yeah. I am. But you let me pick where I'm dying. You're going to let me pick how I'm dying. Can you at least let me know why you killed Sebastian?"

"I think you know why."

"That's just it. I think I know…but I'm not sure."

"I see."

She tapped Kevin and Luna on the shoulders and forced them to the ground. Put your hands where I can see them." Then she motioned for me to do the same. I sat down as close as I could to the mound of dirt.

She leaned against a rusted tractor across from me, the gun still pointing my way. "I'll play your game," she said. "What do you think you know?"

"I think you killed Sebastian because he was having an affair with Jessica."

"Jessica? The front desk slut?" Even in the dark, I could see her bristle. "I couldn't care less. We had an open marriage. I already told you that."

"But none of the other affairs had mattered. None of yours… and none of his."

"You're right. They didn't. They were just flings."

"But this time, Sebastian was acting different…and you noticed."

"Again…open marriage. As long as we came back home,

that's all that mattered."

"But that's the thing," I said. "He wasn't coming back this time. Matter of fact, the papers you waved around in the office the day of his murder were divorce papers. You were there to convince him to change his mind."

"You have a great imagination."

"And you had an iron-clad prenup, so it was in your best interest to stay married. If you divorced, you wouldn't receive half of his business. But if he died before the divorce, you'd inherit his business—or so you thought. The week before the murder, he told you that Jessica hadn't dumped him. He'd sent her to the Bahamas a month earlier. He was planning to take all of his money and start a new life with her. So you made a plan to kill him. The problem was, you didn't know he'd already sold the business to Duncan."

"You are better than I thought. Bravo!" She lowered the gun for just a moment. "But as Anton Chekhov said, 'Knowledge is no good unless you put it into practice.' And you, my dear, will have nowhere to put your knowledge into practice, but here."

"How about just killing me. Let these two go."

"Please! We won't tell anyone!" Kevin begged through tears. "I'll tell them that Niles did everything!"

"Niles got greedy," she said. "Too bad. I tried to end it quickly for him, but he ran. And that never ends well."

Luna clung to Kevin, shaking and sobbing.

"Now, now," Sophia said. "No need to get emotional. Matter of fact, you should leave emotion out of things if you're going to get anywhere in this world."

"Jealousy is an emotion," I said. "But that's another reason that we're in the mess, isn't it? It wasn't just about the money. You couldn't stand the thoughts of Sebastian falling for someone else. Even though you'd cheated on him, his infidelity made you feel insignificant and rejected. And when you found out he was going to divorce you? Well that was the straw that broke the camel's back."

"Shut. Up."

I could hear the frustration in her voice.

"One more thing—What did Anna have to do with anything?"

"Nothing…she was just collateral damage. She happened to be in the wrong place at the wrong time. She just made it easier to divert suspicion away from me."

Mom and Dad wouldn't even know where to look for me. *This was it. No more traveling around the world. No husband. No kids. No chance to open the Nestled Inn and run it my way. Unless God was about to smite Sophia dead here and now, this moment would be my final chapter.*

At once, Aunt Bert's last words in her letter exploded in my brain: *Don't let anyone write your story for you.*

That was all I needed to remember. If I was gonna die, I was going down fighting.

I moved a little, but Sophia noticed. "What are you doing?"

"OWW!" Luna screamed. "Something bit me!"

Sophia immediately turned her gun toward Luna. "Stop that!"

"But something bit me! It hurts so bad!"

"It won't hurt for long. Stand up! All of you!"

I didn't have long. I picked up the biggest rock I could hold and stood up. Sophia started to turn toward me, but I caught Kevin's eye.

"Leave Luna alone, you old bat!" he yelled, drawing Sophia's attention back to him. "She doesn't deserve any of this!"

I lurched forward, making solid contact with Sophia's arm, knocking the gun out of her hand. As she cursed and we scrambled for the gun, Kevin and Luna ran for their lives.

We tumbled around on the ground, but suddenly she had me on my back…and the knife hovering in the air, ready to plunge into my chest. "You really are a pain," she said.

Suddenly, I heard something. And at that moment, it was the most beautiful sound in the world. Holly stood in the doorway, baying at the top of her doggy lungs.

"I hate dogs," Sophia muttered, looking up at the door. "I'll kill her next."

Holly must have understood…and ran at full speed toward Sophia and me.

"NO!" Sophia yelled, shielding herself.

I grabbed the rock that I'd dropped and knocked Sophia has hard as I could from my position on the ground.

She fell to the ground with a thud.

While Holly stood over Sophia, I grabbed the knife, the gun, and my phone…then dialed 911.

Hank and the ambulance crew arrived sooner than I thought they would. Kevin and Luna had run for help, not just run away. To my surprise, Duncan was with him, too.

The EMTs checked me over and tried to get me to go to the hospital, but I refused. "I just want to go home and sleep in my own bed."

Hank agreed, as long as I promised to call him and Jo if I needed anything. Jo wasn't happy with my decision, but she knew I was as headstrong as she was. "Can I go now?" I asked. "I promise to give my full statement tomorrow."

A few nights later, I was still a little sore from the fight with Sophia, but nothing was broken. In celebration of finally solving the case, the long awaited supper was finally happening, but we'd added a few names to the guest list, including Anna and Allison. The boys were busy playing with Holly, Thor, and Loki.

Allison smiled watching them play. "I wish you had more to give away," she said. "I am not sure Loki is going to be happy about being the only dog in my house."

"Hank promised the boys that he'd let them bring Thor over for playdates sometimes," I said.

Hank checked on the brisket. "Only half an hour more," he said. "Then it needs to rest before cutting into it."

"Rest?" Duncan flopped back in his chair. "I sure could use some of that."

"That's why we're here!" I said, carefully placing a stack of plates to the table, alongside a basket of flatware. "This has not been an easy few weeks. I'm glad you are all here."

"Thank you for inviting me," Anna said, sounding the most relaxed I'd heard in a long time. "It's good to just…be."

"And I'm thankful to be here, too," Allison said. "I am learning how to move forward while Kevin is getting the help he needs at the Blue Ridge Recovery Center for Addiction. The DA is cutting him a deal because Kevin has agreed to testify in the trial against Niles and Sophia."

Niles had finally woken up from his coma—and he had a lot of explaining to do.

"Is there anything we can do to help Kevin?" Duncan asked.

"I appreciate the offer," Allison replied, "but I'm not sure. As of right now, all I know is that he'll be there for 6 months—maybe longer." She wiped her eyes, but then smiled. "I'll let you know if he can get care packages. And if he can, he loves mint chocolate, in any form."

"I can help take care of that," Jo said.

"The church will want to support him, too," I said. "I know that Mom will make sure he gets letters and snacks." I thought back to my brother and his failed attempts at getting sober. At least Kevin wanted to get better. That would go a long way toward his recovery.

Luna sat quietly in the corner. I walked over and put a brownie on the plate in front of her. "You were really brave in the barn," I said. "Faking that bite to get Sophia's attention took me by surprise, but I rolled with it."

"Thanks," she said with a half-smile. It was the most of a smile I'd seen on her face since I'd met her. Then she dug into the dessert in front of her.

"Anyone else want one?" I asked. "Life is short, eat dessert first."

"Dessert I recognize, but what is this?" Anna held up a bag of fried pork skins.

"Delicious. That's what it is!" Hank stuck his hand in the bag, grabbed the biggest one he could find, then dipped it in the big bowl of bean dip in the center of the table. Then he held the bag toward Anna. "Try one?"

"Are you trying to gross her out?" I asked.

"Actually, I love them!" Anna laughed and grabbed a handful and put them on her plate. "But we call them scratchings back home...the one place I'm looking forward to returning to."

"Speaking of home," Jo said, squeezing my hand, "Are you gonna tell them?"

My heart was fluttering and I felt happy...very, very happy.

"I suppose," I said, trying sounding as nonchalant as possible—and failing. "Hold on...I'll be right back!"

I ran inside and to my study. Percy was stretched across my desk, his plump belly partially hiding the green folder with the sticker "The Nestled Inn" on the front. I gently scooted him over, grabbed the folder, gave Percy a kiss, then started to run back outside...but Duncan was waiting in the hallway.

"Hey." He ran his hands through his gorgeous hair. "I wanted to talk to you without all those ears listening."

"Me, too." He'd been on my mind since our last conversation. "I'm so sorry about the phone call and being so mean," I said, "I just—"

"Stop. Don't you dare apologize. I should have known something was wrong. I'm just sorry I didn't come over anyway."

"You did what I asked. And I knew you would. I didn't want anyone else in danger."

"Jo said you were stubborn and strong," he said. "She was right."

I didn't ask why he'd been talking to Jo about me. That would have to wait for another time. There were people in my backyard waiting on my announcement.

"What ya got there?" Duncan asked. "It looks important."

"It is," I said. "Hold this sign, but don't look at it yet. I want to tell everyone at the same time."

He followed me back outside and everyone got quiet, except for Jo. "Tell 'em, T!"

"I've finally decided on my new job, and it's been under my nose the whole time." I held up the folder, my heart fluttering.

Then I elbowed Duncan to hold up the "Booking Now" sign in his hand.

"I'll be writing…and renting out the rooms here at the Nestled Inn, just like Aunt Bert did." The butterflies in my stomach were doing loop-de-loops at this point. "In other words…anyone need a place to stay for the weekend?"

Everyone at the table erupted into applause and cheers, I even saw Luna's smile broaden a bit.

Duncan leaned in to whisper. "I'm glad you found your happy place, but I guess you will be too busy for our pineapple pizza adventure?"

At that moment, Holly edged her way between us and sat on his feet, turning her big brown eyes upward.

"I think that's her way of saying you can't get rid of us that easily."

"I'm glad to hear that," he replied softly.

My face felt hot and Percy must have stolen my tongue… because I had no idea how to respond. I caught Jo's eye.

She read my mind, then whispered something to her husband.

Hank cleared his throat. "First of all, the brisket is finally ready! Second, we need to make a few toasts."

"I'll make the first one," Jo said, holding up her cold glass of RC Cola. "To Tori and her new adventure! May the guest list be long and the headaches be short!"

Jo deserved a toast for the best friend award.

After the laughter died down, Anna raised her glass of water.

"To Tori, my hero! You saved me from going to jail and you saved my life…twice."

"I was sure it was Blake," Allison said, "until um…" Her face turned red when she realized what she was about to say.

"I killed him?" Anna said it softly. "It was him or me."

"And we're glad you're the one here at our table, friend." I put my arm around Anna and gave her a side hug. "Jo's dad said you've got a good case—and he's going to represent you."

"And Judd is going to represent Kevin and Luna, free of

charge," Allison replied with a smile. "He told me that it's his way of giving back to the community. Thanks for setting up our meeting, Jo."

I saw Jo's face light up. She had commented on more than one occasion that Judd was too good of a man to remain a single-pringle. *Maybe her match-making skills were on point this time.*

"How did you put everything together?" Anna asked.

"Well, I actually thought it could have been Blake, too. He'd said he was with you at the time of the murder, but he wasn't. So his alibi was a lie. I just don't know where he was."

"About that," Hank said. "I got a call this morning. They had footage of him trying to break a slot machine. They wanted me to charge him, but I explained we were well past that point."

"But you suspected Kevin, too," Allison said. "And I was very worried that you were right."

"That was what threw me. The break-in at Anna's. Nothing was stolen and she didn't have any drugs. It was nothing like the other break-ins in the area. But turns out, it was Blake."

Anna sighed. "Unfortunately."

"Men like him give good men a bad name," Duncan said.

"I agree with you," Hank said. "I really, really wish Blake was alive. I'd like five minutes alone with him to discuss how to treat a woman properly."

His clenched fists weren't exuding "discussion".

"Blake and Sophia were a lot alike," I said. "They were both jealous and controlling. She hated that Sebastian was pushing her out of his life and taking all his money with him. She tried to use her own lawyer as an alibi, but forgot to give him a head's up. That was our first clue."

Our guests were still confused about how everything worked together, so for the next hour or so, I explained the ins and outs of the whole sordid affair. I finally ended the saga with, "...and that's how I wound up in the hospital with a cut to the lower leg, a mild concussion, and enough fodder for dinner conversations the rest of my life."

Duncan held up his glass and smiled. "To the new manager of the Nestled Inn!"

"And," Hank said, "the best non-detective detective I know!"

Holly came up and laid her head on my lap. "And as you know, this sweet girl helped keep me alive. So…to Holly!"

"That reminds me," Hank said. "Fred wants to know if you ever heard from her owner, and if you've decided on her placement yet."

"No one claimed her," I said, "so we are taking down the signs. They lost their chance." Holly pawed at my hand. I obliged her request by giving her more ear rubs. "And she's already got a new home."

"I knew it!" Jo said, clapping her hands. "You made up your mind weeks ago, didn't you?"

"No. I really didn't! I mean, I thought about it, but Percy was a problem."

"Yeah, but even he has come around a bit," Duncan said. "He didn't even hiss when he walked by her yesterday."

On cue, Percy hopped up on the back of the chair near the fireplace and shot daggers toward Holly. She didn't bark or even look his way. Instead, she snuggled up a little closer. I translated that as "in your face, feline!" …but maybe I was wrong.

"What will you do now, Anna?" Jo asked. "Do you plan to open the paper again?"

"Not here, no. If I'm acquitted—which I really hope to be— then I am going home to England. My mom is coming here in a month to help me pack and get things sorted."

The rest of the evening was spent talking about future plans for each of my guests. I was as excited about their plans as I was my own.

A week later, I snuggled under my travel blanket while working on my new website and newsletter for the Nestled Inn.

The official opening day wasn't until January 15, but word was already getting around. Folks had called with inquiries, but no bookings as of yet. I wasn't worried. Matter of fact, I was the surest about this as I'd been of anything in a long time.

"This is going to work," I said. "I can feel it in my bones. Can't y'all?"

Percy was curled up in the chair by the fire place, and Holly was cuddled on the couch beside me. Percy and Holly mostly ignored each other, but at least they could survive in the same room without destroying it.

"If y'all have any suggestions for the opening date, feel free to throw them out there."

Neither of them stirred. "You're both cute, but no help at all."

I had plenty of ideas, I just had to get them implemented by opening day, less than a month away. By then, Mom and Dad would be back from his surgery and he would be done with his radiation treatments. They'd been able to give me more details and help me feel better about the whole thing. They seemed at peace…so I did, too.

Until then, I would keep myself busy with getting my financial plan ready and making sure the rest of the rooms were ready for guests.

The phone rang; it was Jo's dad, Henry Moore. He was not only a lawyer, but also the president of the Craven Historical Society.

"Hi Tori! Your Aunt Bert used to let us rent out the ballroom for the Historical society. And I was wondering if you would allow us to have our first meeting of the year there on January 20th?"

"You would be my first guests," I said. "And that would make history!"

"Got time to discuss the details?" he asked.

I had all the time in the world.

The End

Hot Russian Tea Recipe

Ingredients

- 3 quarts of water
- 1 box of whole cloves
- 1 box of cinnamon sticks
- 2 cups of sugar
- 6 teaspoons of loose leaf tea (or 2 family-size tea bags) and 2 cups of water
- 1 cup of reconstituted lemon juice (can use RealLemon)
- 1-12oz can of frozen orange juice
- 2 orange juice cans of water
- 1 large can unsweetened pineapple juice

Directions

- Mix first three ingredients and bring to a boil.
- Cover and simmer for 10 minutes.

- Strain out the cloves and cinnamon sticks, then add sugar to liquid.
- In separate pot, steep tea in 2 cups of water for 5 min, strain and cool. Add to mixture.
- Add last four ingredients.
- Heat (do not boil) and serve.

About the Author

Donna Earnhardt grew up in the Sandhills of NC reading C.S. Lewis, Nancy Drew, Hardy Boys, and the Queen of clean—Betty Neels. Donna writes clean cozy murder mysteries, but has been published in other genres over the last 15 or so years. And although her cozy mysteries deal with some of the not-so-lovely sides of the human condition, her stories are always filled with hope.

When Donna isn't spending time with her family or writing, then you can find her learning the Irish language, researching local history, or trying to find new ways to avoid housework.

You can find her online here:

Facebook: www.facebook.com/DWEarnhardt
Facebook: www.facebook.com/writerEarnhardt
Instagram: @dwearnhardt
Twitter: @Donna_Earnhardt
Amazon: https://bit.ly/DWEZon

Made in the USA
Columbia, SC
10 December 2021